W9-BXF-646

DETROIT PUBLIC LIBRARY
3 5674 00682957 7

The Dead of Jericho

by the same author

LAST BUS TO WOODSTOCK
LAST SEEN WEARING
THE SILENT WORLD OF NICHOLAS QUINN
SERVICE OF ALL THE DEAD

The Dead of Jericho

Colin Dexter

ST. MARTIN'S PRESS
NEW YORK

For information, write: St. Martin's Press,
175 Fifth Avenue, New York, N.Y. 10010
Manufactured in the United States of America

Library of Congress Cataloging in Publication Data

Dexter, Colin.
The dead of Jericho.

I. Title.
PR6054.E96D4 823'.914 81-5736
ISBN 0-312-18511-1 AACR2

10 9 8 7 6 5 4 3 2 1

First Edition

For

Patricia and Joan,

kindly denizens of Jericho.

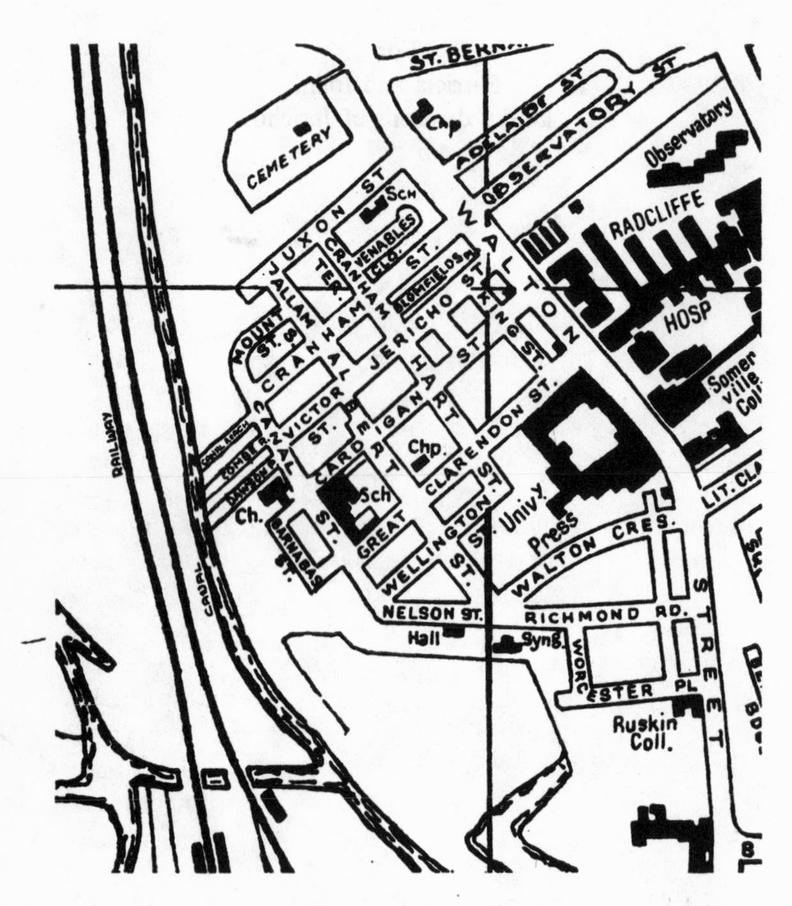

Street Plan of Jericho

Prologue

And I wonder how they should have been together
T. S. Eliot, *La Figlia che Piange*

Not remarkably beautiful, he thought. Not, that is to say, if one could ever measure the beauty of a woman on some objective scale: *sub specie aeternae pulchritudinis*, as it were. Yet several times already, in the hour or so that followed the brisk, perfunctory 'hullos' of their introduction, their eyes had met across the room – and held. And it was after his third glass of slightly superior red plonk that he managed to break away from the small circle of semi-acquaintances with whom he'd so far been standing.

Easy.

Mrs Murdoch, a large, forcefully optimistic woman in her late forties, was now pleasantly but firmly directing her guests towards the food set out on tables at the far end of the large lounge, and the man took his opportunity as she passed by.

'Lovely party!'

'Glad you could come. You must mix round a bit, though. Have you met – ?'

'I'll mix. I promise I will – have no fears!'

'I've told lots of people about you.'

The man nodded without apparent enthusiasm and looked at her plain, large-featured face. 'You're looking very fit.'

'Fit as a fiddle.'

'How about the boys? They must be' (he'd forgotten *what* they must be) 'er getting on a bit now.'

'Michael eighteen. Edward seventeen.'

'Amazing! Doing their exams soon, I suppose?'

'Michael's got his A levels next month.' ('Do please go along and help yourself, Rowena.')

'Clear-minded and confident, is he?'

'Confidence is a much over-rated quality – don't you agree?'

'Perhaps you're right,' replied the man, who had never previously considered the proposition. (But had he noticed a flash of unease in Mrs Murdoch's eyes?) 'What's he studying?'

'Biology. French. Economics.' ('That's right. Please do go along and help yourselves.')

'Interesting!' replied the man, debating what possible motives could have influenced the lad towards such a curiously uncomplementary combination of disciplines. 'And Edward, what's – ?'

He heard himself speak the words but his hostess had drifted away to goad some of her guests towards the food, and he found himself alone. The people he had joined earlier were now poised, plates in their hands, over the assortment of cold meats, savouries, and salads, spearing breasts of curried chicken and spooning up the cole slaw. For two minutes he stood facing the nearest wall, appearing earnestly to assess an amateurishly executed water-colour. Then he made his move. She was standing at the back of the queue and he took his place behind her.

'Looks good, doesn't it?' he ventured. Not a particularly striking or original start. But a start; and a sufficient one.

'Hungry?' she asked, turning towards him.

Was he hungry? At such close quarters she looked more attractive than ever, with her wide hazel eyes, clear skin, and lips already curved in a smile. *Was* he hungry?

'I'm a bit hungry,' he said.

'You probably eat too much.' She splayed her right hand lightly over the front of his white shirt, a shirt he had himself carefully washed and ironed for the party. The fingers were slim and sinewy, the long nails carefully manicured and crimsoned.

'Not too bad, am I?' He liked the way things were going, and his voice sounded almost schoolboyish.

She tilted her head to one side in a mock-serious assessment of whatever qualities she might approve in him. 'Not too bad,' she said, pouting her lips provocatively.

He watched her as she bent her body over the buffet table, watched the curve of her slim bottom as she leant far across to fork a few slices of beetroot – and suddenly felt (as he often felt) a little lost, a little hopeless. She was talking to the man just in front of her now, a man in his mid-twenties, tall, fair-haired, deeply-tanned, with hardly an ounce of superfluous flesh on his frame. And the older man shook his head and smiled ruefully. It had been a nice thought, but now he let it drift away. He was fifty, and age was just about beginning, so he told himself, to cure his heart of tenderness. Just about.

There were chairs set under the far end of the table, with a few square feet of empty surface on the white table-cloth; and he decided to sit and eat in peace. It would save him the indigestion he almost invariably suffered if he sat in an armchair and ate in the cramped and squatting postures that the other guests were happily adopting. He refilled his glass yet again, pulled out a chair, and started to eat.

'I think you're the only sensible man in the room,' she said, standing beside him a minute later.

'I get indigestion,' he said flatly, not bothering to look up at her. It was no good pretending. He might just as well be himself – a bit paunchy, more than a bit balding, on the cemetery side of the semi-century, with one or two unsightly hairs beginning to sprout in his ears. No! It was no use pretending. Go away, my pretty one! Go away and take your fill of flirting from that lecherous young Adonis over there!

'Mind if I join you?'

He looked up at her in her cream-coloured, narrow-waisted summer dress, and pulled out the chair next to him.

'I thought I'd lost you for the evening,' he said after a while.

She lifted her glass of wine to her lips and then circled the third finger of her left hand smoothly round the inner rim at the point from which she had sipped. 'Didn't you want to lose me?' she said softly, her moist lips close to his ear.

'No. I wanted to keep you all to myself. But then I'm a selfish beggar.' His voice was bantering, good humoured; but his clear blue eyes remained cold and appraising.

'You might have rescued me,' she whispered. 'That blond-headed bore across there – Oh, I'm sorry. He's not – ?'

'No. He's no friend of mine.'

'Nor mine. In fact, I don't really know anyone here.' Her voice had become serious, and for a few minutes they ate in silence.

'There's a few of 'em here wouldn't mind getting to know *you*,' he said finally.

'Mm?' She seemed relaxed again, and smiled. 'Perhaps you're right. But they're all such bores – did you know that?'

'I'm a bit of a bore myself,' the man said.

'I don't believe you.'

'Well, let's say I'm just the same as all the others.'

'What's that supposed to mean?' There were traces in her flat 'a's of some north country accent. Lancashire, perhaps?

'You want me to tell you?'

'Uh uh.'

Their eyes held momentarily, as they had done earlier; and then the man looked down at his virtually untouched plate of food. 'I find you very attractive,' he said quietly. 'That's all.'

She made no reply, and they got on with their eating, thinking their own thoughts. Silently.

'Not bad, eh?' said the man, wiping his mouth with an orange-coloured paper napkin, and reaching across for one of the wine bottles. 'What can I get you now, madame? There's er there's fresh fruit salad; there's cream gateau; there's some sort of caramel whatnot – '

But as he made to rise she laid her hand on the sleeve of his jacket. 'Let's just sit here and talk a minute. I never seem to be able to eat and talk at the same time – like others can.'

Indeed, it appeared that most of the other guests were remarkably proficient at such simultaneous skills, for, as the man became suddenly aware, the large room was filled with the chatter and clatter of the thirty or so other guests.

'Drop more wine?' he asked.

'Haven't I had enough?'

'As soon as you've had enough, it's time to have a little drop more.'

She laughed sweetly at him. 'Is that original?'

'I read it on the back of a match-box.'

She laughed again, and for a little while they drank their wine.

'You know what you just said about – about – '

'Finding you attractive?'

She nodded.

'What about it?'

'Why did you say it?'

The man shrugged in what he trusted was a casual manner. 'No call for any great surprise, is there? I expect hundreds of fellers have told you the same, haven't they? It's not your fault. The Almighty just happened to fashion you wondrously fair – that's all. Why not accept it? It's just the same with me: I happen to be blessed with the most brilliant brain in Oxford. I can't help that either, can I?'

'You're not answering my question.'

'No? I thought – '

'When you said you found me attractive, it wasn't just *what* you said. It was – it was the way you said it.'

'Which was?'

'I don't know. Sort of – well sort of nice, somehow, and sort of sad at the same time.'

'You shouldn't say "sort of" all the time.'

'I was trying to tell you something that wasn't easy to put into words, that's all. But I'll shut up if you want me to.'

He shook his head slowly. 'I dunno. You see where honesty gets you? I tell you I find you attractive. You know why? Because it does me good to look at you, and to sit next to you like this. And shall I tell you something else? I reckon you're getting more attractive all the time. Must be the wine.' His glass was empty again and he reached over for a bottle.

'Trouble with most men is that "attractive" just means one thing, doesn't it? Slip in between the sheets. Ta very much! Cheerio!'

'Nothing much wrong with that, is there?'

'Of course there isn't! But there *can* be more to it all than that, can't there?'

'I dunno. I'm no expert on that sort of thing. Wish I were!'

'But you can like a woman for what she *is*, can't you – as well as what she looks like?' She turned her head towards him, the dark hair piled high on top, and her eyes shone with an almost fierce tenderness.

'Will you just tell me – ?' He found himself swallowing hard in the middle of whatever he was going to say and he got no further. She had slipped her right hand under the table and he felt the long soft fingers slowly curling and entwining themselves with his own.

'Can you just pass that wine across a sec, old chap?' It was one of the older guests, red-faced, pot-bellied, and jovial. 'Sorry to barge in and all that, but a chap needs his booze, eh?'

Their hands had sprung guiltily apart and remained so, for the other guests were now returning to the tables to make their choice of dessert.

'Do you think we'd better mix in again?' he asked, without conviction. 'We shall be causing a bit of comment if we're not careful.'

'That worry you?'

The man appeared to give his earnest attention to this question for a good many seconds; and then his face relaxed into a boyish grin. 'Do you know,' he said, 'I don't give a bugger. Why the hell shouldn't we sit together all night? Just tell me that, my girl! It's what *I* want. And if it's what *you* –'

'Which it is – as you know! So why not stop pretending, and go and get me some of that gateau? And *here*!' She gulped down the rest of her wine. 'You can fill this up while you're at it – right to the top.'

After finishing their gateaux, and after twice refusing the

offer of coffee, he asked her to tell him something about herself. And she told him.

She'd been born in Rochdale, had been a hardworking and clever girl at school, and had won a place at Lady Margaret Hall to read modern languages. With a good second-class honours degree behind her, she had left Oxford and worked as the (sole) foreign sales rep of a smallish publishing company at Croydon, a company started from scratch a few years previously by two bright and reasonably ambitious brothers and dealing with text books in English as a foreign language. Just before she'd joined the company an increasing number of contracts had been coming in from overseas, and the need for some more effective liaison with foreign customers was becoming ever more apparent. Hence the appointment. Pretty good job, and not bad money either – especially for someone without the slightest experience in business matters. It had involved a good deal of necessary (and occasionally unnecessary) travel with the elder of the two brothers (Charles, the senior partner), and she had stayed in the job for eight years, enjoying it enormously. Business had boomed, the pay-roll had increased from ten to over twenty, new premises were built, new machinery purchased; and during this time, amid rumours of expenses fiddles and tax avoidance, the workforce had witnessed the arrival of the inevitable Rolls Royce, first a black one, then a light-blue one; and, for a favoured few, there was a spanking little beauty of a yacht moored somewhere up at Reading. Her own salary was each year – sometimes twice a year – increased, and when three years ago she had finally left the company she had amassed a nice little nest-egg of savings, certainly enough for her to envisage a reasonably affluent independence for several years to come. Why had she left? Difficult to say, really. Eight years was quite a long time, and even the most enjoyable job becomes a little less challenging, a little more – more familiar (was that the word?) as the years pass by, with colleagues seeming to grow more predictable and more ... Oh! It didn't much matter *what* they grew! It was far simpler than that: she'd just wanted a change – that was all. So she'd had a change. At

Oxford she'd read French and Italian, and through her work with the company she'd become comprehensively fluent in German. So? So she'd joined the staff of a very large (eighteen hundred!) comprehensive school in the east end of London – teaching German. The school was far rougher than she could have imagined. The boys were doubtless good enough at heart, but were blatantly and impertinently obscene, not infrequently (she suspected) exposing themselves on the back rows of their classes. But it was the girls who had been the real trouble, seeing in their new teacher a rival intruder, likely enough to snatch away the coveted affections of the boys and the male staff alike. The staff? Oh, some of them had tried things on a bit with her, especially the married ones; but they weren't a bad lot, really. They'd certainly been given a Herculean task in trying to cure, or at least to curb, the pervasive truancy, the mindless vandalism, and the sheer bloody-mindedness of those truculent adolescents to whom all notions of integrity, scholarship, or even the meanest of the middle-class virtues were equally foreign and repugnant. Well, she'd stuck it out for four terms; and looking back she wished she'd stuck it longer. The boys and girls in her own form had clubbed together generously to buy her an utterly *hideous* set of wine glasses; and those glasses were the most precious present she'd ever had! She'd cried when they made the presentation – all of them staying behind after final assembly, with one of the boys making a stupidly incompetent, facetious, *wonderful* little speech. Most of the girls had cried a bit, too, and even one or two of the inveterate exposers had been reduced to words of awkward farewell that were sad, and mildly grateful, and quite unbearably moving. Oh dear! Then? Well, she'd tried one or two other things and, finally – two years ago that is – she'd come back to Oxford, advertised for private pupils, got rather more offers than she could cope with, bought a small house – and well, there she was! There she was at the party.

She'd missed something out though – the man knew that. He remembered, albeit vaguely, how Mrs Murdoch had introduced her to him; remembered clearly the third finger on her left hand as she'd wiped the inside of her wine-glass. Had she missed out a few other facts as well? But he said nothing. Just sat there, half bemused and more than half besotted.

It was just after midnight. The Murdoch boys had gone to bed and several of the guests had already taken their leave. Most of those who remained were drinking their second or third cups of coffee, but no one came up to interrupt the oddly assorted pair who still sat amidst the wreckage of the trifles and the flans.

'What about you?' she asked. 'You've managed to get me to do all the talking.'

'I'm not half as interesting as you are. I'm not! I just want to keep sitting here – next to you, that's all.'

He'd drunk a prodigious amount of wine, and his voice (as she noticed) was at last becoming slurred. 'Nesht to you, thas aw,' would be the more accurate phonetic equivalents of his last few words; and yet the woman felt a curiously compelling attraction towards this mellowing drunkard, whose hand now sought her own once more and who lightly traced his fingertips across her palm.

The phone rang at twenty minutes past one.

Mrs Murdoch placed her hand tactfully on his shoulder and spoke very quietly. 'Call for you.' Her keen eyes had noticed everything, of course; and she was amused and – yes! – quite pleased that things were turning out so sweetly for the pair of them. Pity to interrupt. But, after all, he'd mentioned to her that he might be called away.

He picked up the receiver in the hallway. 'What? . . . Lewis? What the hell do you have to . . . ? Oh! . . . Oh! . . . All right.' He looked at his wrist-watch. 'Yes! Yes! I *said* so, didn't I?' He banged down the receiver and walked back into the lounge.

She sat just as he had left her, her eyes questioning him as he stood there. 'Anything wrong?'

'No, not really. It's just that I've got to be off, I'm afraid. I'm sorry – '

'But you've got time to see me home, haven't you? *Please!*'

'I'm sorry, I can't. You see, I'm on er on call tonight and – '

'Are you a doctor or something?'

'Policeman.'

'Oh, God!'

'I'm sorry – '

'You keep *saying* that!'

'Don't let's finish up like this,' he said quietly.

'No. That would be silly, wouldn't it? I'm sorry, too – for getting cross, I mean. It's just that . . .' She looked up at him, her eyes now dull with disappointment. 'Perhaps the fates – '

'Nonsense! There's no such bloody thing!'

'Don't you believe in – ?'

'Can we meet again?'

She took a diary from her handbag, tore out a page from the back, and quickly wrote: 9 Canal Reach.

'The car's here,' said Mrs Murdoch.

The man nodded and turned as if to go. But he had to ask it. 'You're married, aren't you?'

'Yes, but – '

'One of the brothers in the company?'

Was it surprise? Or was it suspicion that flashed momentarily in her eyes before she answered him. 'No, it wasn't. I was married long before that. In fact, I was silly enough to get married when I was nineteen, but – '

A rather thick-set man walked into the lounge and came diffidently over to them. 'Ready, sir?'

'Yes.' He turned to look at her for the last time, wanting to tell her something, but unable to find the words.

'You've got my address?' she whispered.

He nodded. 'I don't know your name, though.'

'Anne. Anne Scott.'

He smiled – almost happily.

'What's *your* name?'

'They call me Morse,' said the policeman.

Morse fastened his safety-belt as the police car crossed the Banbury Road roundabout and accelerated down the hill towards Kidlington.

'Where do you say you're dragging me to, Lewis?'

'Woodstock Crescent, sir. Chap's knifed his missus in one of the houses there. No trouble, though. He came into the station a few minutes after he'd killed her.'

'Doesn't surprise you, Lewis, does it? In the great majority of murder cases the identity of the accused is apparent virtually from the start. You realize that? In about 40 per cent of such cases he's arrested, almost immediately, at or very near the scene of the crime – usually, and mercifully for the likes of you, Lewis, because he hasn't made the slightest effort to escape. Now – let me get it right – in about 50 per cent of cases the victim and the accused have had some prior relationship with each other, often a very close relationship.'

'Interesting, sir,' said Lewis as he turned off left just opposite the Thames Valley Police HQ. 'You been giving another one of your lectures?'

'It was all in the paper this morning,' said Morse, surprised to find how soberly he'd spoken.

The car made its way through a maze of darkened side streets until Morse saw the flashing blue lights of an ambulance outside a mean-looking house in Woodstock Crescent. He slowly unfastened his seat-belt and climbed out. 'By the way, Lewis, do you know where Canal Reach is?'

'I think so, yes, sir. It's down in Oxford. Down in Jericho.'

BOOK ONE

Chapter One

A certain man went down from Jerusalem to Jericho
St Luke x. 30

Oxford's main tourist attractions are reasonably proximate to one another and there are guide books a-plenty, translated into many languages. Thus it is that the day visitor may climb back into his luxury coach after viewing the fine University buildings clustered between The High and the Radcliffe Camera with the gratifying feeling that it has all been a compact, interesting visit to yet another of England's most beautiful cities. It is all very splendid: it is all a bit tiring. And so it is fortunate that the neighbouring Cornmarket can offer to the visitor its string of snack bars, coffee bars, and burger bars in which to rest his feet and browse through his recently purchased literature about those other colleges and ecclesiastical edifices, their dates and their benefactors, which thus far have fallen outside his rather arbitrary circumambulations. But perhaps by noon he's had enough, and quits such culture for the Westgate shopping complex, only a pedestrian precinct away, and built on the old site of St Ebbes, where the city fathers found the answer to their inner-city obsolescence in the full-scale flattening of the ancient streets of houses, and their replacement by the concrete giants of supermarket stores and municipal offices. *Solitudinem faciunt: architecturam appellant.*

But further delights there are round other corners – even as the guide books say. From Cornmarket, for example, the visitor may turn left past the *Randolph* into the curving sweep of the Regency houses in Beaumont Street, and visit the Ashmolean there and walk round Worcester College gardens. From here he may turn northwards and find himself walking along the lower stretches of Walton Street into an area which has, thus far, escaped the vandals who sit on the City's planning committees. Here, imperceptibly at first, but soon quite unmistakably, the University has been left behind, and even the vast building on the left which houses the Oxford University Press, its lawned quadrangle glimpsed through the high wrought-iron gates, looks bleakly out of place and rather lonely, like some dowager duchess at a discotheque. The occasional visitor may pursue his way even further, past the red and blue lettering of the Phoenix cinema on his left and the blackened-grey walls of the Radcliffe Infirmary on his right; yet much more probably he will now decide to veer again towards the city centre, and in so doing turn his back upon an area of Oxford where gradual renewal, sensitive to the needs of its community, seems finally to have won its battle with the bulldozers.

This area is called Jericho, a largely residential district, stretching down from the western side of Walton Street to the banks of the canal, and consisting for the most part of mid-nineteenth century, two-storey, terraced houses. Here, in the criss-cross grid of streets with names like 'Wellington' and 'Nelson' and the other mighty heroes, are the dwellings built for those who worked on the wharves or on the railway, at the University Press or at Lucy's iron foundry in Juxon Street. But the visitor to the City Museum in St Aldates will find no *Guide to Jericho* along the shelves; and even by the oldest of its own inhabitants, the provenance of that charming and mysterious name of 'Jericho' is variously – and dubiously – traced. Some claim that in the early days the whistle of a passing train from the lines across the canal could make the walls come tumbling down; others would point darkly to the synagogue in Richmond Road and talk of sharp and profitable dealings in the former Jewish quarter; yet others lift their eyes to read the legend on a local inn: 'Tarry ye at Jericho until your beards be grown'. But the majority of the area's inhabitants would just look blankly at their interlocutors, as if they had been asked such obviously unanswerable questions as why it was that men were born, or why they should live or die, and fall in love with booze or women.

It was on Wednesday, October 3rd, almost exactly six months after Mrs Murdoch's party in North Oxford, that Detective Chief Inspector Morse of the Thames Valley Police was driving from Kidlington to Oxford. He turned down into Woodstock Road, turned right into Bainton Road, and then straight down into Walton Street. As he drove the Lancia carefully through the narrow street, with cars parked either side, he noticed that *Sex in the Suburbs* was on at the Phoenix; but almost simultaneously the bold white lettering of a street sign caught his eye and any thoughts of an hour or two of technicolour titillation was forgotten: the sign read 'Jericho Street'. He'd thought of Anne Scott occasionally – of course he had! – but the prospect of a complicated liaison with a married woman had not, in the comparatively sober light of morning, carried quite the same appeal it had the night before; and he had not pursued the affair. But he was thinking of her now . . .

That morning, in Kidlington, his lecture on Homicide Procedures to a group of earnest, newly-fledged detectives (Constable Walters amongst them) had been received with a polite lack of enthusiasm, and Morse knew that he had been far from good. How glad he was to have the afternoon free! Furthermore, for the first time in many months he had every reason to be in the precincts of Jericho. As a member of the Oxford Book Association he had recently received advanced notice of a talk (Oct. 3rd, 8 p.m.) by Dame Helen Gardner on *The New Oxford Book of English Verse*; and the prospect of hearing that distinguished Oxford academic was quite sufficient in itself to stir an idle Morse to his first attendance of the year. But, in addition, the Association's committee had appealed to all members for any old books that might be finished with, because before Dame Helen's talk a sale of secondhand books had been arranged in aid of the Association's languishing funds. The previous night, therefore, Morse had decimated his shelves, selecting those thirty or so paperbacks which now lay in a cardboard box in the boot of the Lancia. All books were to be delivered to the Clarendon Press Institute in Walton Street (where the Association held its meetings) between 3 p.m. and 5 p.m. that day. It was now twenty-five minutes past three.

For very good reasons, however, the delivery of Morse's offerings was temporarily postponed. Just before the OUP building, Morse turned right and drove slowly down Great Clarendon Street, crossed a couple of intersections, and noticed Canal Street on his right. Surely she must live somewhere very close? It had been raining intermittently all day, and heavy spots were spattering his windscreen as he turned into the deserted street and looked around for parking space. Difficult, though. Double yellow lines on one side of the street, with a row of notices on the other – a series of white P's set against their blue backgrounds: 'Resident Permit Holders Only'. True, there was a gap or two here and there; but with a stubborn law-abiding streak within him – and with the added risk of a hefty parking fine – Morse drove on slowly round the maze of streets. Finally, beneath the towering Italianate campanile of St Barnabas' Church, he found an empty space in a stretch of road by the canal, marked off with boxed white lines: 'Waiting limited to 2 hours. Return prohibited within 1 hour'. Morse backed carefully into the space and looked around him. Through an opened gate he glimpsed the blues, browns, and reds of a string of house-boats moored alongside the canal, whilst three unspecified ducks, long-necked and black against the late-afternoon sky, flapped away noisily towards a more northerly stretch of water. He got out of the car and stood in the rain awhile, looking up at the dirtyish yellow tower that dominated the streets. A quick look inside, perhaps? But the door was locked, and Morse was reading the notice explaining that the regrettable cause of it all was adolescent vandalism when he heard the voice behind him.

'Is this your car?'

A young, very wet traffic warden, the yellow band round her hat extremely new, was standing beside the Lancia, trying bravely to write down something on a bedrenched page of her notebook.

'All right, aren't I?' mumbled Morse defensively, as he walked down the shallow steps of the church towards her.

'You're over the white line and you'll have to back it up a bit. You've plenty of room.'

Morse dutifully manoeuvred the Lancia until it stood more neatly within its white box, and then wound down the window. 'Better?'

'You ought to lock your doors if you're going to stay here – two hours, remember. A lot of cars get stolen, you know.'

'Yes, I always lock –'

'It wasn't locked just now!'

'I was only seeing if . . .'

But the young lady had walked on, apparently unwilling to discuss her edicts further, and was writing out a sodden ticket for one of the hapless non-permit holders just a little way up the street when Morse called out to her.

'Canal Reach? Do you know it?'

She pointed back up to Canal Street. 'Round the corner. Third on the left.'

In Canal Street itself, two parking tickets, folded in cellophane containers, and stuck beneath the windscreen wipers, bore witness to the conscientious young warden's devotion to her duties; and just across the road, on the corner of Victor Street, Morse thought he saw a similar ticket on the windscreen of an incongruously large, light-blue Rolls Royce. But his attention was no longer focused on the problems of parking. A sign to his left announced 'Canal Reach'; and he stopped and wondered. Wondered why exactly he was there and what (if anything) he had to say to her . . .

The short, narrow street, with five terraced houses on either side, was rendered inaccessible to motor traffic by three concrete bollards across the entrance, and was sealed off at its far end by the gates of a boat-builder's yard, now standing open. Bicycles were propped beside three of the ten front doors, but there was little other sign of human habitation. Although it was now beginning to grow dark, no light shone behind any of the net-curtained windows, and the little street seemed drab and uninviting. These were doubtless some of the cheaper houses built for those who once had worked on the canal: two up, two down – and that was all. The first house on the left was number 1, and Morse walked down the narrow pavement, past number 3, past number 5, past number 7 – and there he was, standing in front of the last house and feeling strangely nervous and undecided. Instinctively he patted the pocket of his raincoat for a packet of cigarettes, but found he must have left them in the car. Behind him, a car splashed its way along Canal Street, its side-lights already switched on.

Morse knocked, but there was no answer. Just as well, perhaps? Yet he knocked again, a little louder this time, and stood back to look at the house. The door was painted a rust-red colour, and to its right was the one downstairs window, its crimson curtains drawn across; and just above it, the window of the first floor bedroom where – Just a minute! There *was* a light. There was a light *here*. It seemed to Morse that the bedroom door must be open, for he could see a dull glow of light coming from somewhere: coming from the other room across the landing, perhaps? Still he stood there in the drizzling rain and waited, noting as he did so the attractive brickwork of the terrace, with the red stretchers alternating in mottled effect with the grey-blue contrast of the headers.

But no one answered at the rust-red door.

Forget it? It was stupid, anyway. He'd swallowed rather too much beer at lunch-time, and the slight wave of eroticism which invariably washed over him after such mild excess had no doubt been responsible for his drive through Jericho that day ... And then he thought he heard a noise from within the house. She *was* there. He knocked again, very loudly now, and after waiting half a minute he tried the door. It was open.

'Hello? Anyone there?' The street door led directly into the surprisingly large downstairs room, carpeted and neatly decorated, and the camera in Morse's mind clicked and clicked again as he looked keenly around.

'Hello? Anne? *Anne?*'

A staircase faced him at the far left-hand corner of the room, and at the foot of the stairs he saw an expensive-looking, light-brown leather jacket, lined with sheep's wool, folded over upon itself, and flecked with recent rain.

But even leaning slightly forward and straining his ears to the utmost, Morse could hear nothing. It was strange, certainly, her leaving the door unlocked like that. But then he'd just done exactly the same with his own car, had he not? He closed the door quietly behind him and stepped out on to the wet pavement. The house immediately opposite to him was number 10, and he was reflecting vaguely on the vagaries of those responsible for the numbering of street houses when he thought he saw the slightest twitch of the curtains behind its upper-storey window. Perhaps he was mistaken, though ... Turning once more, he looked back at the house he had come to visit, and his thoughts lingered longingly on the woman he would never see again ...

It was many seconds later that he noticed the change: the light on the upstairs floor of number 9 was now *switched off* – and the blood began to tingle in his veins.

Chapter Two

Towards the door we never opened
T. S. Eliot, *Four Quartets*

She seemed on nodding terms with all the great, and by any standards the visit of Dame Helen, emeritus Merton Professor of English Literature, to the Oxford Book Association was an immense success. She wore her learning lightly, yet the depths of scholarship and sensitivity became immediately apparent to the large audience, as with an assurance springing from an infinite familiarity she ranged from Dante down to T. S. Eliot. The texture of the applause which greeted the end of her lecture was tight and electric, the crackling clapping of hands seeming to constitute a continuous crepitation of noise, the palms smiting each other as fast as the wings of a humming bird. Even Morse, whose applause more usually resembled the perfunctory flapping of a large crow in slow flight, was caught up in the spontaneous appreciation, and he earnestly resolved that he would make an immediate attempt to come to terms with the complexities of the *Four Quartets*. He ought, he knew, to come along more often to talks such as this; keep his mind sharp and fresh – a mind so often dulled these days by cigarettes and alcohol. Surely that's what life was all about? Opening doors; opening doors and peering through them – perhaps even finding the rose gardens there ... What were those few lines that Dame Helen had just quoted? Once he had committed them to memory, but until tonight they had been almost forgotten:

Footfalls echo in the memory
Down the passage which we did not take
Towards the door we never opened.

That was writing for you! Christ, ah!

Morse recognized no one at the bar and took his beer over to the corner. He would have a couple of pints and get home reasonably early.

The siren of a police car (or was it an ambulance?) whined past outside in Walton Street, reminding him tantalizingly of the opening of one of the Chopin nocturnes. An accident somewhere, no doubt: shaken, white-faced witnesses and passengers; words slowly recorded in constables' notebooks; the white doors of the open ambulance with the glutinous gouts of dark blood on the upholstery. Ugh! How Morse hated traffic accidents!

'You look lonely. Mind if I join you?' She was a tall, slim, attractive woman in her early thirties.

'Delighted!' said a delighted Morse.

'Good, wasn't she?'

'Excellent!'

For several minutes they chatted happily about the Dame, and Morse, watching her large, vivacious eyes, found himself hoping she might not go away.

'I'm afraid I don't know you,' he said.

She smiled bewitchingly. 'I know you, though. You're Inspector Morse.'

'How – ?'

'It's all right. I'm Annabel, the chairman's wife.'

'Oh!' The monosyllable was weighted flat with disappointment.

Another siren wailed its way outside on Walton Street, and Morse found himself trying to decide in which direction it was travelling. Difficult to tell though . . .

A few minutes later the bearded chairman pushed his way through from the crowded bar to join them. 'Ready for another drink, Inspector?'

'No – no. Let me get you one. My pleasure. What will you have – ?'

'You're not getting anything, Inspector. I would have bought you a drink earlier but I had to take our distinguished speaker back to Eynsham.'

When the chairman came back with the drinks, he turned immediately to Morse. 'Bit of a traffic jam outside. Some sort of trouble down in Jericho, it seems. Police cars, ambulance, people stopping to see what's up. Still, you must know all about that sort of thing, Inspector.'

But Morse was listening no longer. He got to his feet, mumbling something about perhaps being needed; and leaving his replenished pint completely ungulped walked swiftly out of the Clarendon Press Institute.

Turning left into Richmond Road, he noticed with a curiously disengaged mind how the street lights, set on alternate sides at intervals of thirty yards, bent their heads over the street like guardsmen at a catafalque, and how the houses not directly illuminated by the hard white glow assumed a huddled, almost cowering appearance, as if somehow they feared the night. His throat was dry and suddenly he felt like running. Yet with a sense of the inevitable, he knew that he was already far too late; guessed, with a heavy heart, that probably he'd always been too late. As he turned into Canal Street – where the keen wind at the intersection tugged at his thinning hair – there, about one hundred yards ahead of him, there, beneath the looming, ominous bulk of St Barnabas' great tower, was an ambulance, its blue light flashing in the dark, and two white police cars pulled over on to the pavement. Some three or four deep, a ring of local residents circled the entrance to the street, where a tall, uniformed policeman stood guard against the central bollard.

'I'm afraid you can't – ' But then he recognized Morse. 'Sorry, sir, I didn't – '

'Who's looking after things?' asked Morse quietly.

'Chief Inspector Bell, sir.'

Morse nodded, his eyes lowered, his thoughts as tangled as his hair. He walked along Canal Reach, tapped lightly on the door of number 9, and entered.

The room seemed strangely familiar to him: the settee immediately on the right, the electric fire along the righthand wall; then the TV set on its octagonal mahogany table, with the two armchairs facing it; on the left the heavy-looking sideboard with the plates upon it, gleaming white with cherry-coloured rings around their sides; and then the back door immediately facing him, just to the right of the stairs and exactly as he had seen it earlier that very day. All these details flashed across Morse's mind in a fraction of a second and the two sets of photographs seemed to fit perfectly. Or almost so. But before he had time to analyse his recollections, Morse was aware of a very considerable addition to the room in the form of a bulky, plain-clothes man whom Morse thought he vaguely remembered seeing very recently.

'Bell's here?'

'In there, sir.' The man pointed to the back door, and Morse felt the old familiar sensation of the blood draining down to his shoulders. 'In there?' he asked feebly.

'Leads to the kitchen.'

Of course it did, Morse saw that now. And doubtless there would be a small bathroom and WC behind that, where the rear of the small house had been progressively extended down into the garden plot at the rear, like so many homes he knew. He shook his head weakly and wondered what to do or say. Oh, god! What *was* he to do?

'Do you want to go in, sir?'

'No – o. No. I just happened to be around here – er, at the Clarendon Institute, actually. Talk, you know. We er we've just had a talk and I just happened . . .'

'Nothing we can do, I'm afraid, sir.'

'Is she – is she dead?'

'Been dead a long time. The doc's in there now and he'll probably – '

'How did she die?'

'Hanged herself. Stood on a – '

'How did you hear about it?'

'Phone call – anonymous one, sir. That's about the only thing that's at all odd if you ask me. You couldn't have seen her from the back unless – '

'She leave a note?'

'Not found one yet. Haven't looked much upstairs, though.' What do you do, Morse? What do you *do*?

'Was – er – was the front door open?'

The constable (Morse remembered him now – Detective Constable Walters) looked interested. 'Funny you should ask that, sir, because it *was* open. We just walked straight in – same as anybody else could've done.'

'Was that door locked?' asked Morse, pointing to the kitchen.

'No. We thought it was though, first of all. As you can see, sir, it's sagging on its hinges and what with the damp and all that it must have stuck even more. A real push, it needed!'

He took a step towards the door as though about to illustrate the aforesaid exertion, but Morse gestured him to stop. 'Have you moved anything in here?'

'Not a thing, sir – well, except the key that was on the middle of the door-mat there.'

Morse looked up sharply. 'Key?'

'Yes, sir. Newish-looking sort of key. Looked as if someone had just pushed it through the letter box. It was the first thing we saw, really.'

Morse turned to go, and on the light-green Marley tiles beside the front door saw a few spots of brownish rain-water. But the black gentleman's umbrella he'd seen there earlier had gone.

'Have you moved anything here, constable?'

'You just asked me that, sir.'

'Oh yes. I – I was just thinking er – well, you know, just thinking.'

'Sure you don't want to have a word with Chief Inspector Bell, sir?'

'No. As I say, I just happened . . .' Morse's words trailed off into feeble mumblings as he opened the door on to the street and stood there hesitantly over the door-sill. 'You haven't been upstairs yet, you say?'

'Well, not really, sir. You know, we just looked in –'

'Were there any lights on?'

'No, sir. Black as night up there, it was. There's two rooms leading off the little landing . . .'

Morse nodded. He could visualize the first-floor geography

of the house as well as if he'd stayed there – as he might well have stayed there once, not all that long ago; might well have made love in one of the rooms up there himself in the arms of a woman who was now stretched out on the cold, tiled floor of the kitchen. Dead, dead, dead. And – oh Christ! – she'd hanged herself, they said. A warm, attractive, living, loving woman – and she'd hanged herself. Why? Why? Why? For Christ's sake *why*?

As he stood in the middle of the narrow street, Morse was conscious that his brain had virtually seized up, barely capable for the moment of putting two consecutive thoughts together. Lights were blazing behind all the windows except for that of number 10, immediately opposite, against which darkened house there stood an ancient bicycle, with a low saddle and upright handle-bars, firmly chained to the sagging drainpipe. Three slow paces and Morse stood beside it, where he turned and looked up again at the front bedroom of number 9. No light, just as the constable had said. No light at all ... Suddenly, Morse found himself sniffing slightly. Fish? He heard a disturbance in the canal behind the Reach as some mallard splashed down into the water. And then he turned and sniffed specifically at the cycle. Fish! Yes, quite certainly it was fish. Someone had brought some fish home from somewhere.

Morse was conscious of many eyes upon him as he edged his way through the little crowd conversing quietly with one another about the excitement of the night. He turned right to retrace his steps and spotted the telephone kiosk – empty. For no apparent reason he pulled open the stiff door and stepped inside. The floor was littered with waste paper and cigarette stubs, but the instrument itself appeared unvandalized. Picking up the receiver, he heard the buzzing tone, and was quietly replacing it when he noticed that the blue telephone directory was lying open on the little shelf to his right. His eyes were no longer as keen as they once had been, and the light was poor; but the bold black print stood out clearly along the top of the pages: Plumeridge – Pollard – Pollard – Popper. And then – he saw the big capitals in the middle of the right-hand page: POLICE. And under the Police entries he could just make out the familiar details, including one that caught and held his eye: Oxford Central, St Aldates, Oxford 49881. And there was something else, too – or was he imagining it? He sniffed closely at the open pages, and again the blood was tingling across his shoulders. He was right – he knew it! *There was the smell of fish.*

Morse walked away from Jericho then, across Walton Street, across Woodstock Road, and thence into Banbury Road and up to his bachelor apartment in North Oxford, where he slumped into an armchair and sat unmoving for almost an hour. He then selected the Barenboim recording of the Mozart Piano Concerto number 21, switched on the gramophone to 'play', and sought to switch his mind away from all terrestrial troubles as the etherial Andante opened. Sometimes, this way, he almost managed to forget.

But not tonight.

Chapter Three

We saw a knotted pendulum, a noose: and a strangled woman swinging there

Sophocles, *Oedipus Rex*

When Constable Walters closed the door, his eyes were puzzled, and the slight frown on his forehead was perpetuated for several minutes as he recalled the strange things that Morse had asked him. He'd heard of Morse many times, of course, albeit Morse worked up at the Thames Valley HQ in Kidlington whilst he himself was attached to the City force in St Aldates. Indeed, that very morning he'd heard Morse giving a lecture: just a little disappointing that had been, though. People said what an eccentric, irascible old sod he could be; they also said that he'd solved more murders than anyone else for many leagues around, and that the gods had blessed him with a brain that worked as swiftly and as cleanly as the lightning.

'Chief Inspector Morse was here a few minutes ago.'

Bell, a tall, black-haired man, looked across at Walters with a mixture of suspicion and distaste. 'What the 'ell did he want?'

'Nothing really, sir. He just asked – '

'What the 'ell was he *doing* here?'

'Said he'd been to some do at the Clarendon Institute or something. I suppose he must have heard about it.'

Bell's somewhat dour features relaxed into a hint of a grin, but he said nothing.

'Do you know him well, sir?'

'Morse? Ye-es, I suppose you could say that. We've worked together once or twice.'

'They say he's an odd sort of chap.'

'Bloody odd!' Bell shook his head slowly from side to side.

'They say he's clever, though.'

'Clever?' The tone of voice suggested that Bell was not firmly convinced of the allegation; but he was an honest man. 'Cleverest bugger I've ever met. I'm not saying he's always right, though – God, no! But he usually seems to be able to see things, I don't know, half a dozen moves ahead of most of us.'

'Perhaps he's a good chess player.'

'Morse? He's never pushed a pawn in his life! Spends most of his free time in the pubs – or listening to his beloved Wagner.'

'He never got married, did he?'

'Too lazy and selfish to be a family man, I reckon. But – ' Bell stopped and his eyes suddenly looked sharp. 'Perhaps you'd like to tell me, would you, Walters, exactly what this sudden interest in Morse is all about?'

As well as he could remember them, Walters repeated the questions that Morse had asked him; and Bell listened in silence, his face showing no outward sign of interest or surprise. The fact of the front door being open was certainly a bit unusual, he realized that; and there was, of course, the question of who it was who'd rung the police and how it was that he (or she?) had come to find the grim little tragedy enacted in the kitchen behind him. Still, these were early hours yet, and many things would soon be clear. And what if they weren't? It could hardly matter very much either way, for everything was so pathetically simple. She'd made a neatly womanish job of fashioning a noose from strands of household twine, fastened the end to a ceiling-hook, fixed deep into the joist above to support a clothes-rack; then stood on a cheap-looking plastic-covered stool – and hanged herself, immediately behind the kitchen door. It wasn't all that uncommon. Bell had read the reports some dozens of times: 'Death due to asphyxia caused by hanging. Verdict: suicide'. And he was an experienced enough officer – a good enough one, too – to know exactly what had happened here. No note, this time; but sometimes there was, and sometimes there wasn't. Anyway, he'd not yet had the opportunity of searching the other rooms at all thoroughly; and there was every chance, especially in that back bedroom, that he'd find something to help explain it all. Just the one thing that was really worrying – just the one thing; and he was going to keep that to himself for the present. He'd said nothing to Walters about it, nothing to the police surgeon, nothing to the ambulance men – and, for the last hour, as things were slowly straightened out inside the kitchen, nothing much to himself, either. But it was very strange: how in heaven's name does a woman stand on a flimsy kitchen stool and then, at that terrible, irrevocable second of decision, kick it away from under her so that it lands, still standing four-square and upright, about two yards (well, 1.72 metres, according to his own careful measurement) from the suspended woman's left foot, itself dangling no more than a few inches above the white and orange floor-tiles? And that's where it *had* been, for it was Bell himself who had exerted his bulk against the sticking door, and there had been no stool immediately behind it:

only a body, swaying slightly under the glaring light of the neon strip that stretched across the ceiling. A fluke, perhaps? Not that it affected matters unduly, though, since Bell was utterly convinced in his own mind (and the post mortem held the next morning was to corroborate his conviction) that Ms Anne Scott had died of asphyxiation caused by hanging. 'The police', as *The Oxford Mail* was soon to report, 'do not suspect foul play.'

'C'mon,' said Bell, as he walked over to the narrow, carpeted stairs. 'Don't touch anything until I tell you, right? Let's just hope we find a note or something in one of the rooms. It'd pull the threads together all nice and tidy like, wouldn't it?'

Bell himself, however, was to find no suicide note in the house that evening, nor any other note in any other place on any other evening. Yet there was at least one note which Anne Scott had written on the night before she died – a note which had been duly delivered and received . . .

From number 10 Canal Reach, George Jackson continued to watch the house opposite. He was now 66 years old, a sparely built man, short in stature, with a sharp-featured face, and rheumy, faded-blue eyes. For forty-two years he had worked at Lucy's iron foundry in neighbouring Juxon Street and then, three years since, with the foundry's order books half empty and with little prospect of any boom in the general economy, he had accepted a moderately generous redundancy settlement, and come to live in the Reach. He had a few local acquaintances – mostly one or two of his former work-mates; but no real friends. To many he appeared to exude an excessive meanness of soul, creating (as he did) the impression of being perpetually preoccupied with his own rather squalid self-interest. But he was not a particularly unpopular man, if only because he was good with his hands and had undertaken a good many little odd-jobs for his Jericho neighbours; and if the charges he made were distinctly on the steep side, nevertheless he was punctual, passably expeditious, and quite certainly satisfactory in his workmanship.

He was a fisherman, too.

Although he seldom drank much, Jackson stood at the back of his darkened front room that evening with a half-bottle of Teacher's whisky on the cupboard beside him and a tiny, grimy glass in his right hand. He had seen the police arrive: first two of them; then a doctor-looking man with a bag; then two other policemen; and after them a middle-aged man wearing a raincoat, a man with windswept, thinning hair, who was almost certainly a policeman, too, since he'd been admitted readily enough through the front door of the house opposite. *A man Jackson had seen before*. He'd seen him that very afternoon, and he felt more than a little puzzled ... After that there'd been the ambulance men; then a good deal of activity with the lights throughout the house flicking on and off, and on and off again. And still he watched, slowly sipping the unwatered whisky and feeling far more relaxed, far less anxious than he'd felt a few hours earlier. Had anyone seen him? – that was his one big worry. But even that was now receding, and in any case he'd fabricated a neat enough little lie to cover himself.

It was 3 a.m. before the police finally left, and although the whisky bottle had long since been drained Jackson maintained his static vigil, his slow-moving mind mulling over many things. He felt hungry, and on a plate in the kitchen behind him lay the fish he'd caught that morning. But when at last he could see no further point in staying where he was, the two rainbow trout remained untouched and he climbed the stairs to the front bedroom, where he pulled the flimsy floral-patterned curtains, jerking them into an ill-fitting overlap across the window, before kneeling down by his bed, putting his hand beneath it, and sliding out a large pile of glossy, pornographic magazines. Then he slipped his hand still further beneath the bed – and drew out something else.

Earlier that same evening, in a posh-addressed and well-appointed bungalow on the outskirts of Abingdon, Mrs Celia Richards at last heard the crunch of gravel as the car drove up to the double garage. He was very late, and the chicken casserole had long been ready.

'Hello, darling. Sorry I'm so late. God! What a foul evening!'

'You might have let me know you were going to be – '

'Sorry, darling. Just said so, didn't I?' He sat down opposite her, reached to his pocket and pulled out a packet of cigarettes.

'You're not going to smoke just before we eat, surely?'

'All right.' He pushed a cigarette carefully back into its packet and stood up. 'Time for a quick drink though, isn't there, darling? I'll get them. What's yours? The usual?'

Celia suddenly felt a little more relaxed and – yes! – almost happy to see him again; felt a little guilty, too, for she had already drunk a couple of jumbo gins herself.

'You sit down, Charles, and have that cigarette. I'll get the drinks.' She forced herself to smile at him, fetched another gin for herself, a whisky for her husband, and then sat down once more.

'You see Conrad today?'

Charles Richards looked preoccupied and tired as he repeated the word absently: 'Conrad?'

'Isn't it the duty of your dear little brother Conrad, as copartner in your dear little company – ?'

'*Conrad!* Sorry, yes, darling. I'm a bit whacked, that's all. Conrad's fine, yes. Sends his love, as always. Enjoyed his trip, he said. But the meeting finished at lunch time – well, the formal part of it – and then I had some er some rather delicate business to see to. That Swedish contract – you remember me telling you about it?'

Celia nodded vaguely over her gin and said nothing. Her momentary euphoria was already dissipated, and with a blank look of resignation she sank back into her armchair, an attractive, smartly-dressed, and wealthy woman on whom the walls were slowly closing in. She knew, with virtual certainty, that Charles had been unfaithful to her in the past: it was an instinctive feeling – utterly inexplicable – but she felt she almost always *knew*. Had he been with another woman today? Dear

God, could she be wrong about it all? Suddenly she felt almost physically sick with worry again: so many worries, and none greater than her awareness that she herself was quite certainly the cause of some of Charles's orgiastic escapades. Sex meant virtually nothing to her – never had – and for various reasons the pair of them had never seriously considered having children. Probably too late now, anyway, with her thirty-eighth birthday shortly coming up ...

Charles had finished his whisky and she went out to the kitchen to serve the evening meal. But before she took the casserole out of the oven she saw the gentleman's black umbrella, opened and resting tentatively on two fragile points, in the broad passage-way that led to the rear door. The place for that (Charles could be so very fussy about some things!) was in the back of the Rolls – just as the place for her own little red one was in the back of the Mini. She furled the umbrella, walked quietly through into the double garage, flicked on the lights, opened a rear door of the Rolls, and placed the umbrella along the top of the back seats. Then she looked around quickly in the front of the car, sliding her hands down the sides of the beige leather upholstery, and looking into the two glove-compartments – both unlocked. Nothing. Not even the slightest trace of any scented lady lingering there.

It was almost half-past eight when they finished their meal – a meal during which Celia had spoken not a single word. Yet so many, many thoughts were racing madly round and round her mind. Thoughts that gradually centred specifically around one person: around Conrad Richards, her brother-in-law.

It was three quarters of an hour later that someone had rung the Police in St Aldates and told them to go to Jericho.

Chapter Four

I lay me down and slumber
  And every morn revive.
Whose is the night-long breathing
  That keeps a man alive?
    A. E. Housman, *More Poems*

At exactly the same time that Bell and Walters were climbing the stairs in Canal Reach, Edward Murdoch, the younger of the two Murdoch brothers, was leaning back against his pillow with the light from his bedside table-lamp focused on the book he held in his hand: *The Short Stories of Franz Kafka*. Edward's prowess in German was not as yet distinguished and his interest in the language (until so recently) was only minimal; but during the previous summer term a spark of belated enthusiasm had been kindled – kindled by Ms Anne Scott. Earlier in the evening he had been planning the essay he had to write on *Das Urteil*, but he needed (he knew) to look more closely at the text itself before committing himself to print; and now he had just finished re-reading the fifteen pages which comprised that short story. His eyes lingered on the last brief paragraph – so extraordinarily vivid and memorable as now he saw it: *In diesem Augenblick ging uber die Brucke ein geradezu unendlicher Verkehr*. In his mind the familiar words slipped fairly easily from German into English: 'In this moment there went across the bridge a' (he had difficulty over that *geradezu* in its context and omitted it) 'a continuous flow of traffic'. Phew! That was while the hero (hero?) of the story was hanging by his faltering finger-tips from the parapet, determined upon and destined for his death by suicide, whilst the rest of the world, unknowing and uncaring, passed him by, driving straight on across – Ah, yes! That was the point of *geradezu*, surely? He pencilled a note in the margin and closed the slim, orange volume, a cheap white envelope (its brief note still inside) serving to mark the notes at the back of the text. He put the book down on the table beside him, pressed the light-switch off, lay on his back, and allowed his thoughts to hover in the magic circle of the night . . .

It was Anne Scott who dominated and monopolized those thoughts. His elder brother, Michael, had told him one or two stories about her, but surely *he*'d been exaggerating and romanticizing everything? It was often difficult to believe what Michael said, and in this particular case quite out of the question until – until last week, that was. And for the hundredth encore Edward Murdoch re-enacted in his mind those few erotic moments . . .

The door had been locked the previous Wednesday afternoon, and that was most unusual. With no bell to ring, he had at first tapped gently in a pusillanimous attempt to make her hear. Then he had rapped more sharply with his knuckles against the upper panel and, with a child-like surge of relief, he was aware of a stirring of activity within. A minute later he heard the scrape of the key in the lock and the noisy twang as the key was turned – and then he saw her there.

'Edward! Come in! Oh dear, I must have overslept for hours.' Her hair, usually piled up high on the top of her head, was resting on her shoulders, and she wore a long, loose-fitting dressing-gown, its alternating stripes of black, beige, brown, and white reminding Edward vaguely of the dress of some Egyptian queen. But it was her face that he noticed: radiant, smiling – and somehow almost *expectant*, as if she was so pleased to see him. Him! She fussed for a further second or two with her hair before standing back to let him in.

'Come upstairs, Edward. I shan't be a minute.' She laid her hand lightly on his arm and shepherdessed him up the stairs and into the back bedroom (the 'study', as she called it) where side by side they invariably sat at the roll-top desk while

Edward ploughed his wobbling furrows through the fields of German literature. She came into the study with him now and, as she bent forward to turn on the electric fire, the front of her dressing-gown gaped wantonly open awhile, and he could see that she was naked beneath it. His thoughts clambered over one another in erotic confusion and the back of his mouth was like the desert as she left him there and walked across the little landing to the front bedroom.

She had been gone for two or three minutes when he heard her.

'Edward? *Edward?*'

Her bedroom door was half open, and the boy stood beside it, hesitant and gauche, until she spoke again.

'Come *in*! I'm not going to *bite* you, am I?'

She was standing, with her back towards him, at the foot of a large double-bed, folding a light-grey skirt round her waist, and for some inconsequential reason Edward was always to remember the inordinately large safety-pin fixed vertically at its hem. With her hands at her waist, tucking, fastening, buckling, he was also to remember her, in those few moments, for a far more obvious cause: above the skirt her body was completely bare, and as she turned her head towards him, he could see the swelling of her breast.

'Be a darling and nip down to the kitchen, will you, Edward? You'll find a bra on the clothes-rack – I washed it out last night. Bring it up, will you?'

As he walked down the stairs like some somnambulant zombie, Edward heard her voice again. 'The black one!' And when he returned to her room she turned fully towards him still naked above the waist, and smiled gratefully at him as he stood there, his eyes seemingly mesmerized as he stared at her.

'Haven't you seen a woman's body before? Now you be a good boy and run along – I'll join you when I've done my hair.'

Somehow he had struggled through that next three-quarters of an hour, fighting to wrench his thoughts away from her, and seeking with all his powers to come to grips with Kafka's tale *Das Urteil*; and he could still recall how movingly she'd dwelt upon that final, awesome, terrifying sentence ...

He turned over on to his right side and his thoughts moved forward to the present, to the day that even now was dying as the clock ticked on to midnight. It had been a huge disappointment, of course, to find the note. The first of the household to arise, he had boiled the kettle, made himself two slices of toast, and listened to the 7 a.m. news bulletin on Radio 4. At about twenty-past seven the clatter of the front letter-box told him that *The Times* had been pushed through; and when he went to fetch it he'd seen the small white envelope, face upwards, lying in the middle of the door-mat. It was unusually early for the mail to have been delivered, and in any case he could see immediately that the envelope bore no stamp. Picking it up he found that it was addressed to himself; and sticking an awkward fore-finger under the sealed flap he opened it and read the few words written on the flimsy sheet inside.

And now, as he turned over once again, his mind wandered back to those words, and he eased himself up on his arm, pressed the switch on the bedside lamp, slid the envelope out of the text-book, and read that brief message once more:

Dear Edward,

I'm sorry but I shan't be able to see you for our usual lesson today. Keep reading Kakfa – you'll discover what a great man he was. Good luck!

Yours,

Anne (Scott)

He had never called her 'Anne' – always 'Miss Scott', and always slightly over-emphasizing the 'Miss', since he was not at all in favour of the 'Ms' phenomenon; and even if he had been he would have felt self-conscious about pronouncing that ugly, muzzy monosyllable. Should he be bold next week – and call her 'Anne'? Next week ... Had he been slightly brighter he might have been puzzled by that 'today', perhaps. Had he been slightly older than his seventeen years, he might, too, have marked the ominous note in that strangely final-sounding valediction. He might even have wondered whether she was thinking of going away somewhere: going away – perhaps for ever. As it was, he turned off the light and soon sank into a not-unpleasing slumber.

Morse awoke at 7.15 a.m. the following morning feeling taut and unrefreshed; and half an hour later, in front of the shaving-mirror, he said 'Bugger!' to himself. His car, he suddenly remembered, was still standing in the court of the Clarendon Institute, and he had to get out to Banbury by 9 a.m. There were two possibilities: he could either catch a bus down into Oxford; or he could ring Sergeant Lewis.

He rang Sergeant Lewis.

To Morse's annoyance, he found that a sticker had been obstinately glued to the Lancia's windscreen, completely obscuring the driver's view. It was an official notice, subscribed by the Publisher of the Oxford University Press:

> This is private property and you have no right to leave your vehicle here. Please remove it immediately. Note has been taken of your vehicle's registration number, and the Delegacy of the Press will not hesitate to initiate proceedings for trespass against you should you again park your vehicle within the confines of this property without official authorization.

It was Lewis, of course, who had to scrape it off, whilst Morse asked vaguely, though only once, if he could do anything to help. Yet even now Morse's mind was tossing as ceaselessly as the sea, and it was at this very moment that there occurred to him an extraordinarily interesting idea.

Chapter Five

The mass of men lead lives of quiet desperation
Henry Thoreau

Detective Constable Walters had been impressed by Bell's professionalism after the finding of Anne Scott. The whole grisly gamut of procedures had been handled with a quiet and practised authority, from the initial handling of the swinging corpse through to the post-mortem and inquest arrangements. And Walters admired professionalism.

Upstairs in the two small bedrooms of 9 Canal Reach, Bell had shown (as it seemed to Walters) an enviable competence in sifting the relevant from the irrelevant and in making a few immediate decisions. The bed in the front room had not, it appeared, been slept in during the previous night, and after a quick look through the drawers of the dressing table and the wardrobe Bell had concluded that there was nothing there to detain him further. In the back room, however, he had stayed much longer. In the two bottom right-hand drawers of the roll-top desk they had found piles of letters in a state of moderate – though far from chaotic – confusion. At a recent stage, it appeared, Anne Scott had made an effort to sort some of the letters into vaguely definable categories and to tie them into separate bundles, since the bank statements from the previous two and a half years, conjoined with her mortgage receipts and electricity bills, were neatly stacked together and fastened with stout household twine, rather too thick for its modest purpose.

'Recognize that, Walters?' Bell had asked quietly, flicking his finger under the knot.

Two or three loops of the twine, also knotted, were to be

seen loose amongst the scores and scores of envelopes, as though perhaps Ms Scott had recently been searching through the pre-tied bundles for some specific letters. Almost an hour had been spent on these two drawers, but Bell had finally left everything where it was. It was under the cover of the roll-top desk that he had found the only three items that held his attention: a recently dated letter headed from a Burnley address and subscribed 'Mum'; an address book; and a desk diary for the current year. Bell had looked through the address book with considerable care, but had finally laid it back on the desk without comment. The desk diary, however, he had handed to Walters.

'Should be helpful, my son!'

He had pointed to the entry for Tuesday, 2 October: 'Summertown Bridge Club 8 p.m.'; and then to the single entry for the following day, Wednesday, 3 October – the day that Anne Scott had died. The entry read: 'E.M. 2.30'.

When Walters reported to Bell on the Friday morning of the same week, he felt he'd done a good job. And so did Bell, for the picture was now pretty clear.

Anne Scott had been the only child of the Revd Thomas Enoch Scott, a minister in the Baptist Church (deceased some three and a half years previously) and Mrs Grace Emily Scott, presently living in Burnley. At the time of Anne's birth and throughout her childhood, the family had lived in Rochdale, where young Anne had been a pupil at Rochdale Grammar School, and where she had shown considerable academic prowess, culminating in her gaining a place at Lady Margaret Hall to read Modern Languages. Then the cream had turned sour. At Oxford, Anne had met a fellow undergraduate, a Mr John Westerby, had fallen in love with him, fallen into bed with him, and apparently forgotten to exercise any of her contraceptual options. The Revd Thomas, mortified by his beloved child's unforgivable lapse, had refused to have anything whatsoever to do with the affair, and had dogmatically maintained to the end his determination never to see his daughter again; never to recognize the existence of any child conceived in such fathoms of fornication. Anne had attended the funeral service when her father's faithful soul had solemnly been ushered into the joyous company of the saints, and she had been corresponding regularly with her mother since that time, occasionally travelling up to Lancashire to see her. Anne and John had been married at a registry office, she 19, he 20; and then, almost immediately it seemed, they had left Oxford at the beginning of one long summer vac – no one knowing where they went – and when Anne returned some three and a half months later she told her few friends that she and John had separated. The gap of the lost months could be filled in only with guesswork, but Walters suggested (and Bell agreed) that the time was probably spent touting some back-street abortionist, followed by miserable weeks of squabble and regret, and finally by a mutual acceptance of their incompatibility as marriage partners. After that, Anne's career had been easy to trace and (in Walters' view) unexceptional to record. John Westerby was more of a mystery, though. A Barnado boy who had made good (or at least started to make good) he had not finished his degree in Geography, and after the break-up of his marriage had lived in a succession of dingy digs in the Cowley Road area, carrying on a variety of jobs ranging from second-hand car salesman to insurance agent. He was well-liked by his landladies, popular enough with the girls, generous with his money; but also somewhat withdrawn, a little unpredictable, and – according to two former employers whom Walters had interviewed – almost totally lacking in drive or ambition. Anyway, that was all hearsay now, for John Westerby, too, was dead. He had been killed just over a year ago in a car crash on the Oxford-Bicester road – one of those accidents where it was difficult to apportion blame, although the inquest findings revealed that the quantity of beer in Westerby's belly placed him just beyond the limits of statutory sobriety. Unlike the young male driver of the other car, he had not been wearing his safety-belt – and his head had gone straight through the windscreen. *Finis.*

'Type it all up,' said Bell. 'Nobody'll read it – but get it typed. There's not much else we can do.'

Bell had a busy day ahead of him. Two more burglaries over-night, one a wholesale clear-out in North Oxford; an appearance before the magistrates' court in half an hour's time; lunch with the Chairman of Oxford United to discuss the recurring hooliganism of the club's ill-christened 'supporters'; and a good deal of unfinished business from the past week. No, he could hardly feel justified in allowing young Walters to worry much more about what might have happened many years ago to a woman who had just put herself out of whatever misery she was in. Anyway, Bell had a secret respect for suicides ... But he couldn't just leave things where they were, he knew that. There was the inquest to think about. *Why* had she done it? – that would be the question nagging away in the minds behind those saddened, tense, and self-recriminating faces. Oh dear! It was always the same old questions. Was there anything that was worrying her? Anything at all? Health troubles? Money troubles? Sex troubles? Family troubles? Any bloody troubles? And the answer to most of these questions was always the same, too: it was 'yes', 'yes', 'yes', and so they all said 'no', 'no', 'no', because it seemed so much the kinder way. Bell shook his head sadly at his own thoughts. The real mystery to him was why so many of them thought fit to soldier on ... He got up and lifted his overcoat from the hook behind the door.

'Any luck with "E.M."?'

'No, sir,' said Walters, with obvious disappointment. That Anne Scott had taken in several private pupils each week had been made perfectly clear to him, but there seemed to have been an *ad hoc* acceptance of fees in cash for the tutorials rendered. Certainly there was no formal record of names and receipts of monies, and doubtless the tax-man was far from well informed about the scope of Anne's activities. The neighbours had spoken of various visitors, usually young, usually with books, and almost always with bicycles. But such visits appeared to have been somewhat spasmodic, and none of the neighbours could promise to recognize any of the callers again, let alone recall their names. Pity! Walters was slowly coming to terms with the sheer volume of work associated with even the most mundane enquiries; beginning, too, to appreciate the impossibility of following up every little clue. Yet, all the same, he would have been much gratified to have come up with a name (if it was a name) for those tantalizing initials.

He found Bell looking at him with a half-smile on his lips.

'Forget it, Walters! It was probably the electricity man! And just let me tell you one thing, my lad. That woman committed suicide – you can take the word of a man who's been finding 'em like that for the last twenty years. There is no way, *no way*, in which that suicide could have been rigged – have you got that? So. What are we left with? *Why* she did it, all right? Well, we may learn a few things at the inquest, but I doubt we're ever going to know for certain. It's usually cumulative, you know. A bit of disappointment and worry over this and that, and you sort of get a general feeling of depression about life that you just can't shake off, and sometimes you feel why the hell should you try to shake it off anyway.' Bell shrugged on his coat and stood holding the door-handle. 'And don't you go running around with the idea that life's some wonderfully sacred thing, my lad – because it ain't. There's thousands of unborn kids lying around in abortion clinics, and every second – *every second*, so they tell me – some poor little sod somewhere round the globe gets its merciful release from hunger. There's floods and earthquakes and disease and plane crashes and car crashes and people killed in wars and shot in prisons and – Agh! Just don't feel too surprised, that's all, if you come across one or two people who find life's a bit too much for 'em, all right? This woman of yours probably put her bank balance on some horse at ten-to-one and it came past the post at twenty-to-six!'

Walters didn't see the joke, although he took the general drift of Bell's philosophy. Would Morse though (he wondered) not have been slightly more anxious to probe more deeply?

'You're not too worried about that chair in the – ?'

The telephone rang on the desk, and whilst the outside call

was switched through, Bell put his hand over the mouthpiece.

'I'm not worried about *anything*. But if *you* are, you go and do something about it. And find me one or two people for the inquest, lad, while you're about it.'

At that point, as Walters walked out into the bright, cold air of St Aldates, he had not the remotest notion of the extraordinary sequence of events which was soon to unfold itself.

Chapter Six

The fatal key,
Sad instrument of all our woe
Milton, *Paradise Lost*

Walters returned to Canal Reach at 2 p.m. the same day. It was the brief conversation with Morse that had given him the idea, and over a pint and a pork pie he had decided on his first move. Although he had already spoken to most of the residents in the Reach, he now knocked once again at the door of number 7, the house immediately adjacent to number 9.

'I just wondered whether Ms Scott ever left a key with you, Mrs Purvis,' he asked of the little, grey-haired widow who stood in the slit of the hall – here leading directly to the staircase.

'Well, as a matter of fact she did, yes. Left it about a year ago, she did. I always keeps it in me little pot on the – Just a minute, me dear.'

Mrs Purvis retreated through one of the doors that led off the hall to the downstairs rooms, and returned with a key which Walters took from her and examined with interest.

'Did she ever ask you for it?'

'No, she didn't. But I know she were locked out once, poor

soul, and it's always just as well to have a fall-back, isn't it? I remember once . . .' Walters nodded understandingly as the old girl recalled some bygone incident from the unremarkable history of the Purvis household.

'Do you remember how many keys you had when you came here?'

'Just the two, me dear.'

Was Walters imagining things, or did Mrs Purvis seem rather more nervous than when he had interviewed her the day before? Imagining things, he decided, as he took his leave of her and walked along Canal Street to Great Clarendon Street where, turning left, he could see the sandstone, temple-like church of St Paul's, its fluted columns supporting the classical portico, facing him at the far end on the other side of Walton Street. Yes, he'd been right, and he felt pleased with himself for remembering. There it was, the corner shop he'd been looking for, only twenty-odd yards up the street on the left: *A. Grimes, Locksmith.*

The proprietor himself, surrounded by a comprehensive array of keys, locks, and burglar-alarm devices, sat behind a yellow-painted counter sorting out into various boxes a selection of metal and plastic numerals such as are used for the numbering of street houses. Putting a large, white '9' into its appropriate box, he extended a dirt-ingrained hand as Walters introduced himself.

'You cut quite a lot of extra keys, I suppose?'

Grimes nodded cautiously, pushing his horn-rimmed glasses slightly further up his porous-looking nose. 'Steady old line, that sort of thing, officer. People are forever losin' 'em.'

Walters held out the three keys now in his possession: the one (that found on the cupboard-top just inside Anne Scott's lounge) a dull, chocolate-brown in colour; the other two of newish, light-grey gun metal, neither of them looking as if it had often performed its potential function.

'You think you cut those two?' asked Walters, nodding to the newer keys.

'Could've done, I suppose.' The locksmith hesitated a

moment. 'From Canal Reach, officer? Number 9, perhaps?'

'Perhaps.'

'Well, I did then.'

'You've got a record of doing the job?'

The man's eyes were guarded. 'Very doubtful, I should think, after all this time. It must have been eighteen months, coupla years ago. She locked herself out one day and came in to ask for help. So I went down there and opened up for her – and I suggested that she had a couple more keys cut.'

'A couple, you say?'

'That's it.'

'I suppose most of the people round here have two to start with, don't they?'

'Most of 'em.'

'So she finished up with four,' said Walters slowly.

'Let's say that one time or another she had four different keys in her possession. Wouldn't that be slightly more accurate, officer?'

Walters was beginning to dislike the man. 'Nothing else you can tell me?'

'Should there be?'

'No, I'm sure there shouldn't.'

But as Walters was half-way through the door, the locksmith decided that there might be a little more to tell after all. 'I shouldn't be surprised if somebody else in the Reach knows something about those keys.'

'Really. Who – ?'

But the locksmith had no further need of words. His right hand selected one of the numerals from the boxes in front of him, his left hand another. Then, like an international judge at a skating championship, he held his arms just above his head, and the number thus signalled was 10.

Walters walked thoughtfully back to Canal Reach and let himself into number 9 with the key that Mrs Purvis had kept for her neighbour. It slipped easily into the socket and the tongue of the lock sprang across with a smooth but solid twang. He walked through into the kitchen, every detail of death now removed, and looked out on to the narrow back garden, where he noticed that the wall fronting the canal had recently (very recently, surely?) been repaired, with thirty or so new rosy-red bricks and half a dozen coping stones – all most professionally pointed. Then he went upstairs into the front bedroom and looked around quietly, keeping as far as he could from the line of the curtainless window. The bed was just as he had seen it before, neatly made, with the edge of the purple quilt running uniformly parallel about three inches from the floor. Would Morse have noticed anything here, he wondered? Then he suddenly stepped boldly right in front of the window – and saw what he was half expecting to see. The floral curtains of the bedroom across in number 10 had moved, albeit very slightly, and Walters felt quite sure that the room in which he stood was under a steady and proximate surveillance. He smiled to himself as he looked more closely at the houses opposite – brick-built, slate-roofed, sash-windowed, with square chimneys surmounted by stumpy, yellow pots. No tunnel-backs to the houses, and so the bicycles had to be left outside: like the bicycle just opposite. Yes ... perhaps it was high time to pay a brief call at number 10, one of only two houses in the Reach at which he'd received no answer to his knocks the day before.

The door was opened almost immediately. 'Yes?'

'I'm a police officer, Mr er – ?'

'Jackson. Mr Jackson.'

'Mind if I come in for a minute or two, Mr Jackson?'

Here the ground floor of the house had (as at number 9) been converted into one large, single room, but in comparison it seemed crowded and dingy, with fishing paraphernalia – rods, baskets, keep-nets, boxes of hooks, and dirty-sided buckets – providing the bulk of the untidy clutter. Removing a copy of *The Angler's Times*, Walters sat down in a grubby, creaking armchair and asked Jackson what he knew about the woman who had lived opposite for the past two years.

'Not much really. Nice woman – always pleasant – but I never knew her personally, like.'

'Did she ever leave her key with you?'

Was there a glimmer of fright in those small, suspicious eyes? Walters wasn't sure, but he felt a little surprised at the man's hesitant reaction; even more surprised at his reply.

'As a matter of fact she did, yes. I do a few little jobs, you know – round about, like – and I did one or two things for Miss Scott.'

'She used to let you have a key for that?'

'Well, you see, she wasn't always in in the afternoons – and with me, well, not in much in the mornings, like – so I'd let meself in if – '

'Was it you who did the brick-work?'

There was no fright this time – Walters was sure of that – and perhaps he'd been wrong earlier. After all, most of the public get a little flustered when the police start questioning them.

'You saw that?' Jackson's ratty-featured face was creased with pleasure. 'Neat little job, wasn't it?'

'When did you do that?'

'This week – Monday and Tuesday afternoons it was – not a big job – about four or five hours, that's all.'

'You finished Tuesday afternoon?'

'That's right – you can ask Mrs Purvis if you don't believe me. She was out the back when I was just finishing off, and I remember her saying what a nice and neat little job it was, like. You ask her!' The man's small eyes were steady and almost confident now.

'You've still got the key?'

Jackson shook his head. 'Miss Scott asked me to give it back to her when I'd finished and – '

'You gave it back to her, then?'

'Well, not exactly, no. She was there on the Tuesday afternoon and while she paid me, like, it must have slipped me memory – and hers, as well. But I remembered on the Wednesday, see. I'd been fishing in the morning and I got back about – oh, I don't know – some time in the afternoon, so I nipped over and – '

'You did?' Walters felt strangely excited.

'– just stuck it through the letter box.'

'Oh.' It was all as simple and straight-forward as that, then; and Walters suspected he'd been getting far too sophistical about the key business. Could Jackson clear up one or two other things, as well, perhaps? 'Was the door unlocked, do you remember?'

Jackson closed his eyes for a few moments, inclining his head as though pondering some mighty problem. 'I didn't try it, I don't think. As I say, I just stuck –'

'What time was that, do you say?'

'I – I can't remember. Let's see, I must have slipped across there about – it must have been about half-past ... No, I just can't seem to remember. When you're out fishing, you know, you lose all track of time, really.' Then Jackson looked up with a more obvious flash of intelligence in his eyes. 'Perhaps one or two of the neighbours might have seen me, though? Might be worth asking round, mightn't it?'

'You mean people here tend to er to pry on what all the others are doing?' Walters had chosen his words carefully, and he could see that his point had registered.

'Only a tiny little street, isn't it? It's difficult not to –'

'What I meant was, Mr Jackson, that perhaps – perhaps *you* might have seen someone – someone else – going over to number 9 when you got back from your fishing.'

'Trouble is,' Jackson hesitated, 'one day seems just like any other when you're getting on a bit like I am.'

'It was only two days ago, you know.'

'Ye-es. And I think you're right. I can't be sure of the time and all that, like – but there *was* someone. It was just after I'd nipped over, I think – and – yes! I'm pretty sure it was. I'd just been up to the shop for a few things – and then I saw someone go in there. Huh! I reckon I'd have forgotten all about it if –'

'This person just walked in?'

'That's it. And then a few minutes later walked out.'

Phew! Things had taken an oddly interesting turn, and

Walters pressed on eagerly. 'Would you recognize him – it was a *man*, you say?'

Jackson nodded. 'I didn't know him – never seen him before.'

'What was he like?

'Middle-age, sort of – raincoat he had on, I remember – no hat – getting a bit bald, I reckon.'

'And you say you'd never seen him before?'

'No.'

Walters was getting very puzzled, and he needed time to think about this new evidence. In a few seconds, however, his puzzlement was to be overtaken by an astonished perplexity, for Jackson proceeded to add a gloss on that categorically spoken 'no'.

'I reckon I seen him later, though.'

'You *what*?'

'I reckon I seen him later, I said. He went in there again while *you* was there, officer. About quarter-past ten, I should think it was. You must have seen him because you let him in yourself, if me memory serves me right. Must have been a copper, I should think, wasn't he?'

After Walters had left, Jackson sat in his back kitchen drinking a cup of tea and feeling that the interview had been more than satisfactory. He hadn't been at all sure about whether he should have mentioned that last bit, but now he felt progressively happier that he had in fact done so. His plan was being laid very carefully, but just a little riskily; and the more he could divert suspicion on to others, the better it would be. How glad he was he'd kept that key! At one point he'd almost chucked it into the canal – and that would have been a mistake, perhaps. As it was he'd just 'stuck it through the letter box' – exactly the words he'd used to the constable. And it was the truth, too! Telling the truth could be surprisingly valuable. Sometimes.

Chapter Seven

I say, 'Banish bridge'; let's find some pleasanter way of being miserable together

Don Herold

The recently formed Summertown Bridge Club had advertised itself (twice already in *The Oxford Times* and intermittently in the windows of the local newsagents) as the heaven-sent answer to those hundreds of residents in North Oxford who had played the game in the past with infinite enjoyment but with rather less than infinite finesse, and who were now a little reluctant to join one of the city's more prestigious clubs, where conversation invariably hinged on trump-coups and squeezes, where county players could always be expected round the tables, and where even the poorest performer appeared to have the enviable facility of remembering all the fifty-two cards at a time. The club was housed in Middle Way, a road of eminently desirable residences which runs parallel to the Banbury Road and to the west of it, linking Squitchey Lane with South Parade. Specifically, it was housed at a large white-walled residence, with light-blue doors and shutters, some half-way down that road, where lived the chairman of the club (who also single-handedly fulfilled the functions of its secretary, treasurer, hostess, and general organizer), a gay and rather gaudy widow of some sixty-five summers who went by the incongruously youthful name of Gwendola Briggs and who greeted Detective Constable Walters effusively under the mistaken impression that she had a new – and quite handsome – recruit to a clientèle that was predominantly (much too predominantly!) female. Never mind, though! A duly identified Walters was anxious, it seemed, to talk about the club, and Gwendola, as publicity agent, was more than glad to talk about it. Ms Scott ('She wore a ring, though,') had been a member for about six months. She was quite a promising, serious-minded player ('You can never play bridge flippantly, you know, constable'), and her bidding was improving all the time. What a tragedy it all was! After a few years (who knows?) she might have developed into a very good player indeed. It was her actual *playing* of the cards that sometimes wasn't quite as sharp as . . . Still, that was neither here nor there, now, was it? As she'd said, it was *such* a tragedy. Dear, oh dear! Who would ever have thought it? Such a *surprise*. No. She'd no idea at all of what the trouble could have been. Tuesday was always their night, and poor Anne ('Poor Anne!') had hardly ever missed. They started at about 8 p.m. and very often played through until way past midnight – sometimes (the chairman almost smiled) until 3 or 4 a.m. Sixteen to twenty of them, usually, although one quite *disastrous* night they'd only had nine. ('*Nine*, constable!') Anne had moved round the tables a bit, but (Gwendola was almost certain) she must have been playing the last rubber with Mrs Raven ('The Ravens of Squitchey Lane, d'you know them?'), old Mr Parkes ('Poor Mr Parkes!') from Woodstock Road, and young Miss Edgeley ('Such a scatter-brain!') from Summertown House.

Walters took down the addresses and walked across the paved patio towards the front gate with the strong impression that the ageing Gwendola was far more concerned about the re-filling of an empty seat at a green-baize table than about the tragic death of an obviously enthusiastic and faithful member of the club. Perhaps even such modest stakes as tuppence a hundred tended to make you mean deep down in the soul; perhaps with all those slams and penalty points and why-didn't-you-play-so-and-so, a bridge club was hardly the happiest breeding-ground for any real compassion and kindliness. Walters was glad he didn't play.

It was not a good start, for Miss Catharine Edgeley was away from home. The young, attractive brunette who shared the flat informed Walters that Cathy had left Oxford that same morning after receiving a telegram from Nottingham: her mother was seriously ill. Declining the offer of a cup of tea, Walters asked only a few perfunctory questions.

'Where does Miss Edgeley work?'

'She's an undergraduate at Brasenose.'

'Do they have women there?'

'They've always had women at Brasenose, haven't they?' said the brunette slowly.

But Walters missed the second joke of the day, and drove down to Squitchey Lane, where he received from Mrs Raven an inordinately long and totally unhelpful account of the bridge evening; and thence to Woodstock Road, where he received from Mr Parkes an extremely brief but also totally unhelpful account of the same proceedings. So that was that.

As it happened Walters had been unusually unlucky that day. But life can sometimes be a cussed business, and even a policeman with a considerably greater endowment of nous than Walters possessed must hope for a few lucky breaks here and there. And, indeed, Walters was no one's fool. As he lay beside his young wife in Kidlington that night, there were several points that now appeared clear to him. Bell was quite right – there was no doubt about it: the Scott woman had hanged herself, albeit for reasons as yet unapparent. But there were several fishy (fishy?) aspects about the affair. The bridge evening (evening?) had finally finished at about 2.45 a.m., and almost certainly Anne Scott had gone home shortly after that. *How*, though? Got a lift with someone? In a taxi? On a bicycle? (He'd forgotten to put the point to the garish Gwendola.) And then something had gone sadly wrong. Time of death could not be firmly established, but the medical report suggested she had been dead at least ten hours before the police arrived, and that meant ... But Walters wasn't quite sure what it meant. Then again there was the business of the front door being left open. Why? Had she forgotten to lock it? Unlikely, surely. Had someone else unlocked it, then? If so, the key on the inside must first have been removed. Wasn't that much more likely, though? He himself always took the key out of his own front door and placed it by the telephone on the hall table. Come to think of it, he wasn't quite sure why he did it. Just habit, perhaps. Three keys . . . three keys . . . and *one* of them must have opened that door. And if it wasn't Anne Scott herself and if it wasn't Mrs Purvis . . . Jackson! What if Jackson had gone in, unlocking the door with his own key, called out for Ms Scott, heard no reply, and so walked through – into the kitchen! Jackson would know all about that sticking door because he'd been through it at least twice on each of the two previous days. And what if . . . what if he'd . . . Yes! The chair must have been in the way and he would almost certainly have knocked it over as he pushed the door inwards . . . would probably have picked it up and placed it by the kitchen table before turning round and – Phew! That would explain it all, wouldn't it? Well, most of it. Yet why, if that had happened, hadn't Jackson phoned the police immediately? There was a phone *there*, in number 9. Had Jackson felt guilty about something? Had there been something – money, perhaps? – in the kitchen that his greedy soul had coveted? It must have been *something* like that. Then, of course, there was that other mystery: Morse! For it *must* have been Morse whom Jackson had seen there that day. What on earth was *he* doing there earlier in the afternoon? Was he taking German lessons? Walters thought back to those oddly tentative, yet oddly searching questions that Morse had asked that night. 'Is she – is *she* dead?' Morse had asked him. Just a minute! How on earth . . . ? Had one of the policemen outside mentioned who it was they'd found? But no one could have done, for there was no one else who knew . . . Suddenly Walters shot bolt upright, jumped out of bed, slipped downstairs, and with fingers all thumbs, riffled through the telephone directory until he came to the M's. Rubbing his eyes with disbelief he stared again and again at the entry he'd been looking for: 'Morse, E, 45 The Flats, Banbury Road'. Morse! 'E.M.'! Was it *Morse* who'd been expected that afternoon? Steady on, though! There were a thousand and one other people with those initials – of course there were. But Morse *had* been there that afternoon – Walters was now quite sure in his own mind of that. It all fitted. Those questions he'd asked about doors and locks and lights – yes, he'd been there, all right. Now if Morse had a key and if *he*, not Jackson, had found his way through into the kitchen . . . Why hadn't he reported it, then? Money wouldn't fit into the picture now, but what if somehow Morse had . . . what if Morse was frightened he might compromise himself in some strange way if he reported things immediately? He'd rung later, of course – that would have been his duty as a police officer . . . Walters returned to bed but could not sleep. He was conscious of his eye-balls darting about in their sockets, and it was in vain that he tried to focus them on some imaginary point about six inches in front of his nose. Only in the early hours did he finally drift off into a disturbed sleep, and the most disturbing thought of all was what, if anything, he was to say to Chief Inspector Bell in the morning.

Chapter Eight

For he who lives more lives than one
   More deaths than one must die
Oscar Wilde, *The Ballad of Reading Gaol*

It was not only Walters who slept uneasily that night, although for Charles Richards the causes of his long and restless wakefulness were far more anguished. The undertow of it all was what he saw as the imminent break-up of his marriage, and all because of that one careless, amateurish error on his own part. Why, oh why – an old campaigner like he! – when Celia had seen that long, blonde, curling hair on the back of his dark brown Jaeger cardigan, hadn't he shrugged her question off, quite casually and uncaringly, instead of trying (as he had) to fabricate that laboured, unconvincing explanation? He remembered – kept on remembering – how Celia's face, for all its fortitude, had reflected then her sense of anger and of jealousy, her sense of betrayal and agonized inadequacy. And that hurt him – hurt him much more deeply than he could have imagined. In the distant past she might have guessed; in the recent past she must, so surely, have suspected; but now she *knew* – of that there now was little doubt.

And as he lay awake, he wondered how on earth he could ever cope with the qualms of his embering conscience. He could eat no breakfast when he got up the next morning, and after a cup of tea and a cigarette he experienced, as he sat alone at the kitchen table, a sense of helplessness that frightened him. His head ached and the print of *The Times* jumped giddily across his vision as he tried to distract his thoughts with events of some more cosmic implication. But other facts were facts as well: he was losing his hair, losing his teeth, losing whatever integrity he'd ever had as a civilized human being – and now he was losing his wife as well. He was drinking too heavily, smoking too addictively, fornicating far too frequently ... Oh God, how he hated himself occasionally!

Saturday mornings were hardly the most productive periods in the company's activities, but there was always correspondence, occasionally an important phone call, and usually a few enquiries at the desk outside; and he had established the practice of going in himself, of requiring his personal secretary to join him, and of expecting his brother Conrad to put in a brief appearance, too, so that before adjourning for a midday drink together they could have the opportunity of discussing present progress and future plans.

On that Saturday morning, as often when he had no longer-ranging business commitments, Charles drove the five minute journey to the centre of Abingdon in the Mini. The rain which had persisted through the previous few days had now cleared up, and the sky was a pale and cloudless blue. Not an umbrella day. Once seated in his office he called in his secretary and told her that he didn't wish to be disturbed unless it were absolutely necessary: he had, he said, some most important papers to consider.

For half an hour he sat there and did nothing, his chin resting on his left hand as he smoked one cigarette after another. *That* could be a start, though! He vowed earnestly that as soon as he'd finished his present packet (Glory be! – it was still almost full) he would pack up the wretched, dirty habit, thereby deferring, at a stroke, the horrid threats to heart and lungs, with the additional sweet benefits of less expense and (as he'd read) a greater sexual potency in bed. Yes! For a moment, as he lit another cigarette, he almost regretted that there were so many left. By lunchtime they'd be gone though, and that would be the time for his monumental sacrifice – yes, after he'd had a drink with Conrad. If Conrad were coming in that morning ... He sank into further fathoms of self-pitying gloom and recrimination ... He had tried so hard over the years. He had reformed and vowed to turn from his sinful ways as frequently as a regular recidivist at revivalist meetings, and the thought of some healing stream that could abound and bring, as it were, some water to the parched and withering roots of life was like the balm of hope and grace. Yet (he knew it) such hope was like the dew that dries so early with the morning sun. So often had his inner nature robbed him of his robe of honour that now he'd come to accept his weaknesses as quite incurable. So he safeguarded those weaknesses, eschewing all unnecessary risks, foregoing those earlier, casual liaisons, avoiding where he could the thickets of emotional involvement, playing the odds with infinitely greater caution, and almost persuading himself sometimes that in his own curious fashion he was even becoming a fraction more faithful to Celia. And one thing he knew: he would do anything not to hurt Celia. Well, almost anything.

At ten-fifteen he rang his brother Conrad – Conrad, eighteen months younger than himself, not quite so paunchy, far more civilized, far more kindly, and by some genetic quirk a little greyer at the temples. The two of them had always been good friends, and their business association had invariably been co-operative and mutually profitable. On many occasions in the past Charles had needed to unbosom himself to his brother about some delicate and potentially damaging relationship, and on those occasions Conrad had always shown the same urbanity and understanding.

'You thinking of putting in any appearance today, Conrad? It's after ten, you know.'

'Twenty past, actually, and I'm catching the London train at eleven. Surprised you'd forgotten, Charles. After all, it was you who arranged the visit, wasn't it?'

'Of course, yes! Sorry! I must be getting senile.'

'We're all getting a little older day by day, old boy.'

'Conrad – er – I want you to do me a favour, if you will.'

'Yes?'

'It'll be the last one, I promise you.'

'Can I have that in writing?'

'I almost think you can, yes.'

'Something wrong?'

'Everything's wrong. But I can sort it out, I think – if you can help me. You see, I'd – I'd like an alibi for yesterday afternoon.'

'That's the *second* time this week!' (Was there an unwonted note of tetchiness in Conrad's voice?)

'I know. As I say, though, I promise it won't – '

'Where were we?'

'Er – shall we say we had a meeting with some prospective – '

'Whereabouts?'

'Er – High Wycombe, shall we say?'

'High Wycombe it shall be.'

'The Swedish contract, let's say.'

'Did I drive you there?'

'Er – yes. I – er – we – er – finished about six.'

'About six, I see.'

'This is all just in case, if you see what I mean. I'm sure Celia wouldn't want to go into details, but – '

'Understood, old boy. You can put your mind at rest.'

'Christ, I wish I could!'

'Look, Charles, I must fly. The train's – '

'Yes, of course. Have a good day! And, Conrad – thanks! Thanks a million!'

Charles put down the phone, but almost immediately it rang, and his secretary informed him that there was a call on the outside line: personal and urgent.

'Hello? Charles Richards here. Can I help you?'

'Charles!' The voice was caressing and sensual. 'No need to sound quite so formal, darling.'

'I told you not to ring – ' The irritation in his voice was obvious and genuine, but she interrupted him with easy unconcern.

'You're on your own, darling – I know that. Your secretary said so.'

Charles inhaled deeply. 'What do you want?'

'I want *you*, darling.

'Look – '

'I just wanted to tell you that I had a call from Keith this morning. He's got to stay in South Africa until a week tomorrow. A week tomorrow! So I just wondered whether to put the electric blanket on for half-past one or two o'clock, darling. That's all.'

'Look, Jenny. I – I can't see you today – you know that. It's impossible on Saturdays. I'm sorry, but – '

'Never *mind*, darling! Don't sound so *cross* about it. We can make it tomorrow. I was just hoping – '

'Look!'

'For God's sake stop saying "look"!'

'I'm sorry; but I can't see you again next week, Jenny. It's getting too risky. Yesterday – '

'What the hell *is* this?'

Charles felt a rising tide of despair engulfing him as he thought of her long, blonde, curling hair and the slope of her naked shoulders. 'Look, Jenny,' he said more softly, 'I can't explain now but – '

'Explain? What the hell is there to *explain*?'

'I can't tell you now.' He ground the words into the mouthpiece.

'When shall I see you then?' Her voice sounded brusque and indifferent now.

'I'll get in touch. Not next week, though. I just can't – '

But the line was suddenly dead.

As Charles sat back breathing heavily in his black-leather swivel chair, he was conscious of a hard, constricting pain between his shoulder-blades, and he reached into a drawer for the *Opas* tablets. But the box was empty.

That day *The Oxford Mail* carried a page-two account (albeit a brief and belated one) of the death of Anne Scott at 9 Canal Reach, Jericho; and at various times in the day the account was noticed and read by some tens of thousands of people in the Oxford area, including the Murdoch family, George Jackson, Elsie Purvis, Conrad Richards, Gwendola Briggs, Detective Constable Walters, and Chief Inspector Morse. It was quite by chance that Charles Richards himself was also destined to read it. After three double scotches at *The White Swan*, he had returned home to find the Rolls gone and a note from Celia saying that she had gone shopping in Oxford. 'Back about five – pork-pie in the frig.' And when she had returned home, she'd brought a copy of *The Oxford Mail* with her, throwing it down casually on the coffee table as Charles sat watching the football round-up.

The paper was folded over at page two.

Chapter Nine

Suicide is the worst form of murder, because it leaves no opportunity for repentance

John Collins

The inquest on Ms Anne Scott was one of a string of such melancholy functions for the Coroner's Court on the Tuesday of the following week. Bell had spent the weekend arranging the massive security measures which had surrounded the visit to Oxfordshire of one of the Chinese heads of state; and apart from exhorting Walters to 'stop bloody worriting' he took no further part in the brief proceedings. He had already been informed of the one new – and quite unexpected – piece of evidence that had come to light, but he had betrayed little surprise about it; indeed, felt none.

Walters took the stand to present a full statement about the finding of the body (including the one or two rather odd features of that scene), and about his own subsequent enquiries. The Coroner had only two questions to ask, which he did in a mournful, disinterested monotone; and Walters, feeling considerably less nervous than he'd expected to be, was ready with his firm, unequivocal replies.

'In your opinion, officer, is it true to say that the jury can rule out any suspicion of foul play in the death of Ms Scott?'

'It is, sir.'

'Is there any doubt in your own mind that she met her death by her own hand?'

'No, sir.'

The hump-backed surgeon was the only other witness to be called, and he (as ever) delighted all those anxious to get away from the court by racing through the technical jargon of his medical report with the exhilarating rapidity of an Ashkenazy laying into Liszt. To those with acute hearing and micro-chip mentalities it was further revealed that the woman had probably died between 7 and 9.30 a.m. on the day she was found – that is, she had been dead for approximately eleven hours before being cut down; that her frame was well nourished and that her bodily organs were all perfectly sound; that she was 8–10 weeks pregnant at the time of death. The word 'pregnant' lingered for a while on the air of the still courtroom as if it had been acoustically italicized. But then it was gone, and Bell as he stared down at the wooden flooring silently moved his feet a centimetre or two towards him.

Only one question from the Coroner this time.

'Is there any doubt in your own mind that this woman met her death by her own hand?'

'That is for the jury to decide, sir.'

At this point Bell permitted himself a saddened smile. The surgeon had answered the same question in the same courtroom in the same way for the last twenty years. Only once, when the present Coroner had just begun his term of office, had this guarded comment been queried, and on that occasion the surgeon had deigned to add an equally guarded gloss, at a somewhat decelerated tempo: 'My job, sir, is to certify death where it has occurred and to ascertain, where possible, the physical causes of that death.' That was all. Bell was sometimes surprised that the old boy ever had the temerity to certify death in the first place; and, to be fair, the surgeon himself had grown increasingly reluctant to do so over the past few years. But, at least, that was his province, and he refused to trespass into territory beyond it. As a scientist, he had a profound distrust of all such intangible notions as 'responsibility', 'motive', and 'guilt'; and as a man he had little or no respect for the work of the police force. There was only one policeman he'd ever met for whom he had a slight degree of admiration, and that was Morse. And the only reason for such minimal approbation was that Morse had once told him over a few pints of beer that he in turn had a most profound contempt for the timid twaddle produced by pathologists.

The jury duly recorded a verdict of 'death by suicide', and the small band of variously interested parties filed out of the court-room. Officially, the case of Ms Anne Scott was filed and finished with.

On the evening of the day of the inquest, Morse telephoned the hump-backed surgeon.

'You fancy a drink in an hour or so, Max?'

'No.'

'What's up? You stopped boozing or something?'

'I've started boozing at home. Far cheaper.'

'No licensing hours, either.'

'That's another reason.'

'When do you start?'

'Same time as you, Morse – just before breakfast.'

'Did this Scott woman commit suicide, Max?'

'Oh God! Not you as well!'

'*Did* she commit suicide?'

'I look at the injuries, Morse – you know that, and in this case the injuries were firm and fatal. All right? Who it is who commits the injuries is no concern of mine.'

'Did she commit *suicide*, Max? It's important for me to have your opinion.'

There was a long hesitation on the other end of the line, and the answer obviously cost the surgeon dearly. The answer was 'yes'.

A little later that evening, Detective Constable Walters, in the course of his variegated duties, was seated by the bedside of a young girl in the Intensive Care Unit of the John Radcliffe Two. She had swallowed two bottles of pills without quite succeeding in cutting the thread – sometimes so fragile, sometimes so tough – that holds us all to life.

'It's getting dreadful, all this drugs business,' said the sister as Walters was leaving. 'I don't know! We're getting them in all the time. Another one besides her today.' She pointed to a closed white door a little further down the corridor, and Walters nodded with a surface understanding but with no real sympathy: he had quite enough to cope with as it was. In fact, as he walked along the polished corridor he passed within two feet of the door that the Sister had pointed out to him. And, if Walters had only known, he was at that very second within those same two feet of finding out the truth of what was later to be called The Case of the Jericho Killings.

BOOK TWO

Chapter Ten

There's not a note of mine that's worth the noting
Much Ado about Nothing Act II, scene iii

On Saturday, 13th October, four days following the inquest on Anne Scott, a man knocked on the door of 2 Canal Reach, and told the heavily pregnant, nervous-looking young woman who answered the door that he was writing an article for the Bodleian archives on the socio-economic development of Jericho during the latter half of the nineteenth century. Not surprisingly, he elicited little information likely to further his researches, and was soon knocking at number 4: this time with no answer. At number 6 he was brusquely told to 'bugger off' by a middle-aged giant of a man, heavily tattooed from wrists to muscular shoulders, who supposed the caller to be some peripatetic proselytiser. But at number 8, the slim, pale-faced, bespectacled young man who opened the door proved a gushing fount of information on the history of the area, and very soon the researcher was filling his amateurish-looking, red-covered Cash Book with rapid notes and dates: 'Key decade 1821–31 – see monograph Eliza M. Hawtrey (? 1954) Bodleian – if they'd ever let me in – variable roof lines, brick built, sash-windowed – I went down to Jericho and fell among thieves – artisan dwellings – there was a young fellow from Spain – Lucy's Iron Works 1825 – who enjoyed a tart – OUP to its pres. site 1826 – now and again – Canal: Oxford-Banbury-Coventry-Midlands, compl. 1790 – not just now and again but – St Paul's begun 1835 – now and again and – St Barnabas 1869 – again and again and again'.

'Marvellous, marvellous!' said the researcher as the young man at last showed the first welcome signs of flagging. 'Most interesting and – and so valuable. You're a local historian, I suppose?'

'Not really, no. I work on the line up at Cowley.'

With further profuse expressions of gratitude for a lengthy addendum on the construction of the railway, the researcher finally saw the door to number 8 close – and he breathed a sigh of relief. Most of the other residents in the Reach would now have seen him, and his purpose was progressing nicely. No answer from number 10; no bicycle there, either. Over the narrow – ridiculously narrow – street, and no answer from number 9, either, in spite of three fairly rigorous bouts of knocking, during the third of which he had surreptitiously tried the door-knob. Locked. At number 7 he introduced himself with a most ingratiating smile, and Mrs Purvis, on hearing of his projected monograph for the Royal Architectural Society on the lay-out of the two-up, two-down, dwellings of the mid-Victorian era, duly invited him into her home. Ten minutes later he was seated in the little scullery at the back of the house drinking a cup of tea and (as Mrs Purvis was to tell her married daughter the next day) proving to be 'such a charming, well-educated sort of person'.

'I see you grow your own vegetables,' said Morse, getting to his feet and looking out onto the narrow garden plot beyond the dark-green doors of what looked like an outside lavatory-cum-coal-shed. 'Very sensible, too! Do you know, I bought a caulie up in Summertown the other day and it cost me . . .'

Willingly, it appeared, Mrs Purvis would have spent the rest of the day discussing the price of vegetables, and Morse had no difficulty in pressing home his advantage.

'What's your soil like here, Mrs Purvis? Sort of clayey, is

it? Or,' – Morse hunted around in his mind for some other vaguely impressive epithet – 'alkaline, perhaps?'

'I don't *really* know too much about that sort of thing.'

'I could tell you if . . .'

They were soon standing in the garden, where Morse scooped up a handful of soil from a former potato furrow and let it trickle slowly through his fingers. His eyes missed nothing. The wall between number 7 and number 9 was a lowish red-brick affair, flaked into lighter patches by the tooth of countless frosts; and beyond that wall . . . Morse could see it all now. What, in Mrs Purvis's house, had been the original low-ceilinged scullery had there been converted into a higher, longer extension, with the line of the slates carried forward, albeit at a shallower angle, to roof it. Beyond that, and shielding the plot from the boat-building sheds which fronted the canal, was a wall some eight feet high – a wall (as Morse could see) which had recently been repaired at one point.

Interesting . . . Tonight, perhaps?

It says something for Morse that he proceeded to knock (though very gently) on the doors of numbers 5, 3, and 1 of the Reach, and he was fortunate to the extent that the first two were either at that moment empty or tenanted by the slightly hard-of-hearing. At number 1 he satisfied his talent for improvisation by asking the very old man who answered the door if a Mr – Mr er – Green lived anywhere about; and was somewhat taken aback to see an arthritic finger pointing firmly across to number 8 – the abode of the polymath from the car-line at Cowley.

'Haven't I seen you somewhere afore, mister?' asked the old man, peering closely at him.

A rather flustered Morse confessed that he'd often been in the district doing a bit of local research ('For the library, you know'), and stayed talking long enough to learn that the old boy spent a couple of hours across at *The Printer's Devil* every evening. 'Eight o'clock to ten o'clock, mister. Reg'lar as clockwork – like me bowels.'

If it was going to be tonight, it had better be between 8 and 10 p.m., then. Why not? Easy!

Morse was more honest (well, a little more honest) with the locksmith – the same locksmith whom Walters had visited and questioned a week earlier. Introducing himself as a chief inspector of police, Morse stated (which was quite true) that he had to get into number 9 Canal Reach again, and (which, of course, was quite untrue) that he'd left his key at the police station. It was a bit of a nuisance, he knew, but could . . . ? Mr Grimes, however, was unable to oblige: there wasn't a single key in the shop that could fit the front door of number 9. He could always open the lock himself, though; could open *any* door. Did Morse want him to . . . ? No! That was the last thing Morse wanted.

'Look,' said Morse. 'I know I can trust you. You see, we've had some outside information about the trouble there – you remember? – the suicide. The big thing is that we don't want the neighbours to be worried or suspicious at all. And the truth is that my incompetent sergeant has er temporarily misplaced both the keys – '

'You mean *three* keys, don't you, inspector?'

The locksmith proceeded to give an account of his earlier visit from Walters, and Morse listened and learned – and wondered.

'I didn't tell him about the back door key, though,' continued the locksmith. 'It didn't seem important, if you follow me, and he didn't ask me, anyway.'

Two minutes and one £5 note later, Morse left the shop with a key which (he was assured) would fit the back door lock of number 9: Grimes himself had fitted the lock some six months earlier and could remember exactly which type it was. 'Keep all this quiet, won't you?' Morse had said, but he'd found no kindred spirit in the locksmith. And how foolish and risky it all was! Yet so much of Morse's life was exactly that, and now, at least, his mind was urgently engaged. It made him feel strangely content. He walked up Great Clarendon Street and saw (as Walters had seen) St Paul's now facing him at the top of Walton Street. 'Begun 1835,' he said to himself. Even his memory was sharpening up again.

Chapter Eleven

He can't write, nor rade writing from his cradle, please your honour; but he can make his mark equal to another, sir

Maria Edgeworth, *Love and Law*

It was the same morning, the morning of Saturday, 13th October, that Charles Richards had received the letter at his home address. The postage stamp (first class) corner of the cover had been doubly cancelled – the first postmark clearly showing 'Oxford, 8 Oct.', with the second, superimposed mark blurred and illegible. Nor was the reason for the delayed delivery difficult to see, for the original address was printed as 61 (instead of 261) Oxford Avenue, Abingdon, Nr. Oxford, and someone (doubtless the householder at number 61) had been aware of the mistake, had re-addressed the envelope correctly, and had put the letter back in the pillar box. The clean, white envelope (with 'Private' printed across the top-left of the cover) was neatly sealed with Sellotape, with the name and address written in capital letters by what seemed a far from educated hand. 'Abingdon' was mis-spelt (the 'g' omitted), and each of the lines gradually veered from the horizontal towards the bottom of the envelope, as if the correspondent were not particularly practised in any protracted activity with the pen. Inside the cover was another envelope, of the same brand, folded across the middle, the name 'Charles Richards' printed on it in capitals, with the words 'Strictly Personal' written immediately above. Richards slit this second envelope with rather more care than he had done the first, and took out the single sheet of good quality paper. There was no address, no signature, and no date:

Dear Mister Richards
Its about Missis Scott who died, I now all about you and her but does Missis Richards. I now ALL about it, I hope you beleive me because if you dont I am going to tell her everything, You dont want that. I am not going to tell her if you agree, You are rich and what is a thousand pounds. If you agree I will not bother to rite again, I keep all promisses beleive that. The police dont now anything and I have never said what I now. Here is what you do, You go down to Walton Street in Jericho and turn left into Walton Well Road and then strate on over the little Canal brige and then over the railway brige and you come to a parking area where you cant go much further, then turn round and face Port Medow and you will see a row of willow trees, the fifth from the left has got a big hole in it about five feet from the ground. So put the money there and drive away, I will be waching all the time. I will give you a ring soon and that will be only once. I hope you will not try anything funny. Please remember your wife.

Although the writing was crudely printed, with several words written out in individual, unjoined characters, the message was surprisingly coherent – and disturbing. Yet as Charles Richards read it, his mind seemed curiously detached: it was almost as if the writing had been submitted to him as a piece of English prose that had to be corrected and commented upon – its message secondary and of comparatively little significance. He read the letter through a second time, and then a third, and then a fourth; but if a hidden observer had recorded the conflicting emotions of puzzlement, anger, and even anxiety, that played upon his face, there was never the slightest hint of panic or despair. For Charles Richards was a clever and resourceful man, and he now refolded the letter, replaced it in its envelope and put it, together with the outer cover, inside his wallet.

Five minutes later he waited for a few seconds by Celia's bedside as she sat up, drew a cardigan round her shoulders, and took the breakfast tray of orange juice, tea, and toast. He kissed her lightly on the forehead, told her that he had to go into Oxford, that he'd take the Mini, and that he'd certainly be home for lunch about one. Was there anything he could get her from the shops? He'd perhaps have to nip into Oxford again in the evening, too.

Celia Richards heard him go, a great burden of anxiety weighing on her mind. How could a man so treacherous seem so kind? It had been an extraordinary coincidence that the first copy of *The Oxford Mail* she'd read for months had contained that account of Anne Scott's death, and she felt quite sure that Charles had read the article, too. Had he been responsible for that terrible thing? She couldn't really know and, to be truthful, she didn't care much either. What she *did* know was that their life together just couldn't go on as it had been. Putting things off was merely aggravating that almost intolerable burden, and she would put it off no longer. He'd said he'd be in for lunch; and after lunch ... Yes! She would tell him *then*. Tell him all she knew; tell him the truth. It was the only way – the only way for *her*. Conrad had counselled against it, but Conrad would understand. Conrad always understood ... She munched the tasteless toast and drank the luke-warm tea. Oxford ... He'd always insisted how important it was for him to put in a few hours at the office on Saturday mornings. So why Oxford? With Anne Scott dead, what could possibly be dragging him to Oxford?

In the Intensive Care Unit at the J.R.2, Doctor Philips walked from the side of the youth lying motionless beneath the startlingly white sheets, and pulled out the chart from the slot at the foot of the bed: temperature still high, pulse still rather disturbingly variable.

'Bloody fool!' he mumbled to the nurse who stood beside him.

'Will he be all right?' she asked.

Philips shrugged his shoulders. 'Doubt it. Once you start on that sort of stuff ...'

'Do we know what stuff it was?'

'Can't be sure, really. Cocaine, I shouldn't wonder, though. High temperature, dilatation of the pupils, sweating, gooseflesh, hypertension – all the usual symptoms. Took it intravenously, too, by the look of things. Which doesn't help, of course.'

'Will he get over *this*, I mean?'

'If he does it'll be thanks to you, nurse – no one else.'

Nurse Warrener felt pleased with the compliment, and just a little more hopeful than she had been. She thought she could perhaps get to like Michael Murdoch. He was only a boy really: well, nineteen according to the records – exactly the same age as she was – and a prospective undergraduate at Lonsdale College. What a tragedy it would be if his life were now to be completely ruined! She thought of Michael's mother, too – a brisk, energetic-looking woman who seemed on the face of it to be taking things none too badly, but who (as Nurse Warrener rightly suspected) was hiding behind that competent, no-nonsense mien the ghost of some distraught despair.

Chapter Twelve

Sophocles lived through a cycle of events spatially narrow, no doubt, in the scale of national and global history, but without parallel in intensity of action and emotion

From the Introduction to *Sophocles, The Theban Plays*, Penguin Classics

The gates of the boat-yard were open as Morse moved swiftly along Canal Reach that night, no lights showing in the fronts of either 9 or 10. It was just before 9 p.m., and the Lancia stood on double yellow lines outside *The Printer's Devil*, into which Morse had slipped a quarter of an hour earlier, not only to establish some spurious *raison d'être* for his presence in the area, but also to down a couple of double Scotches.

Once inside the yard, he turned immediately to his left and felt his way along the brick wall, treading cautiously amid the petrol drums, the wooden spars, and the assorted, derelict débris of old canal barges. There was no one about, and the boatman's hut just ahead of him was securely padlocked. The only noise was a single splash of some water-bird behind the low bulk of the house-boat moored alongside the canal, and the moon had drifted darkly behind the scudding clouds.

With the level of the wharf a foot or so higher than the street behind it, the wall was not going to pose such a problem as Morse had feared, and standing on one of the petrol drums, he peered cautiously over the recently repaired section of the wall. No lights shone in the back rooms of numbers 9, 7 or 5. He hoisted himself up and. keeping his body as close to the top of the wall as he could, dropped down on the other side, feeling a sharp spasm of pain as his right foot crushed a small, terra-cotta flower pot beneath. The noise startled him, and his heart pounded as he stood for several minutes beside the deep shadow of the wall. But nothing moved; no lights came on; and he stepped silently along to the back door, let himself in, stood inside the kitchen, and waited until his eyes could slowly accustom themselves to the darkness. The door immediately to his right would lead, he guessed, to a small bathroom and wc; to his left, the door at the other side of the kitchen would lead (he knew) directly into the lounge. And lifting the latch of the latter, he pulled it open, the bottom of the lower panel scraping raspingly along the floor. Inside the lounge, he felt on familiar territory, and taking a torch from his raincoat pocket he carefully shielded the light with his left hand as he made his way up to the back bedroom. He had already decided that it would be far too risky to venture into the front bedroom, let alone switch on any lights; and so he spent the next half hour by torchlight looking through the drawers of the desk in what had clearly been the woman's study, feeling like some scrawny bird of prey that is left with the offal after the depredations of the jackals and hyenas. Finally he pocketed one book, shone his torch timorously around the room, and nodded with sad approval as the light picked out the black spines of a whole shelf of Penguin Classical Authors, correctly ordered in alphabetical sequence through from Aeschylus to Xenophon. One little gap, though, wasn't there? And Morse frowned slightly as he shone the torch more closely. Yes, a gap between Seneca's *Tragedies* and Suetonius' *Lives of the Caesars*. What could that be? Sophocles, perhaps? Yes, almost certainly Sophocles. So what? So bloody what? Morse shrugged his shoulders, pulled the door to behind him, and stepped carefully down the narrow, squeaking stairs.

Standing motionless for a few seconds in the lounge, he was suddenly aware how very cold the house was, and his mind momentarily settled on the household's heating arrangements. No central heating system, that was clear. No night-storage heaters, either, by the look of things; and the only heating appliance so far encountered was that small electric fire upstairs. A coal fire, perhaps? Surely there'd be a grate here somewhere. His torch still turned off, Morse stepped across the carpeted floor – and there it was in the far wall, surrounded by the lightish-coloured tiles of the fixture. Yes, he remembered it now; and bending down he felt with his right hand along the iron grill. Something there. He switched the torch on right up against the back of the grate, and then slowly allowed the beam to illuminate whatever there was to be seen. It wasn't much: the blackened, curled remains of what had probably been a sheet of notepaper, the flimsy fragments floating down and disintegrating as his delicate fingers touched them. But even as they did so, the torch-light picked out a small piece of something white in the ash-pan below, and Morse pulled away the front and gently picked it out. It seemed to be part of the heading of an official letter, printed in small black capitals, and even now Morse could quite easily make out the letters: ICH. Then he found another tiny piece; and although the flames had obviously curled across it, leaving the surface a smoky brown, it seemed clear to him that it was probably part of the same line of print. KAT, was it? Or RAT, more likely? He inserted the pieces between two pages of the book he had pocketed from upstairs, and his mind was already bounding down improbable avenues. Many of the books and papers he'd looked through upstairs were linked in some way with German literature, and he remembered from his schooldays that '*Ich rat*' meant 'I judged' or 'I thought'. Something like that anyway. He could always look it up later, of course, although it promptly occurred to him that he would hardly be overmuch enlightened if his memory proved to have been reliable. And then as he stood in that cold, dark room beside the fire-less grate another thought occurred to him: what an idiot – what a stupid idiot – he was! It was that first, cowardly evasion of the truth that had caused it all – all because he didn't want it to be known that he'd been floating around in Jericho looking for some necessary sex one afternoon. Suddenly, he felt a little frightened, too ...

He locked the back door behind him, walked down the strip of garden, and looked for a place in the wall where he could get something of a foot-hold in order to scale what, from this side, appeared a most formidable precipice. What if he couldn't manage ... But then Morse saw it. At the foot of the wall was a wooden board, about one foot square, on which someone had recently been mixing small quantities of cement, and beside it a bricklayer's trowel. The shudder that passed through Morse at that moment was not of fear – but of excitement. With his crisis of confidence now passed, his brain was sweetly clear once more. Spontaneously it told him, too, of a dustbin somewhere nearby; and he found it almost immediately, moved it against the wall, and standing on it clambered to the top. Easy! He breathed a great sigh of relief as he landed safely inside the boat-yard, where the gates were still open, and whence he made his exit without further alarum.

As he walked into Canal Reach, keeping tightly to his right, a hand clamped upon his shoulder with an iron grip, and a voice whispered harshly in his ear: 'Just keep walking, mister!'

At about the same time that Morse was entering the house in Canal Reach, a Mini-Clubman turned down into the northern stretch of the Woodstock Road, having travelled into Oxford from Abingdon via the western Ring Road. The car kept closely into the bus-lane, crawling along at about 10 m.p.h. past the large, elegant houses, set back on higher ground behind the tall hedges that masked their wide fronts and provided a quiet privacy for their owners. The driver pulled the car completely over on to the pavement beside a telephone kiosk on his left, turned off the lights, got out, entered the kiosk, and picked up the receiver. The dialling tone told him that the phone was probably in working order, and keeping the instrument to his ear he turned round and looked up and down the road. No one was in sight. He stepped out and, as if searching his pockets for some coinage, carefully examined the surrounds of the kiosk. The stone wall behind it was luxuriantly clad with thick ivy, and he pushed his hands against it, seeming to be satisfied that all was well. He got back into the Mini and drove along the road for about fifty yards, before stopping again and taking note of the name of the road that stretched quite steeply off on his left. He then drove the short distance down to Squitchey Lane, turned left, left at the Banbury Road, left into Sunderland Avenue, and finally left again into the Woodstock Road. For the moment there was no traffic and he drove slowly once more along the self-same stretch of road. Then, nodding to himself with apparent satisfaction, he accelerated away.

The plan was laid.

Michael Murdoch opened his eyes at about ten minutes to ten that evening to find the same pretty face looking down at him. He noticed with remarkable vividness the strong white teeth, a gold filling somewhere towards the extremity of her smile, and he heard her speak.

'Feeling better?'

Momentarily he was feeling nothing, not even a sense of puzzlement, and in a dry-throated whisper he managed to answer 'Yes'. But as he lay back and closed his eyes again, his head was drifting off in a giddying whirl and the body it had left behind seemed slowly to be slipping from the sloping bed.

He felt a cold, restraining hand on his drenched forehead, and immediately he was back inside his skull once more, with a giant, brown rat that sat at the entrance of his right ear, twitching its nose and ever edging menacingly forward, its long tail insinuating itself centimetre by centimetre into the gaping orifice, and the long white slits of teeth drawing nearer and nearer to a vast and convoluted dome of pale-white matter that even now he recognized: it was his own matter, his own flesh, *his own brain.*

He heard himself shriek out in terror.

Miss Catharine Edgeley returned to Oxford that night. Her mother had died of a brain tumour; her mother was now buried. And there was little room in Miss Edgeley's mind that night for any thoughts of the last time she had played bridge in North Oxford. Indeed, she had no knowledge at that time that Anne Scott, too, was dead.

Chapter Thirteen

Sit Pax in Valle Tamesis
Motto of The Thames Valley Police Authority

Morse's mind was curiously detached as he 'kept walking', eyes frozen forward, along the short length of Canal Reach. With Teutonic recollections the order of the night, he recalled that in Germany the situation might have been regarded as serious but not hopeless, in Austria, hopeless but not serious. Or was it the other way round? To his astonishment, however, he found himself being firmly manipulated towards a police car, parked just round the corner, its gaily-coloured emblem illuminated by the orange glare of a street lamp. And as he reached the car and turned about, he found himself looking slightly upwards into the face of a rather frightened-looking young man.

'*You*, sir!' It was Detective Constable Walters who was the first to speak, and Morse's shoulders sagged with a combination of relief and exasperation.

'Are you in the habit of arresting your superior officers, constable?'

A flustered Walters followed the Lancia up to Morse's North-Oxford flat, where over a few whiskies the two of them sat and talked until way after midnight. On his own side, Morse came almost completely clean, omitting only any mention of his bribing of the Jericho locksmith. For his part, Walters admitted to his own anxiety about Morse's behaviour, recounted in detail his own investigations, and revealed that after working late in St Aldates that night he had been on his way to return the few items taken from Canal Reach when he had seen the yellow glow flitting about the dark and silent rooms. Throughout Walters' somewhat discontinuous narrative, Morse remained silent, attentive, and seemingly impassive. When Walters had mentioned the strange discoveries of the chair in the kitchen and the key on the door-mat, Morse had nodded non-committally, as though the incidents were either of little moment or perfectly explicable. Only during Walters' account of his visit to the Summertown Bridge Club had Morse's eyes appeared to harden to a deeper blue.

'You're in a tricky position, young fellow,' said Morse finally. 'You find a superior officer snooping around in an empty house – a house in which he'd poked his nose the day the dead woman was found – an officer who had no more right to be there than a fourth-grade burglar – so what do you do, Walters?'

'I just don't know, sir.'

'I'll tell you what you *ought* to have done.' The sudden sharp edge on Morse's voice made Walters look up anxiously. 'If you had any nous at all you would have asked me how I *got in*. Not really good enough, was it?'

Walters opened his mouth to say something, but Morse continued. 'How long have you been in the Force?'

'Eighteen months altogether, but only three – '

'You've got a lot to learn.'

'I'm learning all the time, sir.'

Morse grinned at the young man. 'Well, you've got something else to learn, and that's exactly what your duty has got to be now. And in case you don't know, I'll tell you. It's your duty to report everything that's happened tonight to Chief Inspector Bell, agreed?'

Walters nodded. The point had been worrying him sorely, and he felt glad that Morse had made things so easy for him. Again he was about to say something, but again he was interrupted.

'But not just yet, understand? I'll see the Assistant Chief Constable first and explain the whole position. You see, Walters, there's something a bit odd about this business; something that needs an older and a wiser head than yours.'

He poured another liberal dose of whisky into Walters' glass, another into his own, and spent the next half hour asking Walters about his training, his prospects and his ambition; and Walters responded fully and eagerly to such sympathetic interest. At half-past midnight he felt the profound wish that he could work with this man; and at a quarter to one, when about to leave, he was only too happy to leave with Morse the items he had originally set out to deposit in the house on Canal Reach.

'How *did* you get in there, sir?' he asked on the doorstep. 'Did you have a key or – '

'When you've been around as long as I have, constable, you'll find you don't need a key to get through most doors. You see, the lock on the back door there is a Yale, and with a Yale the bevel's always facing you when you're on the outside. So if you take a credit card and slip it in, you'll find it's just strong enough and just flexible enough to – '

'I know, sir. I've seen it done on the telly.'

'Oh.'

'And er the lock on the back door there *isn't* a Yale, is it? Goodnight, sir. And thanks for the whisky.'

Morse spent the next hour or so looking through the two

Letts' diaries now in his possession, the one (for the current year) just handed to him by Walters, the other (for the previous year) taken a few hours earlier from Canal Reach. If Walters could be trusted, no letters of even minimal significance had been found in the drawers of the desk; and so the diaries were probably as near as anyone could ever come to unlocking the secret life of the late Anne Scott. Not that the entries seemed to Morse particularly promising. Times, mostly: times of trains; times of social events; times of pupils' lessons – yes, that was doubtless the meaning of those scores of initials scattered throughout the pages, several of them recurring at regular (often weekly) intervals over months, and in a few cases over a year or more. The 'E.M.' entry on the Wednesday she'd died held his attention for a while – as he knew it must have held the attention of Walters and of Bell. But, like them, he could only think of one person with those same initials: himself. And he had never quite forgiven his parents for christening their only offspring as they had.

Morse slept soundly, and woke late next morning, his brain clear and keen. The images and impressions of all he had learned had flashed across his mind but once, yet already the hooks and eyes of his memories were beginning to combine in strange and varied patterns.

Almost all of them wrong.

Chapter Fourteen

Chaos preceded Cosmos, and it is into Chaos without form and void that we have plunged

John Livingston Lowes, *The Road to Xanadu*

Mrs Gwendola Briggs was very soon aware of the different nature of the beast when, on the following Monday, Morse, after a rather skimped day's work at the Thames Valley HQ, finally found time to pursue his unofficial and part-time course of enquiries. This man (it seemed to Gwendola) was quite unnecessarily objectionable and bullying in the series of questions he bombarded her with. Who was there that night? Where had they sat? What were the topics of conversation? Had anyone cancelled? Had anyone turned up at the last minute? Were the bridge-pads still there? Exactly what time had they finished? Where were the cars parked? How many cars? It was all quite flustering for her, and quite unlike the vague and pleasant questions that the big and gentle constable had asked her. *This* man irritated her, making her feel almost guilty about not quite being able to remember things. Yet it was surprising (as she later confessed to herself) how much he'd compelled her to remember; and as Morse prepared to take his leave, holding the list of the names and addresses of those who had attended the bridge evening, he felt adequately satisfied. With the losing pair of each rubber (as he had learned) staying at the same table, and the winning pair moving along, it seemed more than likely that Anne had spoken with everyone there, at least for some intermittent minutes.

'Oh, yes. There *was* something else a little unusual about that night, Inspector. You see, it was our first anniversary, and we had a break about eleven to celebrate. You know, a couple of glasses of sherry to mark the occasion – drink to our future success and – ' Gwendola suddenly broke off, conscious of her tactlessness. But Morse refused to rescue her.

'I'm sorry. I didn't mean to – Oh dear! What a tragedy it all is!'

'Did you meet last week, Mrs Briggs?'

'Yes, we did. We meet every – '

'You didn't feel that because of the er tragedy that – '

'Life must go on, mustn't it, Inspector?'

Morse's sour expression seemed to suggest that there was probably little justification for such continuance in the case of this mean-minded little woman, doubtless ever dreaming of over-tricks and gleefully doubling the dubious contracts of the recently initiated. But he made no answer as his eyes skimmed down the list she had given him. 'Mrs Murdoch'! Was that the same one? The same Mrs Murdoch who had invited him to the party when he and Anne . . . ? Surely it was! His thoughts floated back to that first – no, that only – evening when he and Anne had met; the evening when but for the cussedness of human affairs he – Augh! Forget it! *Should* he forget it, though? Had there been *something* he had learned that evening that he should, and must, remember? Already he had tried to dredge up what he could, but the simple truth was that he'd drunk too much on that occasion. Come to think of it, though, there was that bit of research he'd heard of only the previous week. Some team of educational psychologists in Oxford was suggesting that if you'd revised whilst you were drunk, and turned up sober for the next day's examinations, you'd be lucky to remember anything at all. Likewise, if you'd revised in a comparatively sober state of mind and then turned up drunk, you'd hardly stand much chance of self-distinction. But (and this was the point) if you'd revised whilst drunk, and maintained a similar degree of inebriation during the examination itself, then all was likely to be well. Interesting. Yes . . . Morse felt sure there *was* something he'd heard from Anne that night. Something. Almost he had it as he stood there on the doorstep; but it slipped away and left him frustrated and irritated. The sooner he got drunk, the better!

As he finally took his leave, he realized how less than gracious he'd been to the chairman of the Summertown Bridge Club.

When the door opened, Morse recognized one of the Murdoch boys he'd seen at the party, and his memory struggled for the name.

'Michael, is it?'

'No. I'm Ted.'

'Oh, yes. Is your mother in, Ted?'

'No. She's gone down to the hospital. It's Michael.'

'Road accident?' What made Morse suggest such a possible

cause of hospitalization, he could not have said; but he noticed the boy's quite inexplicable unease.

'No. He's – he's been on drugs.'

'Oh dear! Bad, is he?'

The boy swallowed. 'Pretty bad, yes.'

Things were beginning to stir a little in Morse's mind now. Yes. This was the *younger* brother he was talking to, by quite a few inches the taller of the two and slightly darker in complexion, due to sit his A-level examinations – which year had Mrs Murdoch said that was? Then it hit him. E.M. . . . Edward Murdoch! Wednesday afternoons. And (it flooded back) for the latter part of the previous year and the present year up until June, the initials M.M., too, had appeared regularly in the diaries: Michael Murdoch.

Morse took the plunge. 'Weren't you due for a lesson with Ms Scott the day she committed suicide?' His eyes left the boy's face not for the flutter of an eye-lash as he asked the brutal question; but, in turn, the boy's brown eyes were unblinking as a chameleon's.

'Yes, I was.'

'Did you go?'

'No. She told me the previous week that she – wouldn't be able to see me.'

'I see.' Morse had noticed the hesitation, and a wayward fancy crossed his mind. 'Did you like her?' he asked simply.

'Yes, I did.' The voice, like the eyes, was firm – and oddly gentle.

Morse was tempted to pursue the theme, but switched instead to something different.

'A-levels this year?'

The boy nodded. 'German, French, and Latin.'

'You confident?'

'Not really.'

'Shouldn't worry too much about that,' said Morse in an objectionably avuncular tone. 'Over-rated quality confidence is.' (Weren't those the words of Mrs Murdoch, though? Yes, the memories of the night were stronger now.) 'Hard work – that's the secret. Put your foot through the telly, or something.' Morse heard himself drooling on tediously, and saw the boy looking at him with a hint of contempt in those honest eyes.

'I was working when you called, actually, Inspector.'

'Jolly good! Well, I er I mustn't interrupt you any longer, must I?' He turned to leave. 'By the way, did Ms Scott ever say anything to you about her – well, her private life?'

'Is that what you wanted to see mum about?'

'Partly, yes.'

'She never said anything to me about it.' The boy's words were almost aggressive, and Morse felt puzzled.

'What about your brother? Did he ever say anything?'

'Say anything about what?'

'Forget it, lad! Just tell your mother I called, will you? And that I'll be calling again, all right?' For a few seconds his harsh blue eyes fixed Edward's, and then he turned around and walked away.

It says little for Morse's thoroughness that Miss Catharine Edgeley (next on his list and living so close to the Murdochs) was to be the last of the bridge party destined to be interviewed. Yes, she realized now, there *was* something that might be valuable for him to know: Anne had asked her to drop a note through the Murdochs' letter box, a note in a white, sealed envelope, addressed to Edward Murdoch.

'Why didn't you give it to Mrs Murdoch?'

'I'm not sure, really. I think, yes, I think she left just a bit before the others. Perhaps her table had finished and if she wasn't in line for any of the prizes ... I forget. Anyway, Anne wrote –'

'She wrote it *there*?'

'Yes, she wrote it on the sideboard. I remember that. She had a silver Parker –'

'Did she seem worried?'

'I don't *think* so, no. A bit flushed, perhaps – but we'd all had a few drinks and –'

'What were you all talking about? Try to remember, please!'

Catharine shook her pretty head. 'I can't. I'm sorry, Inspector, but –'

'Think!' pleaded Morse.

And so she tried to think: think what people normally spoke about – the weather, work, inflation, gossip, children ... And slowly she began to form a hazy recollection about an interlude. It was about children, surely ... Yes, they were talking at one stage about children: something to do with the Oxfam appeal for the Cambodian refugees, was it? Or Korean? Somewhere in that part of the world, anyway.

Morse groaned inwardly as she tried to give some sort of coherence to thoughts so inchoate and so confused. But she'd told him about the note, and that was something.

Unfortunately, the item of far greater importance she'd just imparted was completely lost on Morse. At least for the moment.

Chapter Fifteen

Well, time cures hearts of tenderness, and now I can let her go
Thomas Hardy, *Wessex Heights*

Over breakfast on Tuesday morning, Morse read his one item of mail with mild, half-engaged interest. It was the Oxford Book Association's monthly newsletter, giving a full account of Dame Helen's memorable speech, discussing the possibility of a Christmas Book Fair, reporting the latest deliberations of the committee, and then – Morse stopped and stared very hard. *It was with deep regret that we heard of the death of Anne Scott. Anne had served on the committee only since the beginning of this year, but her good humour, constructive suggestions, and invariable willingness to help even in the most routine and humdrum chores – all these will be sadly missed. The chairman represented the Association at Anne's funeral.* Well, that was news to Morse. Perhaps – no, almost certainly – he would have seen Anne at that last meeting if things had turned out differently. And if only he'd been a regular member, he would have seen her often. If only! He sighed and knew that life was full of 'if onlys' for everyone. Then he turned the page and the capital letters of the corrigendum jumped out at him. 'The next meeting NOTE THE CHANGE PLEASE will be on Friday, 19th October, when the speaker (this as previously advertised) will be MR CHARLES RICHARDS. His subject *Triumphs and Tribulations of the Small Publisher* will be of particular interest to many of our members and we look forward to a large attendance. Mr Richards apologizes for the late notification of the change which is necessitated because of business commitments.' Morse made a brief note in his diary: there was nothing else doing that evening. He might go. On the whole, he thought not, though.

When the phone rang at 10.30 a.m. the same morning, Charles Richards was in his office. Normally the call would have filtered from the outer office through his secretary, but she was now sitting opposite him taking down short-hand (interspersed, Richards noticed, with rather too many pieces of long-hand to give him much real confidence in her stenographic skills). He picked up the phone himself.

'Richards here. Can I help you?'

A rather faint, working-class voice replied that he (it was a 'he', surely?) was sure as 'ow Mister Charles Richards *could* 'elp; and at the first mention of his wife, Richards clamped his hand over the mouthpiece, told his secretary to leave him for a few minutes, waited for the door to close, and then spoke slowly and firmly into the phone.

'I don't know who you are and I don't *want* to know, you blackmailing rat! But I believe what you said in your letter and I've made arrangements to get the money – exactly *one quarter* of what you asked for, do you understand me?'

There was no reply.

'There's no chance of my agreeing to the arrangements you made – absolutely none. So listen carefully. Tomorrow night – got that? – tomorrow night I shall be driving slowly down the Woodstock Road – from the roundabout at the top – at half-past eight. Exactly half-past eight. I shall be driving a light-blue Rolls Royce, and I shall stop just inside a road called Field House Drive – two words: "Field House". It's just above Squitchey Lane. I shall get out there and I shall be carrying a brown carrier bag. Then I shall walk up to the telephone kiosk about fifty yards north of Field House Drive, go into the kiosk, and then come out again and put the carrier bag behind the kiosk, just inside the ivy there. *Behind* the kiosk – got that? – not inside it. It will be absolutely safe, you can take my word on that. I shall then walk straight back to the car and drive back up the Woodstock Road. Do you understand all that?'

Still no reply.

'There'll be no funny business on my part, and there'd better be none on yours! You can pick up your money – it's yours. But there'll not be a penny more – you can take that as final. Absolutely final. And if you *do* try anything else like this again, I'll kill you, do you hear that? I'll kill you with my own hands, you snivelling swine!'

Throughout this monologue, Richards had been continuously aware of the harsh, wheezy breathing of the man on the other end of the line, and now he waited for whatever reply might be forthcoming. But there was none.

'Have you got it all straight?'

Finally, he heard the tight voice again. 'You'll be glad you done this, Mister Richards. So will Missis Richards.' With that, the line was dead.

Charles Richards put away the sheet of paper from which he had been reading, and immediately called in his secretary once more.

'Sorry about that. Where were we . . . ?' He sounded completely at ease, but his heart was banging hard against his rib-cage as he dictated the next letter.

Mr Parkes was old, and would soon die. For the last few years he had been drinking heavily, but he had no regrets about that. Looking back over his life, however, he felt it had been largely wasted. Even his twenty years as headmaster of a primary school in Essex seemed to him now a period of little real achievement. A great addict from his early boyhood of all types of puzzles – mathematical problems, crosswords, chess, bridge – he had never found his proper niche. And as he sat drinking another bottle of Diet lager he regretted for the millionth time that no academic body had ever offered him a grant to set his mind to Etruscan or Linear C. He could have cracked those stubborn codes by now! Oh yes!

He had stopped thinking about Anne Scott several days ago.

Mrs Raven was discussing with her husband the final stages of their long-drawn-out (but now at last successful) campaign to adopt a baby. Both of them had been much surprised at the countless provisos and caveats surrounding such an innocent and benevolent-sounding process: the forms in duplicate and triplicate; the statements of incomes, job prospects, religious persuasions, and family history; oaths and solemn undertakings that the prospective parents would 'make no attempt whatsoever to discover the names, dwellings, situations, or any other relevant details of the former parent(s), neither to seek to ascertain' – etc., etc., etc. Oh dear! Mrs Raven had felt almost guilty about everything, especially since it was she herself, according to the gynaecologist, who was thwarting her husband's frequent and frenetic attempts to propagate the Raven species. Still, things were nearly ready now, and she was so looking forward to getting the baby. She'd have to stay at home much more, of course. No more badminton evenings for a while; no more bridge parties.

She had stopped thinking about Anne Scott several days ago.

Catharine Edgeley was busy writing an essay on the irony to be found in Jane Austen's novels, and she was enjoying her work.

There was little room in her mind for a dead woman whom she had met only twice, and of whom she could form only the vaguest visual recollection. She'd rather liked the policeman, though. Quite dishy, really – well, he *would* have been when he was fifteen or twenty years younger.

Gwendola Briggs sat reading *Bridge Monthly*: one or two pretty problems, she thought. She re-read an article on a new American bidding system, and felt happy. Only just over half-an-hour and the bridge players would be arriving. She'd almost forgotten Anne Scott now, though not that 'cocky and conceited officer' as she'd described Morse to her new and rather nice neighbour – a neighbour whom she'd promptly enrolled in the bridge-club's membership. So *fortunate*! Otherwise, they might have been one short.

Mrs Murdoch was another person that evening for whom Anne Scott was little more than a tragic but bearable memory. At a quarter-to-seven she received a telephone call from the J.R.2, and heard from a junior and inexperienced houseman (the young doctor had tried so hard to find some euphemistic guise for 'nearly poked his eyes out') that her son Michael had attempted to do ... to do some damage to his sight. The houseman heard the poor woman's moan of anguish, heard the strangled 'No!' – and wondered what else he could bring himself to say.

Charles Richards was not thinking of Anne Scott when he rang the secretary of the Oxford Book Association at nine o'clock to say that unfortunately he wouldn't be able to get to the pre-talk dinner which had been arranged for him in the Ruskin Room at the Clarendon Institute on Friday. He was very sorry, but he hoped it might save the Association a few pennies? He'd arrive at ten minutes to eight – if that was all right? The secretary said it was, and mumbled 'Bloody chap!' to himself as he replaced the phone.

It was only as he sat in a lonely corner of his local that evening that Morse's mind reverted to the death of Anne Scott. Again and again he came so near to cornering that single piece of information – something seen? something heard? – that was still so tantalizingly eluding him. After his fourth pint, he wondered if he ever *would* remember it, for he knew from long and loving addiction that his brain was never so keen as after beer.

Only Mrs Scott, now back in her semi-detached house in Burnley, grieved ever for her daughter and could not be comforted, her eyes once more brimming with tears as she struggled to understand what could have happened and – most bitter thought of all – how she herself could surely have helped if only she had known. If only . . . if only . . .

Chapter Sixteen

The lads for the girls and the lads for the liquor are there
A. E. Housman, *A Shropshire Lad*

After declining the Master of Lonsdale's invitation to lunch, Morse walked from *The Mitre* along the graceful curve of The High up to Carfax. He had turned right into Cornmarket and was crossing over the road towards Woolworths when he thought he recognized someone walking about fifteen yards ahead of him – someone carrying a brown brief-case, and dressed in grey flannels and a check-patterned sports coat, who joined the bus queue for Banbury Road; and as the boy turned Morse could see the black tie, with its diagonal red stripes, of Magdalen College School. Games afternoon, perhaps? Morse immediately stopped outside the nearest shop, and divided his attention between watching the boy and examining the brown shoes (left foot only) that rested on the 'Reduced' racks.

Edward Murdoch himself seemed restless. He consulted his wrist-watch every thirty seconds or so, punctuating this impatience with a craning-forward to read the numbers on the buses as they wheeled round Carfax into Cornmarket. Five minutes later, he felt inside his sports jacket for his wallet, picked up his brief-case, left the queue, and disappeared into a tiny side street between a jeweller's shop and Woolworths. There, pulling off his tie and sticking it in his pocket, he walked down the steps of the entrance to *The Corn Dolly*. It was just after ten minutes to one.

The bar to his right was crowded with about forty or fifty men, most of them appearing to be in their early twenties and almost all of them dressed in denims and dark-coloured anoraks. But clearly Edward was no stranger here. He walked through a wide porch-way into the rear bar – a more sedate area with upholstered wall-seats and low tables where a few older men sat eating sausages and chips.

'A pint of bitter, please.'

Whether it was his upper-class accent, or the politeness of his request, or his somewhat youthful features, that caused the barmaid to glance at him – it made no difference. She pulled his pint, and the boy sauntered back to the main bar. Here, to his left, was a small dais, about one foot high and measuring some three yards by five, its dullish brown linoleum looking as if a group of Alpine mountaineers had walked across it in their crampons. Only a few chairs were set about the room, and clearly the clientèle here was not the kind to sit quietly and discuss the *Nichomachean Ethics* of Aristotle. And even had any wished to do so, such conversation would have been drowned instantly by the deafening blare of the juke-box. Edward sat on the edge of the dais, sipped his Worthington 'E', stared down at the red-and-black patterned carpet – and waited. Most of the other men pulled fitfully and heavily upon their cigarettes, the smoke curling slowly to a ceiling already stained a deep tobacco-brown. These men were waiting, too.

Suddenly the blue and yellow spotlights were switched on, the juke-box switched off, and a buxom girl in a black cloak, who had hitherto been seated sipping gin in some dim alcove, stepped out on to the miniature stage. Like iron filings drawn towards a powerful magnet, fifty young men who a moment before had been lounging at the bar were now formed into a solid phalanx around the three sides of the dais.

At that second only one man in the room had his eyes on the large blackboard affixed to the white-washed wall behind the dais – a blackboard whereon the management proudly proclaimed the programme for the week: go-go dancing every lunch time; live pop groups each evening; with 'Bar snacks always available' written in brackets at the bottom as an afterthought. But now a softer, more sensuous music filled the semi-subterranean vaults, and the girl billed as the 'Fabulous Fiona' was already unfastening the clasp at the top of her cloak. All eyes (without exception now) were riveted upon her as amateurishly but amiably enough she pranced about the floor, exhibiting a sequence of sequined garments, slowly divested and progressively piled on top of the cloak beneath the blackboard, until at last she was down to her panties and bra. A roar of approval greeted the doffing of this latter garment; but the former, its sequins glittering in the kaleidoscopic lights, remained staunchly in place, in spite of several quite unequivocal calls for its removal. She was a daring girl. With the palms of her hands supporting her weighty breasts, she paraded herself under the noses of several of the more proximate voyeurs – like a maiden holding up a pair of giant bowls in a ten-pin bowling alley. Then the record stopped, the synthetic smile was switched off, and with the cloak now covering all once more, the fabled girl retired to her alcove where she joined two bearded men whose functions in the proceedings had not been immediately apparent.

Most of the audience drifted back to the bar; some of them left; and one of them resumed his seat on the dais. In five minutes the girl would be repeating her routine, Edward was aware of that – as he was also aware of someone who had just sat down beside him.

'Fancy another pint?' asked Morse.

Edward looked as guilty as someone just accused of stealing from a supermarket; but he nodded: 'Yes, please.' Morse was a little surprised at this; and as he stood waiting for two further pints he wondered if the boy would take his chance to get away. Somehow, though, he knew he wouldn't. He just managed to beat the second lunge of bodies to the dais, where he managed a considerably closer view of a now more sinuously synchronized Fiona. The beer, too, was beginning to encourage a rather more positive reaction amongst the ringside viewers, for this time there was even a smattering of applause as she finally turned away to find her cloak.

'Do you come here often?' asked the boy.

'Not *every* lunch time,' Morse said lightly. 'What about you?'

'I've been once or twice before.'

'Shouldn't you be at school?'

'I've got the afternoon off. What about you?'

Morse was beginning to like the boy. 'Me? I do what I want to do every afternoon: watch the girls, drink a pint or two – anything. You see, I'm over eighteen, like you, lad. You *are* over eighteen, aren't you? For those who *aren't*, you know, "the girls and pints are out of order" – if you see what I mean. It's an anagram. "Striplings" – that's the answer. You interested in crosswords?'

But Edward ignored the question. 'Why did you follow me here?'

'I wanted to know why you lied to me, that's all –'

'*Lied?*'

'– about the note Ms Scott left for you.'

The boy took a deep breath. 'Hadn't we better sit somewhere else?'

For a start he was evasive; truculent even. But he had little chance against Morse. In some strange way (the boy felt) Morse's eyes were looking straight into his thoughts, alerted immediately to the slightest deviation from the truth. It was almost as if the man had known this truth before he'd asked, and was doing little more than note the lies. So, in the finish, he told Morse everything about Anne Scott: told him about his brother's boasts; about that week before she died when he'd seen her semi-naked and lusted after her; about the note he'd found on the door mat; even about his own thoughts, so adolescently confused and troublous. And, progressively, he found himself liking Morse; found himself taking to a man who seemed humane and understanding – a man who listened carefully and who seemed so ready to forgive. Perhaps he was almost like a father ... and Edward had never known his own.

Two things surprised Morse about his time with Edward Murdoch. The first was to discover what a pleasant and engaging lad he was, and to realize that others must have found this, too: his mother, his friends, his teachers – including Ms Anne Scott ... The second cause of Morse's surprise was a more immediately personal one: during the energetic gyrations of the fair Fiona, he had felt not the slightest twinge of mild eroticism – and what would Freud have made of that? On second thoughts, however, he didn't much care; he'd come round to the view that Freud would have been a far more valuable citizen if he'd stuck to his research on local anaesthetics. Yet it was a bit worrying, all the same. As a boy, the apogee of any voyeuristic thrill had been the static nude, demurely sitting sideways on, and found about two-thirds of the way through the barber's copy of *Lilliput*. But now? The nudes were everywhere: on calendars, on posters, in fashion adverts, in newspapers – even on the telly. And the truth seemed to be that the naked female body was losing its magic. Understandable, yes; but for Morse, most disappointing. After all, he was only just past his fiftieth birthday.

The boy had gone now, and Morse debated whether he should stay on for Act V of the stripper's scheduled stint. But even the anticipation had now grown as cold as the experienced reality. And he left.

Chapter Seventeen

Go on; I'll follow thee
Hamlet Act I, scene iv

At eight-thirty that evening, George Jackson was crouching behind a hedge, his bicycle lying a few yards away in the dark undergrowth. He had carefully reconnoitred the area, and chosen a large house standing well back from the western side of the Woodstock Road. No lights had shown in the front of the house on his two previous visits, and there were none tonight. No dogs, either. The hedge was high and thick, but where it reached the adjoining property it grew more thin and bedraggled. Ideal – affording a perfect view of the entrance to Field House Drive about thirty yards to the right and the telephone kiosk about twenty yards to the left, both illuminated adequately by the street lamp immediately opposite. Occasionally a solitary person strolled by. Once a young couple, their arms round each other's waists. A few cyclists, and an intermittent flow of traffic either way.

The light-blue Rolls Royce appeared from the direction of the A40 roundabout, travelling slowly along the bus lane. Jackson could see the driver fairly clearly, and he felt the pulses jumping in his wrists as he moved slightly forward and watched intently. The Rolls was doing no more than ten miles-per-hour as it passed the kiosk and covered the short distance to Field House Drive, its left blinker startlingly bright as it turned into the Drive and stopped – still almost completely visible. The driver got out, slammed the door to, and locked it. With the car keys still in his hand, he walked to the boot of the car, unlocked it, peered inside, and closed and re-locked it, without removing anything. Then he disappeared (though for no more than a few seconds) from Jackson's view, and must obviously have opened something on the obscured near-side of the car, for almost immediately another door was closed with an aristocratically engineered 'clunk'. The man was in full view again now, and this time he carried a brown carrier bag in his right hand. He appeared quite calm, glancing neither to his left nor right in curiosity or apprehension.

As he came directly opposite, Jackson could see him plainly beneath the street lamp: a thick-set man of medium height, about forty to forty-five, his thick, dark hair going grey at the temples. He was dressed in an expensive dark-blue suit, and looked exactly as Jackson thought he would – fortunate and prosperous. Not for a second did the staring eyes behind the hedge leave the man as he walked up to the kiosk, went inside, lifted the receiver, came out again, thrust a hand in his pocket as if to find loose change, and then re-entered the kiosk as a grey-haired woman went slowly by with her white-haired terrier. Jackson's body suddenly felt numb with panic as the man in the kiosk appeared to be speaking into the telephone receiver. Was he ringing the police? But, just as suddenly, all was normal again. The man came out of the kiosk, thrust the carrier bag swiftly into the ivy behind it, and then walked back to the Rolls, fingering his car keys as he did so. The Rolls turned in a slow and dignified sweep and, with a momentary flash from the polished silver of the bonnet's grill, accelerated away and disappeared towards the northern roundabout. The road was as still as the grave.

Jackson was now in a dilemma which his limited mental capacities had not foreseen. Was he to leave his vantage-point immediately, grab the bag, and cycle off as fast as he could down the nearest back streets into Jericho? Or was he to wait, take things coolly, saunter over the road when he could convince himself the coast was completely clear, and then cycle sedately down the well-lit reaches of the lower part of Woodstock Road as if nothing were amiss? He decided to wait. Five minutes; ten minutes; fifteen minutes. And still he waited. Suddenly a light flashed on in the front room of the house behind him, and he crouched down further as a young woman pulled the curtains across the window. He had to move. Feeling his way carefully along the inner side of the hedge, he reached the gate and walked down the grassy slope to the pavement. Cold sweat stood out on his brow, and he felt a prickling sensation along his shoulders as he crossed the road and walked the few yards to the kiosk. No one was in sight, and no car passed as he put his hand behind the kiosk and found the bag at once. He recrossed the road, put the bag inside the fishing-basket secured to the rack on his cycle, and rode down towards Jericho. Below South Parade the traffic was busier, and Jackson felt his confidence growing. He turned round as two youngsters behind him zoomed nearer on their L-plated motor-bikes, and saw them almost force off the road a middle-aged don – gown billowing out behind him, his left hand clutching a pile of books. But they were soon gone, searing through the streets and leaving a wake of comforting silence behind them. At *The Horse and Jockey* Jackson turned right and rode down Observatory Street; then straight over Walton Street and down into the familiar grid of the roads in Jericho. Outside 10 Canal Reach he padlocked the rear wheel of his cycle to the drain-pipe, unfastened the fishing-basket, and took out his door key. It had been more nerve-racking than he'd expected; easier, though, in a way. He looked up the Reach briefly before letting himself in. A few youngsters were fooling about outside *The Printer's Devil*, one of them jerking the front wheel of his cycle high into the air as he circled slowly round; two women pushed their way through the door marked 'Saloon'; a man was trying to back his car into a narrow space. Quite a bit of activity, really. But none of them had noticed *him* – Jackson was confident of that. And what if someone *had*?

Jackson was quite right in believing that none of the people he had noticed so casually had noticed him, in turn. Yet *someone* had noticed him; someone whom Jackson could not possibly have seen; someone bending low behind one of the cars parked outside *The Printer's Devil*, getting his hands very dirty as he fiddled with the greasy chain of his bicycle – a chain that had been, and still was, in perfect working order.

The gown this person had been wearing, together with the pile of books he had been carrying, were now stowed away in the basket affixed to the front of the new, folding bicycle which he held upright on the pavement as he watched the door of 10 Canal Reach close.

Chapter Eighteen

An experienced, industrious, ambitious, and often quite picturesque liar

Mark Twain, *Private History of a Campaign that Failed*

The Chairman of the Oxford Book Association was relieved to see the Rolls Royce edge slowly through the narrow entrance to the Clarendon Institute car park. It was six minutes to eight, and he was having an anxious evening all round. Only about fifteen members had so far turned up, and already two of the committee were hastily removing many of the chairs in the large upstairs hall reserved for the meeting. Friday was never a good night, he knew that, and the late change of date could hardly have helped; but it was embarrassing, for everyone, to have an attendance as meagre as this.

Morse counted twenty-five in the audience when he tip-toed into the back row at five-past eight. After listening to *The Archers* he had felt restless, and the thought that he might be able to have a word with the chairman of the OBA about Anne Scott had finally tilted the balance in favour of 'Charles Richards: *Triumphs and Tribulations of the Small Publisher*'. It took only a few minutes for Morse to feel glad he had made the effort to attend. It was not (in Morse's eyes) that this thickishly set man, of medium height, had a particularly forceful presence – although, to be fair, his expensively-cut dark-blue suit lent a certain air of elegance and rank. It was his *manner* of speaking that was impressive. In his quietly spoken, witty, tolerant, self-deprecatory way, Richards spoke of his early days as a schoolmaster, his life-long interest in books, the embryonic idea of starting up for himself as a small publisher, his first, fairly disastrous months, his ladling of luck as time went by, with a few minor coups here and there, and finally the expansion of his company and the recent move to Abingdon. In his peroration he quoted Kipling (much to Morse's delight), and exhorted his listeners to treat that poet's 'twin imposters' with the same degree of amused – or saddened – cynicism.

He'd been good – there was no doubt of that – possessing as he did that rare gift of speaking to an audience in an individualized, personal sort of way, as if he were somehow interested in each of them. Afterwards there were a lot of questions, as if the audience, in its turn, was directly interested in the man who had thus addressed them. Too many questions, for Morse's liking. It was already half-past nine, and he hadn't drunk a pint all day.

'One more question – we really must make this the last, I'm afraid,' said the chairman.

'You said you were a schoolmaster, Mr Richards,' said a woman in the front row. 'Were you a *good* schoolmaster?'

Richards got to his feet and smiled disarmingly. 'I was rather hoping no one would ask me that. The answer is "no", madam. I was *not* a roaring success as a schoolmaster, I'm afraid. The trouble was, I'm sorry to say, that I just wasn't any good at keeping discipline. In fact, my lessons sounded rather like those recordings on the radio of Mrs Thatcher addressing the House of Commons.'

It was a good note on which to end, and the excellent impression the speaker had made was finally sealed and approved. The audience laughed and applauded – all the audience except one, that was, and that one man was Morse. He sat, the sole occupant of the back row, frowning fiercely, for the suspicion was slowly crossing his mind that this man was talking a load of bogus humbug.

At the bar downstairs, the chairman greeted Morse and

said how glad he was to see him again. 'You've not met our speaker before, have you? Charles Richards – Chief Inspector Morse.'

The two men shook hands.

'I enjoyed your talk – ' began Morse.

'I'm glad about that.'

' – except for the last bit.'

'Really? Why – ?'

'I just don't believe you were a lousy schoolmaster, that's all,' said Morse simply.

Richards shrugged his shoulders. 'Well, let's put it this way: I soon realized I wasn't really cut out for the job. But why did you mention that?'

Morse wasn't quite sure. Yet the truth was that Richards had just held a non-captive audience for an hour and a half with ridiculous ease – an audience that had listened to this virtually unknown man with a progressively deeper interest, respect, and enthusiasm. What could the same man have done with the receptive, enquiring minds of a class of young schoolboys?

'I think you were an excellent schoolmaster, and if I were a headmaster now, I'd appoint you tomorrow.'

'I may have exaggerated a bit,' conceded Richards. 'It's always tempting to play for a laugh, though, isn't it?'

Morse nodded. That was one way of putting it, he supposed. The other way was that this man could be a formidable two-faced liar. 'You've not been here – near Oxford – very long?'

'Three months. You couldn't have been listening very carefully, Inspector – '

'You knew Anne Scott, didn't you?'

'Anne?' Richards' voice was very gentle. 'Yes, I knew Anne all right. She used to work for us. You know, of course, that she's – dead.'

The chairman apologized for butting in, but he wished to introduce Richards to the other committee members.

'You won't perhaps know . . . ?' Morse heard the chairman say.

'No, I'm afraid I don't get over to Oxford much. In fact . . .'

Morse drifted away to drink his beer alone, feeling suddenly bored. But boredom was the last thing that Morse should have felt at that moment. Already, had he known it, he had heard enough to put him on the right track, and, indeed, even now his mind was beginning to stir in the depths, like the opening keys of *Das Rheingold* in the mysterious world of the shadowy waters.

When Richards took his leave, just on ten o'clock, Morse insinuated himself into a small group gathered round the bar, and lost no time in asking the bearded chairman about Anne Scott.

'Poor old Anne! She wasn't with us long, of course, but she was a jolly good committee member. Full of ideas, she was. You see, one of our big problems is getting some sort of balance between the literary side of things – you know, authors, and so on – and the technical side – publishing, printing, that sort of thing. We're naturally a bit biased towards the literary side, but an awful lot of our members are more interested in the purely technical, business side – and it was Anne, actually, who suggested we should try to get Charles Richards. She used to work for him once and she – well, we left it to her. She fixed it all up. I thought he was good, didn't you?'

Morse nodded his agreement. 'Very good, yes.' But his mind was racing twenty furlongs ahead of his words.

'Pity we didn't get a decent turn-out. Still, it was their loss. Perhaps with the change of date and everything . . .'

Morse let him go on, then drained his beer, and stood silently at the corner of the bar with a replenished pint. His mind, which had been so obtuse up until this point in the case, was now extraordinarily clear – and he felt excited.

It was then that he heard the whine of the police and ambulance sirens. *Déja acouté*. How long was it since Charles Richards had left? Quarter of an hour, or so? Oh God! What a fool he'd been not to have woken up earlier! The light-blue Rolls Royce he'd seen outside *The Printer's Devil* that day when he'd tried to call on Anne, the parking ticket on the windscreen; the reminder of that incident the following morning (that had *almost* clicked!), with the notice pasted on the Lancia's windscreen in the car park of the Clarendon Institute; the recollection (only now!) of what it was that Anne had told him . . . All these thoughts now shifted into focus, all projecting the same clear picture of Charles Richards – that fluently accomplished liar he'd been listening to less than an hour ago. It was *Charles Richards* who had visited 9 Canal Reach the day Anne Scott had died, for when Morse had parked in the comparatively empty yard of the Clarendon Institute more than a couple of hours ago he had reversed the Lancia into a space next to a large and elegantly opulent Rolls. A light-blue Rolls.

Morse pushed a 5p piece into the pay-phone in the foyer and asked for Bell. But Bell wasn't in, and the desk sergeant didn't know exactly where he was. He knew where Bell was making for though: there'd been a murder and –

'You got the address, sergeant?'

'Just a minute, sir. I've got it here . . . it was somewhere down in Jericho . . . one of those little roads just off Canal Street, if I remember . . .'

But Morse had put down the phone several words ago.

'Don't tell me you've had another meeting at the Clarendon Institute, sir,' said Walters.

Morse ignored the question. 'What's the trouble?'

'Jackson, sir. He's dead. Been pretty badly knocked about.' He pointed a thumb towards the ceiling. 'Want to see him?'

'Bell here yet?'

'On his way. He's been over to Banbury for something, but he knows about it. We got in touch with him as soon as we heard.'

'Heard?'

'Another anonymous phone call.'

'When was that?'

'About a quarter-past nine.'

'You sure of that?' Morse sounded more than a little puzzled.

'It'll be booked in – the exact time, I mean. But the message was pretty vague and . . .'

'Nobody took much notice, you mean?'

'It wasn't that, sir. But you can't expect them to follow up everything – you know, just like that. I mean . . .'

'You mean they're all bloody incompetent,' snapped Morse. 'Forget it!'

Morse ascended the mean, narrow, little flight of stairs and stood on the miniature landing outside the front bedroom. Jackson's body lay across the rumpled bed-clothes, his left leg dangling over the side, his bruised and bleeding head turned towards the door. The floor of the small room at the side of the single bed was strewn with magazines.

'I've not really had a good look around, sir,' ventured Walters. 'I thought I'd better wait for the inspector. Not much we could have done for him, is there?'

Morse shook his head slowly. The man's head lay in a large sticky-looking stain of dark red blood, and to Morse George Jackson appeared very, very dead indeed.

'I'll tell you exactly when he died, if you like,' volunteered Morse. But before he could fill in the dead man's timetable, the door below was opened and slammed, and Bell himself was lumbering up the stairs. His greeting was predictable.

'What the 'ell are you doing here, Morse?'

For the next hour the biggest difficulty was for the three policemen, the two fingerprint men, and the photographer to keep out of one another's way in the rooms of the tiny house. Indeed, when the hump-backed police surgeon arrived, he flatly refused to look at the corpse unless everyone else cleared out and went downstairs; and when he finally descended from his splendid isolation, his findings appeared to have done little to tone down his tetchiness.

'Between half-past seven and nine, at a guess,' he replied to Bell's inevitable question.

Walters looked quizzically at Morse, who sat reading one of the glossy 'porno' magazines he had brought from upstairs.

'You still sex-mad, I see, Morse,' said the surgeon.

'I don't seem to be able to shake it off, Max.' Morse turned over a page. 'And you don't improve much, either, do you? You've been examining all our bloody corpses for donkey's years, and you still refuse to tell us when they died.'

'When do *you* think he died?' From his tone the surgeon seemed far more at ease than at any time since he'd entered.

'Me? What's it matter what I think? But if you want me to try to be a *fraction* more precise than you, Max, I'd say – mm – I'd say between a quarter-past seven and a quarter-to eight.'

The surgeon allowed himself a lop-sided grin. 'Want a bet, Morse?'

'You can't loose with your bloody bets, can you? What's your bet? He died sometime *tonight* – is that it?'

'I think – *think*, mind you, Morse – that he might well have died a little later than you're suggesting; though why anyone should take an atom of notice of your ideas, God only knows. What really astounds me is that with your profound ignorance of pathology and its kindred sciences you have the effrontery to have any ideas *at all*.'

'What's your bet, Max?' asked Morse in the mildest tones.

The surgeon mused. 'Off the record, this is – agreed? I'll say between er – No! You only allowed yourself half an hour, didn't you? So, I'll do the same. I'll say between a quarter-past *eight* and a quarter-to *nine*. Exactly one hour later than you.'

'How much?'

'A tenner?'

The two men shook hands on it, and the surgeon left.

'Very interesting!' mumbled Bell, but Morse appeared to have resumed his reading. In fact, however, Morse's mind was peculiarly active as he turned the pages of the lurid and crudely explicit magazine. After all, he was at least contemplating one of the few clues furnished at the scene of the crime: mags (pornographic); mags (piscatorial); fingerprints (Jackson's); body (Jackson's) – and little else of much importance. A bare, stark murder. No obvious motive; no murder weapon; a crudely commonplace scene; well, that was what Bell would be thinking. With Morse it was quite different. He was confident he knew the solution even before the problem had been posed, and his cursory look round Jackson's bedroom had done little more than to corroborate his convictions: he knew the time of the murder, the weapon of the murder, the motive of the murder—even the name of the murderer. Poor old Bell!

Morse was still thinking, ten minutes later, that he had probably missed the boat in life and should have been a very highly paid and inordinately successful writer of really erotic pornography—when Walters came back into the room and reported to Bell.

Jackson, it appeared, had been seen around in Jericho that evening: at half-past five he had called in the corner grocery store for a small loaf of brown bread; at a quarter-to seven he had gone across to Mrs Purvis's to try to normalize the flushing functions of her recently installed water closet; at above five-past eight—

'*What?*' cried Morse.

'—at about five-past eight, Jackson went across to *The Printer's Devil* and bought a couple of pints of—'

'*Nonsense!*'

'But he *did*, sir! He was *there*! He played the fruit-machine for about ten minutes and finally left about twenty-past eight.'

Morse's body sank limply into the uncomfortable armchair. Had he got it all wrong? *All* of it? For if Jackson was blowing the froth off his second pint and feeding 10p's into the slot after eight o'clock, then without the slimmest shadow of doubt it could assuredly *not* have been Charles Richards who murdered George Alfred Jackson, late resident of 10 Canal Reach, Jericho, Oxford.

'Better have that tenner ready, Morse!' said Bell.

Chapter Nineteen

Alibi: (L. 'alibi', elsewhere); the plea in a criminal charge of having been elsewhere at the material time

Oxford English Dictionary

In the current telephone directory, neither Richards (C.) nor Richards Publishing Company (or whatever) of Abingdon was listed, and Morse realized he would have saved himself the bother of looking if he had remembered Richards' recent arrival in Oxfordshire. But the supervisor of Telephone Enquiries was able, after finally convincing herself of Morse's *bona fides*, to give him two numbers: those of Richards, C., 261 Oxford Avenue, Abingdon, and of Richards Press, 14 White Swan Lane, Abingdon. Morse tried the latter first, and heard a recorded female voice inform him that in gratitude for his esteemed enquiry the answering machine was about to be activated. He tried the other number. Success.

'I was just on my way to the office, Inspector, but I don't suppose you've rung up about a printing contract, have you?'

'No, sir. I just wondered if you'd heard about the trouble in Jericho last night.'

'Trouble? You don't mean my vast audience rioted after my little talk?'

'A man was murdered in Jericho last night.'

'Yes?' (Had Charles Richards' tone inserted the question-mark? The line was very crackly.)

'Pardon?'

'I didn't say anything, Inspector.'

'His name was Jackson – George Jackson, and I think you may have known him, sir.'

'I'm afraid you're mistaken, Inspector. I don't know any Jackson in Jericho. In fact, I don't think I know *anyone* in Jericho.'

'You used to, though.'

'Pardon, Inspector?' (Surely the line wasn't all *that* bad?)

'You knew Anne Scott – you told me so.'

'What's that got to do with this?'

'Jackson lived in the house immediately opposite her.'

'Really?'

'You didn't know where she lived?'

'No, I didn't. You tell me she lived in Jericho but – well, to be truthful, I thought Jericho was somewhere near Jerusalem until . . .' Charles Richards hesitated.

'Until what?'

'Until I heard of Anne's – suicide.'

'You were, shall we say, pretty friendly with her once?'

'Yes, I was.'

'Too friendly, perhaps?'

'Yes, you could say that,' said Richards quietly.

'You never visited her in Jericho?'

'No, I did not!'

'But she got in touch with you?'

'She wrote – yes. She wrote on behalf of the Book Association, asking me if I'd talk about – well, you know that. I said I would – that's all.'

'She must have known you were coming to Abingdon.'

'We're beating about the bush, aren't we, Inspector? Look, I was very much in love with her once, and we – we nearly went off together, if you must know. But it didn't work out like that. Anne left the company – and then things settled down a bit.'

'A *bit*?'

'We wrote to each other.'

'Not purely casual, chatty letters, though?'

Again Richards hesitated and Morse heard the intake of breath at the other end. 'I loved the girl, Inspector.'

'And she loved you in return.'

'For a long time, yes.'

'You've no idea why she killed herself?'

'No, I haven't.'

'Do you remember where you were on the afternoon of the day she died?'

'Yes, I do. I read about her death in *The Oxford Mail* and – '

'Where were you, sir?'

'Look, Inspector, I don't want to tell you that. But, please believe me, if it really – '

'Another girl friend?'

'It could have been, couldn't it? But I'm – '

'You deny your car was parked in Jericho at the bottom of Victor Street that afternoon?'

'I certainly do!'

'And what if I told you I could prove that it was?'

'You'd be making one almighty mistake, Inspector.'

'Mm.' It was Morse's turn to hesitate now. 'Well, let's forget that for the minute, sir. But it's my official duty, I'm afraid, to ask you about er about this person you saw that afternoon. You see – '

'All right, Inspector. But you must promise me on your honour that this whole thing won't go an inch further if – '

'I promise that, sir.'

Morse rang the girl immediately, and she sounded a honey – although a progressively angrier honey. She was reluctant to answer any of Morse's questions for a start, but she slowly capitulated. Yes, if he must know, she'd been in bed with Charles Richards. How long for? Well, she'd *tell* him how long for. From about eleven-thirty in the morning to after five in the afternoon. All the bloody time! So there! As he put down the phone Morse wondered what she was like, this girl. She sounded sensuous and passionate, and he thought perhaps that it might be in the long-term interests of justice as well as to his own short-term benefit if he kept a note of her address and telephone number. Yes. Mrs Jennifer Hills who lived at Radley – just between Oxford and Abingdon: Jennifer Hills ... yet another part of the new picture that was gradually forming in his mind. It was rather like the painting by numbers he'd seen in the toy shops: some areas were numbered for green, some for orange, some for blue, some for red, some for yellow – and, suddenly, there it was! The picture of something you'd little chance of guessing if you hadn't known: 'Sunset over Galway Bay', perhaps – or 'Donald Duck and Goofy'.

If Morse had but known it, Jennifer Hills was thinking along very similar lines. Her husband, Keith, a representative for the Gulf Petroleum Company, was still away in South Africa, and she herself, long-legged, lonely, randy and ready enough this featureless Saturday morning, had liked the sound of the chief inspector's voice. Sort of educated – but sort of close, too, and confidential – if only she could have explained it. Perhaps he might call and give her some 'inter-' something. Interrogation, that was it! And possibly some inter-something-else as well ... How silly she'd been to get so cross with him! It was all Charles Richards' fault! She'd heard nothing from him since that exasperating phone call, and instinct told her to keep well away – at least for the time being. Yes ... it might be nice, though, if the inspector called, and she found herself willing the phone to ring again.

But it didn't.

Chapter Twenty

Certum est quia impossibile est
Tertullian, *De Carne Christi*

'You were quite right, you know,' conceded Bell, when Morse looked into his office in the middle of that Saturday afternoon. 'Jackson had been bashed about the head quite a bit, it seems, but nothing all *that* serious. Certainly not serious enough to give him his ticket. The real trouble was the edge of that head-post on the bed – just like you said, Morse. Someone must have tried to shake his teeth out and cracked his skull against the upright.'

'You make it sound like a football match.'

'Boxing match, more like.'

'Blood all over the other fellow?'

'Pretty certainly, I'd think. Wouldn't you?'

Morse nodded. 'Accidental, perhaps?'

'Accidentally bloody deliberate, Morse – and don't you forget it.'

Morse nodded again. As soon as the surgeon had mentioned 'a squarish sharp-edged weapon', it had merely corroborated the suspicion he'd originally formed when he'd examined the bed-post, only about a foot from Jackson's head. To his naked eye, at the time, there had been nothing to confirm the suspicion, but he was as happy as the rest of them to rely upon the refinements of forensic tests. The weapon was settled then, and Morse felt he ought to put his colleague on the right lines about motive, too.

'Whoever killed him was pretty obviously looking for something, don't you think, Bell? And not just the address of some deaf-and-dumb nymphomaniac, or the results of the latest pike-angling competition.'

'You think he found what he was looking for?'

'I dunno,' said Morse.

'Well, I'll tell you one thing. We've been over the house with a nit-comb, and – nothing! Nothing that's going to help us. Fishing tackle galore, tools, drills, saws – you name it, he's got it in the do-it-yourself line. So what, though? He goes fishing most days, and he does a few handyman jobs round the streets. Good luck to him!'

'Did you find a trowel?' asked Morse quietly.

'Trowel? What's that got to –'

'He mended the Scott woman's wall – did you know that?'

Bell looked up sharply. 'Yes, as a matter of fact, I did. And if I may say so, Morse. I'm beginning to wonder –'

'What about bird watching?'

'What the 'ell's – '

'There was a pair of binoculars in the bedroom, you knew that.'

'All right. He went fishing, and he occasionally had a look at the kingfishers.'

'Why keep 'em in the bedroom, though?'

'You tell *me*!'

'I reckon he used to have a look at the bird across the way every now and then.'

'You mean, he – '

'No curtains, were there?'

'The dirty little sod!'

'Come off it! I'd have done the same myself.'

'Funny, isn't it? The way you just happened to be in Jericho. Both times, too.'

'Coincidence. Life's full of coincidences.'

'Do you appreciate, Morse, what the statistical chances are of you – '

'Phooey! Let me tell you something, Bell. *Statistically*, a woman should have her first baby at the age of nineteen, did you know that? But she shouldn't really start copulating before the age of twenty-six!'

Bell let it go, and his shoulders sagged as he sat at his desk. 'It's going to be one helluva job getting to the bottom of this latest business, you know. Nothing to go on, really. No one saw anybody go into the house – no one! It's that bloody boat-yard, you see. All of 'em there just get used to seeing people drifting in and out all the time. Augh! I don't know!'

'You interviewed the people who saw Jackson in the pub that night?'

'Most of 'em. The landlord sets his clock about five minutes fast, but you can take it from me that Jackson was there until about twenty-past eight.'

Morse pursed his lips. Charles Richards certainly seemed to have provided himself with a Kruger-rand alibi, for *he* – Morse himself – had been sitting in the audience *listening* to the beggar, from about five-past eight to way gone half-past nine. It was absolutely and literally impossible for Richards to have murdered Jackson! Shouldn't he accept that indisputable fact? But Morse enjoyed standing face-to-face with the impossible, and his brain kept telling him he could – and must – begin to undermine that impregnable-looking alibi. It was the second telephone call that worried him: someone had been anxious for the police to have a very definite idea indeed of the time when Jackson had died – a time that put Charles Richards completely in the clear. And who was it who had made that call? It couldn't, quite definitely, have been Jackson this time. But, just a minute. *Could* it just conceivably have been Jackson? What if . . . ?

Bell's thoughts had clearly been following along a parallel track. 'Who do you think phoned us about it, Morse? Do you think it was the same person who rang us about the Scott woman?'

'I don't think so, somehow.'

'Morse! Have you got *any* ideas about this whole business?'

Morse sat silently for a while, and then decided to tell Bell everything he knew, starting with the evening when he'd met Anne Scott, and finishing with his telephone call to Jennifer Hills. He even told Bell about the illicit fiver handed over to the Jericho locksmith. And, in fact (could the two men but have realized it) several of the colours in the pattern were already painted in, although the general picture seemed obstinately determined not to reveal itself.

'If you can help me in any way,' said Bell quietly, 'I'll be grateful – you know that, don't you.'

'Yes, I know that, my old friend,' said Morse. 'And I'll tell you what I'll do. I'll try to *think* a bit more. Because there's something, *somewhere*, that we're all missing. God knows what it is, though – *I* don't.'

Chapter Twenty-one

'I have already chose my officer'
Othello Act I, scene i

Sunday-working was nothing particularly unusual for Bell, but as he sat in his office the following afternoon he knew that he would have been more gainfully employed if he had stayed at home to rake the autumn leaves from his neglected lawn. Reports were still filtering through to him, but there seemed little prospect of any immediate break in the case. After the initial spurt of blood and splurge of publicity, the murder of George Jackson was stirring no ripples of any cosmic concern. Apart from a few far-flung cousins, the man had left behind him neither any immediate family nor any traceable wake of affection. To those who had known him vaguely, he had been a mean and unloved little man, and to the police the manner of his death had hardly risen to the heights of inglorious wickedness. Yet several facts were fairly clear to Bell. Someone had managed to get into number 10 between half-past eight and nine that Friday evening, had probably argued with Jackson in a comparatively pacific way, then threatened and physically intimidated the man, and finally – accidentally or deliberately – cracked his thinly-boned skull against the bed-post in his bedroom. The evidence strongly suggested, too, that Jackson's visitor had been looking for something specific, since the contents of all the drawers and cupboards in the house had been methodically and neatly examined; only in the bedroom were there the signs of frenetic haste and agitation. But of the identity of this visitor, or of the object of his quest, the police as yet had no real ideas at all. No one in the Reach or in the neighbouring streets appeared either to have seen or heard anything or anyone suspicious, and the truth was that only the sudden and disastrous blowing of a TV valve would have caused the majority of Jackson's fellow-citizens to look out into the darkened streets that night: for from 8.30 to 10.30 p.m. that evening, viewing all over Bitain was monopolized by the Miss World Competition. Poor Jackson, alas, had missed the final adjudication, and faced instead the final judgement.

Walters called in at the office in mid-afternoon, after yet another fruitless search for the smallest nugget of gold. He was fairly sure in his own mind that they were trying to drive a motorway through a cul-de-sac, and that the solution to Jackson's murder was never going to be discovered in isolation from the death of Ms Scott. He told Bell so, too, but the answer he received was callous and unkind.

'You don't need to be a bloody genius to come to that conclusion, lad.'

Bell was weary and dejected, Walters could see that, and there seemed little point in staying. But there was one further point he thought he might mention:

'Did you know, sir, that there wasn't a single book in Jackson's house?'

'Wasn't there?' said Bell absently.

Mr Parkes felt happy that Sunday afternoon. One of the social workers from the Ferry Centre had brought a cake for him, and there were tears of gratitude in his old eyes as he asked the young lady inside and poured two glasses of dry sherry. It had been several years since anyone had remembered his birthday. After his visitor had left, he poured himself a second glass and savoured his little happiness. How had she known it was his birthday? And suddenly something clicked – birthdays! That's what they'd been talking about when Gwendola had laid on her little treat with the sherry. Talk of the Bridge Club's anniversary must have led on to birthdays, he was sure of it now – although it seemed a trivial remembrance. Yet the police had asked him to let them know if he could recall anything about that night, and he rang up St Aldates immediately.

'Ah, I see,' said Bell. 'Yes, that's very interesting. Birthdays, eh?'

The old man elaborated as far as he could, and Bell thanked him with a fair show of simulated gratitude. It was good of the old boy to ring up, really. Birthdays! He made a note of the call and put the sheet of paper in his tray: Walters could stick it with the rest of the stuff.

In fact, the note just written was to be the final contribution of Chief Inspector Bell to the riddle of the Jericho Killings.

Morse had been a little surprised when earlier in the week, after seeking an interview with his Assistant Chief Commissoner, he learned that the ACC, in turn, would welcome a little chat with Morse, and that 'a cup of tea up at my little place up at Beckley' would make a pleasant rendezvous. At four-thirty, therefore, on that sunny October afternoon, the two men sat on a weedless lawn overlooking the broad, green sweep of Otmoor, and Morse recounted to his senior officer the irregularities and improprieties of his own investigations over the previous fortnight. The ACC was silent for a long time, and the answer, when it finally came from those rather bloated lips, was unexpected.

'I want you to take over the case, Morse. You're quite good at that sort of thing; Bell isn't.'

'But I didn't come to ask –'

'It's what you've got.'

'Well, I'm sorry, sir, but I can't accept the case. It's just not fair to belittle Bell –'

'Belittle?' The ACC smiled curiously, and Morse knew he'd missed a point somewhere. 'Don't worry about Bell! I'll ring him and put things straight myself.'

'But I just –'

'Shut your mouth a minute, Morse, will you?' (That maddening smile again!) 'You see, you've done me a good turn in a way. I know you didn't apply for the vacant super's post, but I was er thinking of recommending you, actually. On second thoughts, though, I don't think I shall bother. The job's going to involve an awful lot of public relations – very important these days, Morse! – and er I just don't think you're cut out for that sort of thing. Do you?'

'Well, I don't know, really.'

'Anyway, Bell applied – and he's senior to you anyway, isn't he?'

'Only just,' mumbled Morse.

'He's a good man. Not the greatest intellect in the Force – but neither are you, Morse. So I can work things very sweetly for you, can't I? I can let Bell know he's got promotion and tell him to drop this Jericho business straightaway.'

'I'd rather think things over, sir, if you don't mind.'

'No sense, old chap. We made the appointment yesterday, actually.'

'Oh.' Morse felt a twinge of envy and regret; but all that public relations stuff would have bored him to death, he knew that.

The ACC interrupted his thoughts. 'You know, Morse, you don't go about things in the right way, do you? With your ability you could have been sitting in my chair, and earning a sight more – '

'I've got a private income, sir – and a private harem.'

'I thought your father was a taxi driver?'

Morse stood up. 'That's right, sir. He used to drive the Aga Khan.'

'You got any of your private harem to spare?'

'Sorry, sir. I need 'em all.'

'You'll need Lewis, too, I suppose?'

For the first time that afternoon Morse looked happy.

BOOK THREE

Chapter Twenty-two

Those milk-paps
That through the window-bars bore at men's eyes
Timon of Athens Act IV, scene iii

Even if, in his boyhood, Sergeant Lewis's parents had been twinly blessed with privilege and wealth, it seems unlikely that their son would have won a scholarship to Winchester. As it was – after leaving school at fifteen – Lewis had worked his way up through a series of day-release courses and demanding sessions at night schools to a fair level of competence in several technical skills. At the age of twenty he had joined the police force and had never really regretted his decision. Promoted to the rank of sergeant ten years ago, he was as sensibly aware of his potential as of his limitations. It was six years ago that he had first come within Morse's orbit, and in retrospect he felt honoured to have been associated with that great man. In retrospect, let it be repeated. During the many, many hours he had spent in Morse's company on the several murder cases that had fallen within their sphere of duty, there had been frequent occasions when Lewis had wished him in hell. But there were infinitely worth-while compensations – were there not? – in being linked with a man of Morse's almost mythical methodology. For all his superior's irascibility, crudity, and self-indulgence, Lewis had taken enormous pride

– yes, *pride* – in his friendship with the man whom almost all the other members of the Thames Valley Constabulary had now come to regard as a towering, if somewhat eccentric, genius. And in the minds of many the phenomenon of Morse was directly associated with *himself* – yes, with *Lewis*! They spoke of Morse and Lewis almost in the same vein as they spoke of Gilbert and Sullivan, or Moody and Sanky, or Lennon and McCartney. Thus far, however, in the case of the Jericho killings, Lewis's sole contribution had been to drive his chief down to the Clarendon Institute car park about a fortnight ago. And why, oh why (as Lewis had then wondered) hadn't the idle beggar taken a bus? Surely that would have been far, far quicker.

It was, therefore, with a lovely amalgam of treasured reminiscence and of personal satisfaction that Lewis listened to Morse's voice on the phone at 7.30 a.m. the following morning.

'Yes, sir?'

'I want your help, Lewis.'

'How do you mean, sir? I can't help much today. I'm running this road-safety campaign in the schools and – '

'Forget it! I've had a word with Strange. As I say, I need your help.'

Suddenly the uplands of Lewis's life were burnished with the autumn sun. *He* was needed.

'I'll be glad, sir – you know that. When do you want me?'

'I'm in my office. Just get your bloody slippers off and get the car out!'

For the first time for many months, Lewis felt preternaturally happy; and his Welsh wife, cooking the eggs and bacon, could sense it all.

'I know 'oo that was – I can see it from your face, boy. Inspector Morse. Am I right?'

Lewis said nothing, but his face was settled and content, and his wife was happy for him. He was a good man, and his own happiness was a source of hers, too. She was almost glad to see him bolt his breakfast down and go: he had that look about him.

Lewis saw the stubs of filter-tipped cigarettes in the ash-tray when he knocked and entered the office at ten-past eight. He knew that it was Morse's habit either to smoke at an extravagantly compulsive rate or not at all, and mentally he calculated that the chief must have been sitting there since about six-thirty. Morse himself, showing no sign of pleasure or gratitude that Lewis had effected such an early appearance, got down to business immediately.

'Listen, Lewis. If I left my car on a double yellow line in North Oxford and a traffic warden copped me, what'd happen?'

'You'd get a ticket.'

'Oh, for Christ's sake, man! I know that. What's the *procedure*?'

'Well, as I say, you'd get a ticket under your wipers, and then after finishing work the warden would have to put the duplicates –'

'The what?'

'The duplicates, sir. The warden sticks the top copy on the windscreen, but there are two carbons as well. The first goes to the Fixed Penalty Office, and the second goes to the Magistrates' Clerk.'

'How do you come to know all this?'

'I'm surprised *you* don't, sir.'

Morse nodded vaguely. 'What if I wanted to pay the fine straight-away? Could I take the money – or sign a cheque – and, well, just pay it?'

'Oh, yes. Not at the Penalty Office, though. You'd have to take it to the Magistrates' Office.'

'But if the warden hadn't taken the carbon in –'

'Wouldn't matter. You'd take your ticket in, pay your fine – and then things would get matched up later.'

'They'd have a record of all that, would they? I mean, what the fine was for, who paid it, and so on?'

'Of course they would. On the ticket there'd be the details of the date, the time, the street, the registration number, as well as the actual offence – double yellows or whatever it was.

And there'd be a record of who paid the fine, and when it was paid.'

Morse was impressed. 'You know, Lewis, I never realized how many bits and pieces a traffic warden had in that little bag of hers.'

'A lot of them are men.'

'Don't treat me like an idiot, Lewis!'

'Well, you don't seem to know much about ...'

But Morse wasn't listening: he needed just a little confirmation, that was all, and again he nodded to himself – this time more firmly. 'Lewis, I've got your first little job all lined up.'

In fact Lewis's 'first little job' took rather longer than expected, and it was just before noon when he returned and handed Morse a written statement of his findings.

> Parking fine made out on Wed. 3rd Oct. for Rolls Royce, Reg. LMK 306V, parked on corner of Victor St. and Canal St. at 3.25 p.m. in area reserved for resident permit holders only. Fine paid by cheque on Friday 5th Oct. and the Lloyds a/c of Mr C. Richards, 216 Oxford Avenue, Abingdon, duly debited.

'Well, well, well!' Morse beamed hugely, wondered whether the last word was mis-spelt, reached for the phone, and announcing himself rather proudly by his full official title asked if he could speak to Mr Charles Richards. But the attractive-sounding voice (secretary, no doubt) informed him that Mr Richards had just gone off to lunch. Could Morse perhaps try again – in the morning?

'The *morning*?' squeaked Morse. 'Doesn't he work in the afternoons?'

'Mr Richards works very hard, Inspector' (the voice was somewhat sourer) 'and I think er I think he has a meeting this afternoon.'

'Oh, I see,' said Morse. 'Well, that's obviously much more important than co-operating with the police, isn't it?'

'I could *try* to get hold of him.'

'Yes, you could – and I rather hope you *will*,' said Morse quietly. He gave the girl his telephone number and said a sweet 'goodbye'.

The phone rang ten minutes later.

'Inspector Morse? Charles Richards here. Sorry I wasn't in when you called. Can I help you?'

'Yes, you can, sir. There are one or two things I'd like to talk to you about.'

'Really? Well, fire away. No time like the present.'

'I'd rather *see* you about things, if you don't mind, sir. Never quite the same over the phone, is it?'

'I don't see why not.'

Nor did Morse. 'One or two rather – delicate matters, sir. Better if we meet, I think.'

'As you wish.' Richards voice sounded indifferent.

'Tomorrow?'

'Why not?'

'About ten o'clock?'

'Fine.'

'Any parking space outside your office?' Morse asked the question innocently enough, it seemed.

'I'll make sure there's a space, Inspector. Damned difficult parking a car these days, isn't it?' His voice sounded equally innocent.

Outside the inn the legend was printed 'Tarry ye at Jericho until your beards be grown'. Inside the inn, Joe Morley hoisted his vast-bellied frame on to the high stool at the corner of the public bar, and the landlord was already pulling a pint of draught Guinness.

'Evenin', Joe.'

'Evenin'.'

'Bit of excitement, we hear, down your criminal neck of the woods.'

Joe wiped the creamy froth from his thick lips. 'Poor old George, you mean?'

'You knew him pretty well, didn't you?'

'Nobody knew George very well. He were a loner, were George. Bloody good fisherman, though.'

'Bird watcher as well, wasn't he?'

'Was he?'

The landlord polished another glass and leaned forward. 'Used to watch the birds, Joe – and not just the feathered variety. Used to watch that woman opposite as killed herself – with a pair of bloody binoculars!'

' 'Ow do you know?'

'Mrs Purvis was tellin' old Len – you know old Len as comes in sometimes. No curtains in the bedroom, either!'

'Very nice, too, I should think.'

The landlord leaned forward again. 'Do you want to know summat else? George weren't doin' too badly with all the odd jobs he used to do, neither. Two hundred and fifty quid he put in the post office last Thursday – some OAP bonds or something.'

' 'Ow do you know?'

'You know old Alf as comes in. Well, his missus was talkin' to, you know, that woman, whatsername, who works in the post office and – '

A group of youths came in, and the landlord reached up for two sets of darts and handed them over. 'The usual, lads?'

The middle-aged man who had been sitting silently at one of the tables moved over to allow the dartboard area to be cleared. He was beginning to feel very hungry indeed, for Morse had insisted (when he'd divided the Jericho pubs into two lists) that the early evening was the best time for pub gossip. 'Just *listen*, if you like,' Morse had said. 'I'll bet most of 'em there will be talking about Jackson.' And Lewis's hearing was good.

Morse himself, however, had heard nothing whatsoever about Jackson: it seemed that darts, football, and the price of beer had resumed their customary conversational priorities. Life went on as before – except for Anne Scott and George Jackson.

When, considerably over-beered, Morse looked back in his office at 9 p.m., he found an interesting report awaiting him. He had insisted that the fingerprint men should go and have another look round 10 Canal Reach; and they had found something new. Two prints – two fairly clear ones, too. And they weren't Jackson's.

Morse felt he'd had a pretty good day.

Chapter Twenty-three

And he made him a coat of many colours

Genesis, xxxvii. 3

Morse allowed himself half an hour along the A34 from Kidlington; and it was ample, for he spotted White Swan Lane as soon as he approached the town centre. *Richards Brothers, Publishing & Printing*, marked only by a brass plate to the right of the front door, was a converted nineteenth-century red-brick house, set back about ten yards from the street, with four parking lots marked out in white paint on the recently tar-macadamed front. One of the spaces was vacant, and as Morse pulled the Lancia into it he was aware that someone standing by the first-floor window had been observing his arrival. A notice inside the open front door directed him up the wide, elegant staircase where the frosted-glass panel in the door to his right repeated the information on the plate downstairs, with the addendum *Please Walk In*.

A woman looked up from behind a desk littered with papers. A very attractive woman, too, thought Morse – though considerably older than she'd sounded on the phone.

'Inspector Morse, isn't it?' she asked without enthusiasm. 'Mr Richards is expecting you.'

She walked across to a door (*Charles Richards, Manager*, in white plastic capitals), knocked quietly, and ushered Morse past her into the carpeted office, where he heard the door click firmly to behind him.

Richards himself got up from his swivel-chair, shook hands, and beckoned Morse to take the seat opposite him.

'Good to see you again, Inspector.'

But Morse ignored the pleasantry. 'You lied to me, sir, about your visit to Jericho on Wednesday, 3rd October, and I want to know why.'

Richards looked across the desk with what seemed genuine surprise. 'But I *didn't* lie to you. As I told you – '

'So if your car picked up a parking ticket that afternoon, someone *else* must have taken it to Oxford – is that right?'

'I – I suppose so, yes. But – '

'And if you paid the fine a couple of days later, someone must have pinched your cheque book and forged your signature? Is that it, sir?'

'You mean – you mean the cheque ...' Richard's voice trailed off rather miserably, and Morse pounced again.

'Of course, I fully realize that it must have been someone else, because you yourself, sir, were not in Oxford that afternoon – I checked that. The young lady – '

Richards leaned over the desk in some agitation, and waved his right hand from side to side as though wiping the last three words from a blackboard with some invisible rubber. 'Could we forget that, please?' he said earnestly. 'I – I don't want to get anyone else involved in this mess.'

'I'm afraid someone else already *is* involved, sir. As far as I'm concerned, you've got a water-tight alibi yourself – and all I want to know is who it was who drove your car to Jericho that afternoon.'

'Inspector!' Richards sighed deeply and contemplated the carpet. 'I should have had more sense than to lie to you in the first place – especially over that wretched parking ticket. Though goodness knows how ...' He shook his head as if in disbelief. 'You must have some sharp-eyed policemen in the force these days.'

But Morse was too involved to look unduly smug, and Richards continued, his shoulders sagging as he breathed out heavily.

'Let me tell you the truth, Inspector. Anne Scott worked for me for several years, as you know. She was a very attractive girl – in her personality as well as in physical looks – and when we went away on trips together – well, I don't need to spell it all out, do I? I was happily married – in a vague sort of way, if you know what I mean – but I fell for Anne in a big way, and when we were away we used to book into hotels as man and wife. Not that it was all that often, really – I suppose about five or six times a year. She never made any great demands on me, and there was never really a time when we seriously thought of, you know, my getting a divorce and all that.'

'Did your wife know about it?'

'No, I honestly don't think she did.'

'So?'

'Well, I suppose like most people we – we perhaps began to feel after a while that it wasn't all quite so marvellously exciting as it had been; and when Anne decided it would be better if she left – well, I didn't object too strongly. In fact, to tell you the truth, I remember feeling a huge sense of relief. Huh! Odd, isn't it, really?'

'But you wrote to each other.'

Richards nodded. 'Not all that often – but we kept in touch, yes. Then last summer, when I moved up here, we suddenly found we were pretty near each other again, and she wrote and told me she could usually be free at least one afternoon a week and I – I found the temptation altogether too alluring, Inspector. I went to see her – several times.'

'You had a key?'

'Key? Er, no. I didn't have a key.'

'Was the door unlocked on the afternoon we're talking about?'

'Unlocked? Er, yes. It must have been, mustn't it? Otherwise –'

'Tell me what you did *then*, sir. Try to remember *exactly* what you did.'

Richards appeared to be reading the runes off the carpet once more. 'She wasn't in – well, that's what I thought. I called out, you know, sort of quietly – called her name, that is . . .'

'Go on!'

'Well, the place seemed so quiet and I thought she must have gone out for a few minutes, so – I went upstairs.'

'Upstairs?'

Richards smiled sadly, and then looked squarely into Morse's eyes. 'That's right. Upstairs.'

'Which room did you go in?'

'She had a little study in the back bedroom – Look! You know all this anyway, don't you?'

'I know virtually everything,' said Morse simply.

'Well, we normally had a little drink in there – a drop of wine or something – before we – we went to bed.'

'Wasn't that a bit risky – in broad daylight?'

There was puzzlement and unease in Richard's eyes for a moment now, and Morse pondered many things as he waited (far too long) for the answer.

'It's always risky, isn't it?'

'Not if you pull the curtains, surely?'

'Ah, I see what you mean!' Richards seemed suddenly relaxed again. 'Funny, isn't it, that she hadn't got round to putting any curtains up there?'

(One up to Richards!)

'What happened then, sir?'

'Nothing. After about twenty, twenty-five minutes or so, I began to get a bit anxious. It must have been about half-past three by then, and I felt something – something odd must have happened. I just left, that's all.'

'You didn't look into the kitchen?'

'I'd never been into the kitchen.'

'Had it started raining when you left, sir?'

'*Started*? I think it had been raining all the afternoon –

well, drizzling fairly heavily. I know it was raining when I got there because I left my umbrella just inside the front door.'

'Just on the right of the door as you go in, you mean?'

'I can't be sure, Inspector, but – but wasn't it on the *left,* just *behind* the door? I may be wrong, though.'

'No, no, you're quite right, sir. You must forgive me. I was just testing you out, that's all. You see, somebody else saw the umbrella that afternoon – somebody who'd poked his nose into that house during the time you were there, sir.'

Richards looked down at his desk and fiddled nervously with a yellow ruler. 'Yes, I know that.'

'So, you see, I just had to satisfy myself it *was* you, sir. I wasn't sure even a minute ago about that; but I am now. As I say, your car was seen there, your black umbrella just behind the door, your dark-blue mackintosh over the banisters, and the light in the study. It wouldn't have been much good lying to me, sir.'

'No. Once I knew you'd found out about the car, I realized I might as well come clean. I was a fool not to –'

'You're *still* a fool!' snapped Morse.

'*What?*' Richards's head jerked up and his mouth gaped open.

'You're still lying to me, sir – you know you are. You see, the truth is that you weren't in Jericho at all that afternoon!'

'But – but don't be silly, Inspector! What I've just told you –'

Morse got to his feet. 'I shall be very glad if you can show me that mackintosh you were wearing, sir, because whoever it was who was in Anne Scott's house that afternoon, he was quite certainly *not* wearing a blue mackintosh!'

'I – I may have been mistaken –'

'You've got a dark blue mackintosh?'

'Yes, as a matter of fact, I have.'

'Excellent!' Morse appeared very pleased with himself as he picked up his own light-fawn raincoat from the arm of the chair. 'Have you also got a dark-grey duffle-coat, sir? Because that's the sort of coat that was seen on the banister in Anne Scott's house. And it was wet: somebody'd just come into the house out of the rain, and you told me – unless I misunderstood you, sir? – that there was no one else in the house.'

'Sit down a minute!' said Richards. He rested his chin on the palms of his hands and squeezed his temples with the ends of his fingers.

'You've been lying from the beginning,' said Morse. 'I knew that all along. Now –'

'But I *haven't* been lying!'

Suddenly Morse's blood surged upwards from his shoulders to the back of his neck as he heard the quiet voice behind him.

'Yes you have, Charles! You've been lying all your life. You've lied to me for years about everything – we both know it. The odd thing is that now you're lying to try to *save* me! But it's no good, is it?' The woman who had been seated behind the table in the office outside now walked into the room and sat on the edge of the desk. She turned to Morse: 'I'm Celia Richards, the wife of that so-called "husband" behind the desk there. He told me – but he'd no option really – that you were coming here today, and he didn't want Josephine, his normal secretary – and for all I know yet another of his conquests,' she added bitterly, 'he didn't want her to know about the police, and so he got *me* to sit out there. You needn't worry: it was all perfectly amicable. We had it all worked out. He'd told me you'd be asking about Jericho, and we decided that he'd try to bluff his way through. But if he didn't quite manage it – you did *pretty* well, you know, Charles! – then I agreed to come in. You see, Inspector, he left the intercom on all the time you've been speaking, and I've listened to every word that's been said. But it's no good any longer – is it, Charles?'

Richards said nothing: he looked an utterly defeated man.

'Have you got a cigarette, Inspector?' asked Celia as she unfolded her elegant legs and walked over to stand behind the desk. 'My turn, I think, Charles.'

Richards got up and stood rather awkwardly beside her as

she took her seat on the executive chair, and drew deeply on one of Morse's cigarettes.

'I don't want to dwell on the point unduly, Inspector, but poor Charles here isn't the only accomplished liar in the room, is he? I think, if I may say so, that it was a pretty cheap and underhand little trick of *yours* to go on about those coats like you did. Mackintoshes and duffle-coats, my foot! You see, Inspector, it was *me* who went to see Anne Scott that afternoon, and I was wearing a brown leather-jacket lined with sheep-wool. It's in the cupboard next door, by the way.' For a moment her voice was vibrant with vindictiveness: 'Would you like to see it, Inspector Morse?'

Chapter Twenty-four

Some falsehood mingles with all truth
Longfellow, *The Golden Legend*

As he drove back to Oxford that lunch time, Morse thought about Celia Richards. She had told her tale with a courageous honesty and Morse had no doubt whatsoever that it was true. During her husband's earlier liaisons with Anne Scott, Celia had no shred of evidence to corroborate her suspicions, although there had been (she knew) much whispered rumour in the company. She *could* have been mistaken – or so she'd told herself repeatedly; and when Anne left she had felt gradually more reassured. At the very least, whatever there might have been between the pair of them had gone for good now – surely! Until, that is, that terrible day only a few weeks earlier when, with Charles confined to bed with 'flu, she had gone into the office to see Conrad, Charles's younger brother and co-partner, who worked on the floor above him. On Charles's desk, beneath a heavy, glass paper-weight, lay a letter, a letter written in a hand that was known to her, a letter marked 'Strictly Personal and Private'. And even at that very moment she had known, deep inside herself, the hurtful, heart-piercing truth of it all, and she had taken the letter and opened it in her car outside. It was immediately clear that Charles had already seen Anne Scott several times since the move to Abingdon, and the letter begged him to go to see her again – quickly, urgently. Anne was in some desperate sort of trouble and he, Charles, was the only person she could turn to. Money was involved – and this was stated quite explicitly; but above all she had to *see* him again. She had kept (she claimed) all the letters he had written to her, and suggested that if he didn't do as she wished she might have (as far as Celia could recall the exact words) 'to do something off her own bat which would hurt him'. She hated herself for doing it, but if threats were the only way, then threats it had to be. Celia had destroyed the letter – and taken her decision immediately: she herself would go to visit her husband's former lover. And she had done so. On Wednesday, 3rd October, Charles said he had a meeting and had taken the Mini to work, telling her not to expect him home before about 6.30 p.m. The Rolls had been almost impossible to park – even the double yellow lines were taken up; but finally she had found a space and had walked up Canal Reach, up to number 9, where she found the door unlocked. ('Yes, Inspector, I'm absolutely sure. I had no key – and how else could I have got in?') Inside, there was no one. She had shouted. No one. Upstairs she had found the study immediately, and within a few minutes found, too, a pile of letters tied together in one of the drawers – all written to Anne by Charles. Somehow, up until that point, she had felt an aggression and a purpose which had swamped all fears of discovery. But now she felt suddenly frightened – and then, oh God! the next two minutes were an unbearable nightmare. For someone had come in; had shouted Anne's name; had even stood at the foot of the stairs! Never in the whole of her life had she felt so petrified with fear!

And then, it was all over. Whoever it was, had gone as suddenly as he had come; and after a little wait she herself, too, had gone. The parking ticket seemed an utter triviality, and she had paid the fine the next day – by a cheque drawn on her own account. (' "C" for "Celia", Inspector!') So, that was that, and she had burned all the letters without reading a single word. It was only later, when she read of Anne's suicide, that the terrible truth hit her: *she* had been in the house where Anne was hanging dead and as yet undiscovered. She became so fluttery with panic that she just *had* to speak to someone. At first she thought she would unbosom herself to her brother-in-law, Conrad – always a kind and loyal friend to her. But she'd realized that in the end there could be only one answer: to tell her husband everything. Which she had done. And it was *Charles* who had insisted that *he* should, and would, shoulder whatever troubles his own ridiculous escapades had brought upon her. It all seemed (Celia confessed) too stupid and melodramatic now: their amateurish attempts at collusion; those lies of Charles; and then his pathetic attempts to tip-toe a way through the mine-field of Morse's explosive questions.

Throughout Celia's story, Richards himself had sat silently; and after she had finished, Celia herself lapsed into a similar, almost abject, silence. How the pair would react – how they *did* react – after his departure, Morse could only guess. They had refused his offer of a drink at *The White Swan*, and Morse himself stoically decided that he would wait for a pint until he got back to Kidlington. For a couple of minutes he was held up along Oxford Avenue by temporary traffic lights along a short stretch of road repairs, and by chance he found himself noticing the number of the house on the gate-post to his left: 204. He remembered that he must be very close indeed to the Richards' residence, and as he passed he looked carefully at number 216 – set back some thirty yards, with a gravelled path leading up to the garage. Not all that palatial? Certainly there were other properties a-plenty nearby that could more appropriately have housed a successful businessman and his wife; and it suddenly occurred to Morse that perhaps Charles Richards was not quite so affluent as he might wish others to believe. It was a thought, certainly, but Morse could see little point in pursuing it. In fact, however, it would have repaid him handsomely at that point to have turned the Lancia round immediately and visited the Abingdon Branch of Lloyds Bank to try to seek some confidential insight into the accounts of Mr and Mrs Charles Richards, although not (it must be said) for the reason he had just considered. For the moment a mystery had been cleared up, and that, for a morning's work, seemed fair enough. He drove steadily on, passing a turning on his right which was sign-posted 'Radley'. Wasn't that where Jennifer Something, Charles Richards' latest bedfellow, was dispensing her grace and favours? It was; but even that little loose end was now safely tucked away – if Celia Richards was telling the truth . . .

At that point a cloud of doubt no bigger than a man's hand was forming on Morse's mental horizon; but again he kept straight ahead.

Back in Charles Richards' office, Celia stood by the window staring down at the parking area for many minutes after Morse had left – just as she had stood staring down when he had arrived and parked the Lancia in the carefully guarded space. Finally she turned round and broke the prolonged silence between them.

'He's a clever man – you realize that, don't you?'

'I'm not sure.'

'Do you think – ?'

'Forget it!' He stood up. 'Feel like a drink?'

'Yes.' She turned round again and stared down at the street. She'd told only one big lie, but she'd felt almost sure that Morse had spotted it. Perhaps she was mistaken, though. Perhaps he wasn't quite as clever as she'd thought.

Chapter Twenty-five

The life of a man without letters is death
Cicero

In the light of a bright October morning the streets assumed a different aspect, and the terraced houses seemed less squeezed and mean. Along the pavements the women talked and polished the door fixtures, visited the corner shops and in general reasserted, with the men-folk now at work, their quiet and natural birthright. A sense of community was evident once more and the sunlight had brought back the colour of things.

Yes, Sergeant Lewis had spent an enjoyable and reasonably profitable morning in Jericho, and after lunch he reported to Morse's office in the Thames Valley Police HQ buildings in Kidlington. Discreet enquiries had produced a few further items of information about Jackson. Odd jobs had brought him a considerable supplement to his pension, and such jobs had hardly been fitful and minor. Indeed, it was quite clear that the man was far from being a pauper. The house had been his own, he had almost £1,500 in the Post Office Savings Bank, a very recent acquisition of £250 in Retirement Bonds, and (as Lewis guessed) perhaps some £1,000 of fishing equipment. Yet his business dealings with the Jericho traders had been marked by a grudging frugality, and the occasional granting of credit. But it seemed that he always met his debts in the end, and he was up to date with the Walton Tackle Shop on his instalments of £7.50 for a carbon-fibre fishing rod. He had no immediate relatives, and the assumption had to be that Jackson was the last of an inglorious line. But Lewis had met no real ill-feeling against the man: just plain indifference. And somehow it seemed almost sadder that way.

Morse listened with interest, and in turn recounted his own rather more dramatic news.

'Did you get a statement from her?' asked Lewis.

'Statement?'

'Well, we shall need one, shan't we?'

So it was that Lewis rang the number Morse gave him, discovered that Mrs Celia Richards was at home, and arranged to meet her that same afternoon. It seemed to Lewis an unnecessary duplication of mileage, but he forbore to make the point. As for Morse, his interest in the Richards' clan appeared to be waning, and at 3.40 p.m. he found himself entering 10 Canal Reach – though he couldn't have told anyone exactly why.

The blood-stained sheets had been removed from the bedroom in which Jackson had died, but the blankets were still there, neatly folded at the foot of the bare, striped mattress. On the floor the magazines had been stacked in their two categories, and Morse sat down on the bed and picked up some of the pornographic ones once more, flipping through the lewd and lurid photographs. One or two pages had an accompanying text in what looked to him like Swedish or Danish, but most of the magazines had abdicated the requirement of venturing into the suburbs of literature to enhance their visual impact. The Angling magazines remained untouched.

Downstairs, the kitchen boasted few of the latest gadgets, and the tiny larder was ill-stocked. Some copies of *The Sun* lay under the grimy sink, and the crockery and cutlery used by Jackson for his last meagre meal on earth still stood on the dingy, yellow rack on the draining-board. Nothing, really.

In the front room, similarly, there seemed little of interest. A small brass model of a cannon from the Boer War era was the only object on the dusty mantelpiece, and the sole adornment to the faded green wallpaper was a calendar from one of the Angling Associations, still turned to the month of September. A small transistor radio stood on a pile of oddments on the cupboard, and Morse turned on the switch. But the batteries appeared to have run out. There were one or two things in the pile which Morse had vaguely noted on his previous visit, but now he looked at them again: an out-of-date mail-order catalogue; a current pension-book; an unopened gas bill; an old copy of *The Oxford Journal*; an illustrated guide to 'Fish of the British Isles'; two leaflets entitled *On The Move*; a slim box containing two white handkerchiefs; a circular – Suddenly Morse stopped and turned back to the leaflets. Yes. He remembered reading about the successful TV series *On The Move*, catering, as it did, for those viewers who were illiterate – or virtually so. Would illiteracy account for the lack of reading material in the Jackson household? Many a pornographic pose, but hardly a line of pornographic prose? What a different set-up across the way at number 9, where Anne Scott had surrounded herself with books galore! That long line of Penguin Classics, for example – many of them showing the tell-tale white furrows down their black spines: Homer, Plato, Thucydides, Aeschylus, Sophocles, Horace, Livy, Virgil ... If poor old Jackson could only have seen ... He *had* seen though: he'd almost certainly seen more than he should have done, both of the house itself and of the woman who regularly unbuttoned her blouse at the bedroom window.

Morse went upstairs to the front bedroom once more, took the binoculars that hung behind the door, and focused them upon the boudoir opposite. Phew! It was almost like being inside the actual room! He walked into the tiny back bedroom and looked out in the fading light along the narrow strip of garden to the shed at the far end, about thirty yards away. He focused the binoculars again, but finding the dirty panes hardly conducive to adequate delineation he took the catch off the window and pushed up the stiff, squeaky frame. Then he saw something, and his blood raced. He put the binoculars to his eyes once more – and he was sure of it: *someone was looking around in Jackson's shed*. Morse hurriedly made his way downstairs, put the key quietly into the kitchen door, took a deep breath, flicked open the lock, and rushed out.

Unfortunately, however, his right shin collided with the dustbin standing just beside the coalhouse, and he suppressed a yowl of pain as the lid fell clangingly onto the concrete and rolled round like an expiring spinning-top. It was more than sufficient warning, and Morse had the feeling that his quarry had probably been alerted in any case by the opening of the window upstairs. A quick glimpse of a man disappearing over the low wall that separated number 10 from the bank of the canal, and that was all. The garden was suddenly still again in the gathering darkness. If Lewis had been there, Morse would have felt more stomach for the chase. But, alone, he felt useless, and just a little scared.

The hut was a junk-house. Fishing gear crowded every square inch that was not already taken up by gardening tools, and it seemed impossible to take out anything without either moving everything else or sending precariously balanced items clattering to the floor. Against the left-hand wall Morse noticed seven fishing rods, the nearest one a shiny and sophisticated affair – doubtless the latest acquisition from the tackle shop. But his attention was not held by the rods, for it was perfectly clear to see where the intruder had been concentrating his search. The large wicker-work fisherman's basket lay open on the top of a bag of compost, its contents scattered around: hooks, tins of bait, floats, weights, pliers, reels, lengths of line, knives ... Morse looked around him helplessly. Who was it who had been so anxious to search the basket, and why? It was seldom that Morse had no inkling whatsoever of the answers to the questions that he posed himself, but such was the case now.

Before leaving Canal Reach, he walked across to number 9, unlocked the door, and turned on the wall switch immediately to his left. But clearly the electricity had been disconnected, and he decided that his nerves were in no fit state to look around the empty, darkened house. On the mat he saw a cheap brown envelope, with the name and address of Anne Scott typed behind the cellophane window. A bill, no doubt, that probably wouldn't be settled for a few months yet – if at all. Morse picked it up and put it in his jacket pocket.

He drove along Canal Street and found himself facing the green gates of Lucy's Iron Works, where he turned right and followed Juxon Street up to the top. As he waited to turn left into the main thoroughfare of Walton Street, his eyes casually noticed the signs and plaques on the new buildings there: The Residents' Welfare Club; The Jericho Testing Laboratories; Welsh & Cohen, Dentists ... Yet still nothing clicked in his mind.

Lewis was already back from Abingdon. He had seen Celia Richards alone at the house, and Morse glanced cursorily through her statement.

'Get it typed, Lewis. There are three "r"s in "corroborate", and it's an "e" in the middle of "desperate". And make sure you've got the address right.'

Lewis said nothing. Spelling, as he knew was not his strongest suit.

'How much exactly did that new rod of Jackson's cost?' asked Morse suddenly.

'I didn't ask, sir. These modern ones are very light, sort of hollow – but they're very strong, I think.'

'I asked you how much it cost – not what a bloody miracle it was!'

Lewis had often seen Morse in this mood before – snappy and irritable. It usually meant the chief was cross with himself about something; usually, too, it meant that it wasn't going to be long before his mind leaped prodigiously into the dark and hit, as often as not, upon some strange and startling truth.

Later that same evening Conrad Richards drove his brother Charles to Gatwick Airport. The plane was subject to no delay, either technical or operational, and at 9.30 p.m. Charles Richards took his seat in a British Airways DC 10 – bound for Madrid.

Chapter Twenty-six

Some clues are of the 'hidden' variety, where the letters of the word are in front of the solver in the right order

D. S. Macnutt, *Ximenes on the Art of the Crossword*

The next morning, two box files, the one red and the other green, lay on the desk at Kidlington, marked 'Anne Scott' and 'George Jackson' respectively. They remained unopened as Morse sat contemplating the task before him. He felt it most unlikely that he was going to discover many more significant pieces to the puzzle posed by the deaths of two persons separated only by a few yards in a mean little street in Jericho. That the two deaths were connected, however, he had no doubt at all; and the fact that the precise connection was still eluding him augured ill for the cheerful Lewis who entered the office at 8.45 a.m.

'What's the programme today, then, sir?'

Morse pointed to the box files. 'It'll probably not do us any harm to find out what sort of a cock-up Bell and his boys made of things.'

Lewis nodded, and sat down opposite the chief. 'Which one do we start with?'

Morse appeared to ponder the simple question earnestly as he stared out at the fleet of police vehicles in the yard.

'Pardon?'

'I said, which one do we start with, sir?'

'How the bloody hell do I know, man? Use a bit of initiative, for Christ's sake!'

Lewis pulled the red file towards him, and began his slow and industrious survey of the documents in the Scott case. Morse, too, after what seemed an inordinately prolonged survey of the Fords and BMWs, reluctantly reached for the green file and dumped the meagre pile of papers on to his blotting-pad.

For half an hour neither of them spoke.

'Why do you think she killed herself?' asked Morse suddenly.

'Expecting a baby, wasn't she.'

'Bit thin, don't you reckon? It's not difficult to get rid of babies these days. Like shelling peas.'

'It'd still upset a lot of people.'

'Do you think she knew she was pregnant?'

'She'd have a jolly good idea – between ten to twelve weeks gone, it says here.'

'Mm.'

'Well, I know my missus did, sir.'

'Did she?'

'She wasn't exactly sure, of course, until she went to the, you know, the ante-natal clinic.'

'What do they do there?'

'I'm not sure, really. They take a urine specimen or something, and then the laboratory boys sort of squirt something –'

But Morse was listening no longer. His face was alight with an inner glow, and he whistled softly before jumping to his feet and shaking Lewis vigorously by the shoulders.

'You-are-a-bloody-genius, my son!'

'Really?' replied an uncomprehending Lewis.

'Find it! It's there somewhere. That plastic envelope with a couple of bits of burnt paper in it!'

Lewis looked at the evidence, the 'ICH' and the 'RAT', and he wondered what cosmic discovery he had inadvertently stumbled upon.

'I passed the place yesterday, Lewis! Yesterday! And still I behave like a moron with a vacuum between the ears! Don't you see? It's part of a letterheading: the JerICHo Testing LaboRATories! Ring 'em up quick, Lewis, and offer to take 'em a specimen in!'

'I don't quite see –'

'They *tested* her, don't you understand? And then they wrote and – '

'But we *knew* she was having a baby. And so did she, like as not.'

'Ye-es.' For a few seconds Morse's excitement seemed on the wane, and he sat down once again. 'But if they wrote to her the day before she – Lewis! Ring up the Post Office and ask 'em what time they deliver the mail in Jericho. You see, if – '

'It'll be about quarter-to-eight – eightish.'

'You think?' asked More, rather weakly.

'I'll ring if you want, sir, but – '

'Ten to twelve weeks! How long has Charles Richards been in Abingdon?'

'I don't think there's anything about that here – '

'Three months, Lewis! I'm sure of it. Just ring him up, will you, and ask – '

'If you'd come off the boil a minute, sir, I might have a chance, mightn't I? You want me to ring up these three – '

'Yes. Straightaway!'

'Which one shall I ring first?'

'Use a bit of bl – ' But Morse stopped in mid-sentence and smiled beatifically. 'Whichever, my dear Lewis, seems to you the most appropriate. And even if you ring 'em up in some cock-eyed order, I don't think it'll matter a monkey's!'

He was still smiling sweetly as Lewis reached for the phone. The old brain was really working again, he knew that, and he reached happily for the documents once more. It was the start he'd been waiting for.

Within half an hour, Lewis's trio of tasks had been completed. Anne Scott had called at the Jericho Testing Laboratories on the afternoon of Monday, 1st October, to ask if there was any news and she had been told that as soon as the report was through a letter would be in the post – which it had been on Tuesday, 2nd October: pegnancy was confirmed. The Jericho post was delivered somewhat variably, but during the week in question almost all letters would have been delivered by

8.30 a.m. Only with the Richards' query had Lewis experienced any difficulty. No reply from Charles's private residence; and at the business number, a long delay before the call was transferred to Conrad Richards, the junior partner, who informed Lewis that the company had indeed moved to Abingdon about three months ago: to be exact, twelve weeks and four days.

Morse had sat silently during the phone calls, occasionally nodding with quiet satisfaction. But his attention to the documents in front of him was now half-hearted, and it was Lewis who finally picked up the small pink slip of rough paper which had fallen to the floor.

'Yours or mine, sir?'

Morse looked at the brief note. '"Birthdays", Lewis. It seems that one of the old codgers at the bridge evening remembers they were talking about birthdays.'

'Sounds pretty harmless, sir.' Lewis resumed his study of his documents, although a few seconds later he noticed that Morse was sitting as still as the dead, the smoke from a forgotten cigarette drifting in curling whisps before those unblinking, unseeing eyes.

Later the same morning, Conrad Richards dialled a number in Spain.

'That you, Charles? *Buenas* something or other! *Come está?*'

'Fine, fine. Everythink OK with you?'

'The police rang this morning. Wanted to know how long we'd been in Abingdon.'

'Was that all?'

'Yes.'

'I see,' said Charles Richards slowly. 'Celia all right?'

'Fine, yes. She's gone over to Cambridge to see Betty. She'll probably stay overnight, I should think. I tried to persuade her, anyway.'

'That's good news.'

'Look, Charles. We've had an enquiry from one of the Oxford examination boards. They want five hundred copies of some classical text that's gone out of print. No problem over royalties or copyright or anything. What do you think?'

The brothers talked for several minutes about VAT and profit margins, and finally the decision was left with Conrad.

A few minutes later Charles Richards walked out into the bright air of the Calle de Alcatá and, entering the Cafe Léon, he ordered himself a Cuba Libre. On the whole, things seemed to be working out satisfactorily.

All the way, Celia Richards's mind was churning over the events of the past two weeks, and she was conscious of driving with insufficient attention. At Bedford she had incurred the honking displeasure of a motorist she had not noticed quite legitimately overtaking her on the inside in the one-way system through the centre; and on the short stretch of the A1 she had almost overshot the St Neots' turn, where the squealing of her Mini's brakes had frightened her and left her heart thumping madly. What a terrible mess her life had suddenly become!

In the early days at Croydon, when she had first met the Richards brothers, she had almost immediately fallen for Charles ... Charles with his charm and vivacity, his sense of enjoyment, his forceful masculinity. Yet, even then, before they agreed to marry, she was conscious of other sides to his nature: a potential broodiness; a weakness for false flattery; a slightly nasty, hard streak in his business dealings; the suspicion – yes, even then – that his eye would linger far too long on the lovely limbs and the curving breasts of other women. But for several years they had been as happy as most couples: probably more so. Social events had brought her into an interesting circle of friends, and on more than one occasion other men had shown more interest in her own young and attractive body than their wives would have wished. Just a few times she had been *fractionally* disloyal to her marriage vows, but never once had she entertained the idea of any compromising entanglement. But Charles? He had been unfaithful, she knew that now: knew it for certain, because at long last – when there was no longer any hope of screening his impulsive affairs with his fond, if wayward, affection towards her – he had told her so . . . And then there was Conrad. Poor, faithful, lovely Conrad! If only she'd been willing to get to know him better when, in the early days, his own love for her had blazed as brightly as that of Charles . . . But he'd never had the sparkle or the drive of his elder brother, and he'd never really had a chance. A bit ineffectual, a bit passive – a bit 'wet', as she'd once described him to Charles. Oh dear! As things had turned out, he'd always been wonderful to her. No one could have been more kind to her, more thoughtful, more willing to forget himself; and she thought again now of that mild and self-effacing smile that reflected a dry, fulfilled contentment in the happiness of others . . . What would it have been like if she'd married Conrad? Not that he'd ever asked her, of course: he was far too shy and diffident to have joined the lists with Charles. Physically he and Charles looked very similar, but that was only on the surface. Underneath – well, there was no electric current in Conrad . . . or so she'd thought until so very recently.

In Cambridge she turned into the Huntingdon Road and drove out to Girton village, where her sister lived.

When Betty brought a glass of sherry into the lounge, she found her sister in tears – a series of jerky sobs that stretched her full and pretty mouth to its furthest extent.

'You can tell me about it later, Celia, if you want to. But I shan't mind if you don't. A drop of booze'll do you good. Your bed's aired, and I've got a couple of tickets for the theatre tonight. Please stay!'

Dry-eyed at last, Celia Richards looked sadly at her sister and smiled bleakly. 'Be kind to me, Betty! You see – you see – I can't tell you about it, but I've done something terribly wrong.'

Chapter Twenty-seven

The time is out of joint
Hamlet Act I, scene v

Although Morse insisted (that lunch time) that a liquid diet without blotting-paper was an exceedingly fine nutrient for the brain cells, Lewis opted for his beloved chips – with sausages and egg – to accompany the beer. 'Are we making progress?' he asked, between mouthfuls.

'Progress? Progress, Lewis, is the law of life. You and I would be making progress even if we were going backwards. And, as it happens, my old friend, we are actually going *forward* at this particular stage of our joint investigations.'

'We are?'

'Indeed! I think you'll agree that the main facts hang pretty well together now. Anne Scott goes to a bridge evening the night before she kills herself, and I'm certain she learns something there that's the final straw to a long and cumulative emotional strain. She writes a note to Edward Murdoch, telling him she can't see him for a lesson the next afternoon, and from that point the die is cast. She gets home about 3 a.m. or thereabouts, and we shall never know how she spends the next few hours. But whatever doubt or hesitation she may have felt is finally settled by the Wednesday morning post, when a letter arrives from the birth clinic. She burns the letter and she – hangs herself.

'Now Jackson has been doing some brickwork for her, and he goes over to have a final look at things – and to pick up his trowel. He lets himself in, pushes the kitchen door open, and in the process knocks over the stool on which Anne Scott has stood to hang herself – and finds her swaying there behind the door after he's picked up the stool and put it by the table. Now, just think a minute, Lewis. Anyone, virtually *anyone,* in those circumstances would have rung up the police immediately. So why not Jackson? He's got nothing to worry about. He does lots of odd jobs in the neighbourhood and it must be common knowledge that he's patching up the wall at number 9. So why doesn't he ring the police *at that point*? – because I'm sure it *was* Jackson who rang up later. It's because he *finds* something, Lewis – apart from the body: something which proves too tempting for his cheap and greedy little soul.

'I thought for a start it may have been money, but I doubt it now. I think she'd written some sort of letter or note and left it on the kitchen table – a letter which Jackson takes. He's anxious to get out of the house quickly, and he forgets to lock the door behind him. Hence all our troubles, Lewis! You see, since Jackson has been coming over regularly – sometimes when she was still in bed – she's got in the habit of locking her front door, then taking the key out, and leaving it on the sideboard, so that he can put his own key in.'

'Surely she wouldn't have done that if she'd already decided to kill herself?'

But Morse ignored the objection and continued. 'Then Jackson goes over to his own home and reads the letter – '

'But you told me he *couldn't* read!'

'It's addressed, Lewis, to one of two people: either to the police; or to the man who's been her lover – the man she's recently written to, and the man who's probably been the only real passion in her life – Charles Richards. And there's something in that letter that gives Jackson some immediate prospect of personal gain – a situation he's decided to take full advantage of. But let's get back to the sequence of events that day. Someone else goes into number 9 during the afternoon – Celia Richards. Pretty certainly Jackson sees her going in – as he later sees *me*, Lewis – but he can't have the faintest idea that she's the wife of the man he's going to blackmail. He realizes one thing, though – that he's forgotten to lock the door; and so when everything's quiet he goes over and puts his key through the letter box. That's the way it happened, Lewis – you can be sure of that.'

'Perhaps,' mumbled Lewis, wiping up the last of the egg yolk with a final, solitary chip.

'You don't sound very impressed?'

'Well, to be honest, I'd thought very much the same myself, sir, and I'm pretty sure Bell and his boys – '

'Really?' Morse drained his beer and pushed the glass in front of Lewis's plate. 'Bags of time for another.'

'I got the last one, sir. Just a half for me, if you don't mind.'

'Now,' resumed Morse (glasses replenished), 'we've got to link the death of Anne Scott with the murder of Jackson, agreed? Well, I reckon the connection is fairly obvious, and from what you've just said I presume that your own nimble mind has already jumped to a similar conclusion, right?'

Lewis nodded. 'Jackson tried to blackmail Charles Richards because of what he learned from the letter, and it seems he succeeded because he took £250 to the Post Office the day before he was murdered. I reckon he'd written to Richards, or rung him up, and that Richards decided to cough up to keep him quiet. He could have arranged to meet Jackson to give him the money and then just followed him home. And once he knew who he was, and where he lived – well, that was that. Perhaps he didn't really mean to kill him at all – just scare him out of his wits and get the letter, or whatever it was.'

Morse shook his head. It *might* have happened the way Lewis had just outlined things; but it *hadn't*. 'You may be right most of the way, Lewis, but you can be absolutely certain about one thing: *it wasn't Charles Richards who murdered Jackson*. And until somebody proves to us that the earth is round or a triangle hasn't got three sides, we'd better bloody face it! He was giving a lecture – with *me* in the audience!'

'Don't you think, perhaps – ?'

'Nonsense! Jackson was in the *pub* at gone eight and the police found his body while Richards was still talking. And he didn't leave that platform for one *second*, Lewis!'

'I'm not saying he did, sir. But he could have got someone else to go and rough Jackson up, couldn't he?'

Morse nodded. 'Carry on!'

'He's got a wife, sir.'

'I can't exactly see her pushing Jackson upstairs, can you? He was no youngster, but he was a tough and wiry little customer, I should think. Though perhaps it might not be a bad idea to find out exactly where she was that night . . .' His voice drifted off, and characteristically he married a few stray drops of beer on the table with the little finger of his left hand, his eyes seeming to stare into the middle distance.

'He's got a brother, too,' added Lewis quietly.

Morse's eyes refocused on his colleague immediately and a faint smile formed round his mouth. 'The brother? Yes, indeed! I wondered when you were going to get around to him. I've been giving our Conrad a little bit of thought myself this morning, and I reckon it's time we had a quiet little word with him.'

'We've got some jolly good prints, sir – as good as anything the boys have seen for quite some time. And it wouldn't be much trouble getting Conrad's dabs, would it?'

'No trouble at all.'

'Well' – Lewis looked at Morse rather hesitantly – 'shall we go and see him?'

'Why not? We'll just have another pint and then –'

'No more for me, sir. Do you want –'

'Pint, yes please. You're very kind.'

'I've been thinking, sir,' began Lewis when he came back from the bar.

'So have I. Listen! We'll nip over there together. There are two calls we'd better make. Conrad Richards for one, and then there's that girl-friend Charles Richards told me he was with when –'

'But why see her? You've already –'

'Let's toss up, Lewis. You can drive us out there. Heads you go to see Conrad – tails I do. All right?' Morse took out a 10p piece, flipped it in the air, and then peered cautiously underneath his palm before immediately returning the coin to his pocket. 'Heads it is, Lewis. What was it we agreed? Heads was you to see Conrad, wasn't it? Excellent! I shall have to take it upon myself to visit Mrs Whatsername.'

'Hills, sir.'

'Ah yes.' Morse relaxed and lovingly relished the rest of his beer. Someone had left a copy of the *Daily Mirror* on the next table and he picked it up and turned to the racing page. 'Ever have a flutter these days, Lewis?'

Lewis placed his empty glass in the middle of the plate and lay his knife and fork neatly to the side of it. 'Very seldom, sir. I'm not quite so lucky at gambling as you are.'

As they got up to go, Morse suddenly remembered his bet with the police surgeon. 'Do you think there's *any* way, Lewis, in which Jackson could have been murdered *before* eight o'clock that night?'

'No way at all, sir.'

Morse nodded. 'Perhaps you're right.'

Chapter Twenty-eight

•

If you have great talents, industry will improve them; if you have but moderate abilities, industry will supply their deficiency

Sir Joshua Reynolds

Almost immediately Lewis found himself liking Conrad Richards, the junior partner who worked in an office no smaller than that of his brother's below, though designated by no nameplate on the door. Lewis explained the purpose of his visit, and his reasonable requests met with an amiable co-operation. Conrad had exhibited (as Lewis was later to tell Morse) some surprise, perhaps, when the subject of fingerprints was broached, but he had willingly enough pressed the fingers and thumbs of both hands upon the ink-pad, and thence onto the cards.

'Just a matter of elimination,' Lewis explained.

'Yes, I realize that but . . .'

'I know, sir. It sort of puts you on the record, doesn't it? Everyone feels the same.'

Conrad now held his hands out awkwardly, like a woman just disturbed at the kitchen sink who is looking around for a towel. 'Do you mind if I just go and wash –'

'It's all right, sir. I'll be off now. There's only one more thing – just for the record again, of course. Can you tell me where you were between 8 and 9 p.m. on the evening of the 19th October?'

Conrad looked vague and shook his head. 'I can't, I'm afraid. I can try to find out for you – or try to remember, but I – I don't know. Probably at home reading, I should think, but . . .' Again he shook his head, his voice level and seemingly unconcerned.

'You live alone, sir?'

'Confirmed bachelor.'

'Well, if you can have a think and let me know.'

'I will. I expect I'll be able to come up with something, but I've got an awful feeling I'm not going to produce any convincing alibi.'

'Few people do, sir. We don't expect it.'

'Well, that's good news.'

Lewis got up to go. 'There *is* just one more thing. I'd like to have a quick word with your brother. Is he –'

'He's in Spain, officer. He's there on business for a week or so.'

'Oh! Well, never mind! We shall have to try to see him when he gets back.'

For five minutes after Lewis had gone, Conrad Richards sat

silently at his desk, his features betraying no sign of emotion or anxiety. Then he reached for the phone.

Morse, too, sat waiting, depressed, impatient, and irritated, on a low wooden bench beside the church in Radley. He had told himself (with a modicum of honesty) that he *was* still vaguely worried about Charles Richards' whereabouts on the day of Anne Scott's death; but he could only half convince himself on the point. Perhaps the simple truth was that he liked interviewing women whose voices over the phone promised a cloud nine of memorable mouths and leggy elegance. But whichever way it was, his visit had been fruitless. The house was locked firmly front and back, the shrill bell echoing through an ominously vacant property. Pity! A lovely female firmly sunk in fathoms of leisure – and just at this moment she had to be out! A bit more than out, too, according to the neighbours. Away. Abroad.

Morse was still staring glumly at the ground when the white police car finally drew alongside.

'Any luck?' asked Lewis, as Morse got in beside him.

'Interesting!' Morse feigned a vague indifference and fastened his seat-belt.

'Nice-looker, sir?' ventured Lewis after a couple of miles.

'I didn't bloody see her, did I?' growled Morse. 'She's in Spain.'

'Spain?' Lewis whistled loudly. 'Well, well, well! The birds seem to be flying from their nests, don't they?' He recounted the details of his own eminently more successful mission and the impression he'd formed of Conrad Richards; and Morse listened in silence. Lewis had often noticed it before: over a beer table it was usually difficult to get the chief to shut up at all, but in a car he was invariably a taciturn companion.

'What d'you think, then, Lewis?'

'Well, we can get those prints checked straightaway – and I've got the feeling we may just about be there, sir. As I see it, Charles Richards must have brought his brother along with him when he came to give his talk; then dropped him somewhere in Jericho and told him to go and scare the living daylights out of Jackson.'

'He must have taken him completely into his confidence, you mean?'

Lewis nodded as he turned on to the A34 and headed north. 'Charles Richards must have traced Jackson – he probably followed him after leaving the money somewhere – and then, as I say, he must have asked Conrad to help him. Quite neat, really. Charles is completely in the clear and nobody's going to think Conrad had anything to do with it. Anyway, things must have gone wrong, mustn't they? I doubt whether Conrad ever actually meant to kill Jackson – I reckon he'd have been far more careful about leaving any prints if he had. In fact, I doubt if he knew what to do, poor chap. Jackson's bleeding like mad, and Conrad just panics up there in the bedroom. He gets out quick and rings the police. Perhaps his one big worry was to save the old fellow.'

'Mm.' The monosyllable sounded sceptical.

'How else, sir?'

'I dunno,' said Morse. It might have happened the way Lewis had suggested, but he doubted it. From the look of the dead Jackson's face it seemed quite clear that someone had definitely meant business: something more than mere gentle persuasion followed by an accidental bang against a bed-post. The man had been clouted and punched about the head by someone made of much sterner stuff than Conrad Richards, surely, for (from the little Morse had learned of him) Conrad was considered by all to be one of the mildest and most amenable of men. Everyone, as Morse supposed, was just about capable of murder, but why should Conrad be put forward as the likeliest perpetrator of such uncharacteristic malice? He ought to see Conrad, though: ought to have seen him that afternoon instead of –

'Turn the car round!'

'Pardon, sir?'

'We're going back there – and put your foot down!'

But Conrad Richards was no longer in his upper-storey office.

According to the young receptionist, he had brought two suitcases with him that morning, and he had gone off in a taxi about ten minutes ago. He had mentioned something about a business trip, but had given no indication of where he was going or when he would be returning.

Morse was angry with himself and his displeasure was taken out on the receptionist, she appearing to be the only other person on the premises. After impressively invoking the aweful majesty of the law, and magisterially demanding whatever keys were available, he stood with Lewis in Charles Richards' office and looked around: bills in the in-trays, ash in the ash-trays, and the same serried ranks of box files on the shelves he had seen before. It seemed a daunting prospect, and leaving Lewis to 'get on with it' he himself climbed the stairs to Conrad Richards' office.

One way and another, however, it wasn't to be Morse's day. In the (unlocked) drawers of Conrad's desk he found nothing that could raise a twitch from a hyper-suspicious eyebrow: invoices, statements, contracts, costings – it all seemed so futile and tedious. The man had hidden nothing; and might that not be because he had nothing to hide? There were box files galore here, too, but Morse sat back in Conrad's chair and gave up the unequal struggle. On the walls of the office were two pictures only: one a coloured reproduction of a delicate wall-painting from Pompeii; the other a large black-and-white aerial photograph of the mediaeval walled city of Carcassone. And what the hell were *they* supposed to tell him?

It was Lewis who found it – underneath a sheaf of papers in the bottom (locked) drawer of Charles Richards' desk; and as he climbed the stairs he sought to mask the beam of triumph on his face. Putting his nose round the door, he saw Morse seated at the desk, scowling fecklessly around him.

'Any luck, sir?'

'Er, not for the minute, no. What about you?'

Lewis entered the office and sat down opposite his chief. 'Almost all of it business stuff, sir. But I did find *this*.'

Morse took the folded letter and began to read:

Dear Mister Richards

Its about Missis Scott who died, I now all about you and her but does Missis Richards . . .

As they walked out of the office below, Morse spoke to the receptionist once more.

'You weren't here when I called on Tuesday, were you?'

'Pardon, sir?' The young girl seemed very flustered and a red flush spread round her throat.

'You took the day off, didn't you? Why was that?'

'Mr Richards told me I needn't – '

'Which Mr Richards was that?'

'Mr Charles, sir. He said – '

But Morse dismissed her explanation with a curt wave of his hand, and walked down to the street.

'Bit short with her, weren't you, sir?'

'They're all a load of liars, Lewis! Her, too, I shouldn't wonder. Let's get back!'

Morse said nothing on the return drive. The letter that Lewis had found lay on his lap the whole time, and occasionally he looked down to read it yet again. It perplexed him sorely, and by the time the police car pulled into the HQ yard at Kidlington, whatever look of irritation had earlier marked his face had changed to one of utter puzzlement.

'D'you know, Lewis,' he said as they walked into the building together, 'I'm beginning to think we're on the wrong track completely!'

'Pardon, sir?'

'Is everybody going bloody deaf all of a sudden?'

Lewis said no more, and the two men called into the canteen for a cup of tea.

'I'll just be off and see about these prints, sir. Keep your fingers crossed for me. What's the betting?'

'I thought you weren't a gambling man, Lewis? And if you were, I shouldn't put more than a coupla bob on it.'

Lewis shrugged his shoulders, and left his chief staring glumly down at the muddy-brown tea – as yet untouched. He'd frequently seen Morse in this sort of mood, and it worried him no more. Just because one of the chief's fanciful notions took a hefty knock now and then! A bit of bread-and-butter investigation was worth a good deal more than some of that top-of-the-head stuff, and the truth was that they'd found – *he'd* found! – the blackmail letter. Morse might be a brilliant fellow but ... Well, it hardly called for much brilliance, this case, did it? With the prints confirmed, everything would be all tied up, and Lewis was already thinking of a nationwide alert at the airports, because Conrad Richards couldn't have got very far yet, surely. Luton? Heathrow? Gatwick? Wherever it was, there'd be plenty of time.

Half-an-hour later Lewis was to discover that between the excellent facsimiles of the fingerprints lifted from Jackson's bedroom and those taken only that afternoon from Conrad Richards, *there was not a single line or whorl of correspondence anywhere.*

Chapter Twenty-nine

And Isaac loved Esau, because he did eat of his venison: but Rebekah loved Jacob

Genesis, xxv. 28

Edward Murdoch felt ill-tempered and sweaty as he cycled homewards late that Wednesday afternoon. Much against his will, he had been roped into making up the number for his house rugby team, and his own ineffectualness and incompetence had been at least partly to blame for their narrow defeat. He was almost always free on Wednesday afternoons, and here was one afternoon he could have used profitably to get on with those two essays to be handed in the next morning.

The traffic in Summertown was its usual bloody self, too, with cars seeking to pull into the precious parking bays, their near-side blinkers flashing as they waited for other cars to back out. Twice he had to swerve dangerously as motorists, seemingly oblivious to the rights of any cyclist, cut over in front of him. It was always the same, of course; but today everything seemed to be going wrong, and he felt increasingly irritated. He came to the conclusion that his bio-rhythms were heterodyning. The two words were very new to him, and he rather liked them both. He was getting hungry, too, and he just hoped that his mother had got something decent in the oven – for a change! The last ten days or so, meals had been pretty skimpy: it had been mince, stew, and baked beans in a dreary cyclical trio, and he longed for roast potatoes and thinly sliced beef. Not, he knew, that he ought to blame his mother too much – considering all that she'd been going through. Yet somehow his own selfish interests seemed almost invariably to triumph over his daily resolutions to try to help, even fractionally, during these tragic and traumatic days in the life of the Murdoch family.

He pushed his bike roughly into the garden shed, ignored the tin of nails which spilt on to the floor as his handle-bars knocked it over, unfastened his brief case from the rack over the back wheel, and slammed the shed door noisily to.

His mother was in the kitchen ironing one of his white shirts.

'What's for tea?' His tone of voice suggested that whatever it was it would be viewed with truculent disfavour.

'I've got a nice bit of stew on, with some –'

'Oh Christ! Not stew again!'

Then something happened which took the boy completely by surprise. He saw his mother put down the iron; saw, simultaneously, her shoulders heave and the backs of her two fore-fingers go up to her tight mouth; and he saw in her eyes a look that was utterly helpless and hopeless, and then the tears soon streaming down her cheeks. A second later she was sitting at the kitchen table, her breath catching itself in short gasps as she fought to stave off the misery that threatened to swamp her. Edward had never for a second seen his mother like this, and the knowledge that she – she, his own solid and ever-dependable mother – was liable, just like anyone else, to be engulfed by waves of desperation, was a deeply felt shock for him. His own troubles vanished immediately, and he was conscious of a long-forgotten love for her.

'Don't be upset, mum! Please don't! I'm sorry, I really am. I didn't mean . . .'

Mrs Murdoch shook her head vigorously, and wiped her handkerchief across her eyes. 'It's not – ' But she couldn't go on, and Edward put a hand on her shoulder, and stood there, awkward and silent.

'I've not helped much, have I, mum?' he said quietly.

'It's *not* that. It's – it's just that I can't *cope*. I just can't! Everything seems to be falling to bits and I – I – ' She shook her head once more, and the tears were rolling freely again. 'I just don't know what to *do*! I've tried *so* hard to – ' She put her own hand up on to her son's, and tried to steady her quivering voice. 'Don't worry about me. I'm just being silly, that's all.' She stood up and blew her nose noisily into the paper handkerchief. 'You have a good day?'

'It's Michael – isn't it, mum?'

Mrs Murdoch nodded. 'I went to see him again this afternoon. He's lost one eye completely and – and they don't really know – they don't really know . . .'

'You don't mean – he'll be *blind*?'

Mrs Murdoch picked up the iron again and seemed to hold it is front of her like some puny shield. 'They're doing the best they can but . . .'

'Don't let's lose hope, mum! I know I'm not much of a one for church and all that, but hope *is* one of the Christian virtues, isn't it?'

If Mrs Murdoch had followed her instincts at that moment, she would have thrown her arms around her son and blessed him for the words he'd just spoken. But she didn't. Somehow she'd never felt able to express her feelings with any loving freedom, either with Michael or with Edward, and something restrained her even now. She turned off the iron and put two plates under the grill to warm. Where had she gone wrong? Where? If only her husband hadn't died ... If only they'd never decided to ... Oh God! Surely, *surely*, things could never get much worse than this? And yet she knew in her heart that they *could*; and as she put on the oven-glove to take out the stew-pot, she guiltily clutched her little secret even closer to herself: the knowledge that she would never be able to love Michael as she had always loved the boy who was now setting the table in the dining-room.

Later that evening the senior ophthalmic surgeon lifted, with infinite care, the bandage round Michael Murdoch's head. Then he took off his wrist-watch and held it about six inches in front of his patient's left eye.

'How are you, Michael?'

'All right. I feel tired, though – ever so tired.'

'Hungry?'

'No, not really. I've had something to eat.'

'That was a little while ago, though, and you've been asleep since then. Have you any idea of the time now?' He still held the watch steadily in front of the boy's remaining eye.

'Must be about teatime, is it? About five?'

The wrist-watch said 8.45, and still the surgeon held it out. But the boy's horridly blood-shot eye stared past the watch, unseeing still, and as the surgeon replaced the bandage he shook his head sadly at the nurse who was standing anxiously beside him.

On his way back from *The Friar Bacon* at ten minutes to eleven that night, Morse chanced to meet Mrs Murdoch, her labrador straining mightily from her; and for the first time he learned of the tragic fate of her elder boy. He listened dutifully and compassionately, but somehow he couldn't seem to find the appropriate words of comfort, mumbling only the occasional 'Oh dear!', the occasional 'I *am* sorry', as he stood staring blankly at the grass verge. Fortunately the dog came to his rescue, and Morse felt relieved as the sandy coloured beast finally wrenched his mistress off to pastures new.

As he walked the remaining few hundred yards to his home, he pondered briefly upon the Murdoch family and their links with Anne Scott. But he was tired and over-beered, and nothing was to click in Morse's rather muddled mind that night.

Chapter Thirty

An illiterate candidate gives his thoughts. The spelling, punctuation, and sentence structure are chaotic. Examiners should feel no reluctance about giving no marks for such work

Extract from *Specimen Essays at 16+*

Thursday saw Morse late into his office, where he greeted Lewis with a perfunctory nod. He had slept badly, and silently vowed to give the booze a rest that day. Whilst Lewis amateurishly tapped the keys as he typed up a report, Morse forced his attention back to the blackmail note discovered in Charles Richards' desk. At one reading, it seemed a typically semi-literate specimen of the sort of note so often received by blackmail victims – ill-spelt, ill-punctuated, and ill-expressed. And yet, at another reading, it seemed not to fall into the conventional category at all. He handed the note across to Lewis.

'What do you make of it?'

'His spelling's even worse than mine, isn't it? Still, we knew all along he'd never been to Eton.'

'By "he", you mean Jackson, I suppose?'

Lewis turned from the typewriter and frowned. 'Who else, sir?'

'You think Jackson wrote this?'

'Don't *you*?'

'No, I don't. In fact, I'm absolutely sure that Jackson himself couldn't have written one line of this – let alone the whole caboodle. You'll find in Jackson's pathetic little pile of possessions a couple of pamphlets about that telly programme *On the Move* – and that wasn't a programme for your actual *semi*-literates, Lewis: it was for your *complete* illiterates, who've never managed to read or write and who get embarrassed about ever admitting it to anyone. So I reckon Jackson must have got somebody – '

'But it's pretty *bad*, that letter, sir. Probably get about Grade Five CSE, if you ask me.'

'Really? Well, if you honestly think that, I'm sure the nation is most relieved to know that you're not going to be called up to exercise your ignorant prejudices upon the essays written by most of our sixteen-year olds! You see, you're quite *wrong*. Here! Look at it again!' Morse thrust the letter across once more, and sat back in his chair like some smug pedagogue. 'What you want a letter to do, Lewis, is to *communicate* – got that? Now the spelling there is a bit weak, and the punctuation's infantile. *But*, Lewis, I'll tell you this: the upshot of that particular letter is so clear, so unequivocal, so *clever*, that no one who read it could have misunderstood one syllable! Mistakes galore, I agree; but when it comes down to telling Richards exactly where and exactly when and the rest of it – why, the letter's a bloody model of clarity! *Look* at it! Is your understanding held up by some dyslexic correspondent who spells "receive" the wrong way round? Never!'

'But – '

'Yes, I know. If you've got some little typist next door who can't spell, you give her the sack. And quite right, too. That's her job, and none of us wants to sign illiterate letters. But I'll say it again: whoever wrote this letter knew *exactly* what he was up to. And it's just the same with the punctuation, if you look a little more closely. Full stops and question marks are all cock-eyed – but they don't affect what's being *said*.' Morse banged the table with a rather frightening intensity. 'No! *Jackson did not write that letter*.'

He wrote two words on the pad in front of him and passed the sheet over. 'What do you make of those?'

Lewis looked down at *egog* and *metantatopi*, but managed to decipher neither of these orthographic monstrosities.

'You've no idea, have you?' continued Morse. 'And I don't blame you, because that's the sort of thing your illiterate johnnies sink to. The first word's supposed to be "hedge-hog", and the second's "meat-and-potato-pie" – and they're both genuine! Chap from the examination board told me. Do you see what I mean?'

Yes, Lewis was beginning to wonder if the chief hadn't got something; but wasn't he assuming that Jackson *was* illiterate? If someone found a book on your shelves entitled *Teach Yourself to Spell*, it didn't automatically mean ...

But Morse was still going on. 'And then there's this business of the money, isn't there? If Jackson thought he'd got a soft touch for a nice little bit of blackmail, I reckon he'd have asked for one helluva sight more than a measly –'

'Perhaps he did, sir.'

The interjection stopped Morse in his tracks, and he nodded in reluctant agreement. 'Ye-es. You know, I hadn't thought of that.'

'Don't you think, anyway, that it might be better to find out about this? Find out whether Jackson could write?'

'You're right! Get on to that woman at the Post Office down there, Mrs Whatsername –'

'Mrs Beavers.'

'That's her. Get on to her and ask her how Jackson signed for his OAP. And since she's such a nosy old bugger, ask her who Jackson was doing a bit of work for before he died – apart from Anne Scott. Do you know what, Lewis? I reckon you'll find that Jackson was doing one or two other little jobs as well.'

Three-quarters of an hour later Lewis learned that Jackson was able, just, to render in alphabetical characters a tentative resemblance to 'G. Jackson' on his OAP slips. But it wouldn't much have mattered if he'd not even been able to manage that – so Mrs Beavers asserted. There were one or two of the old 'uns who got by with an 'X', provided that it was inscribed on PO premises in view of one of the staff, or vouched for by some close relative or friend. Mrs Beavers herself had often had to read or explain to Jackson some notification of change or renewal, or some information about supplementary benefit or rate rebate. And Jackson had readily understood such things – and acted upon them. He was, it seemed, far from unintelligent. The fact remained, however, that to all intents and purposes Jackson *was* illiterate.

Mrs Beavers was just as well up with the odd-job needs of the local community as with the literary competences of her clientèle. Mrs Jones in Cardigan Street, had found occasion to hire Jackson's services in planing and re-hanging several doors that were sagging and sticking; Mrs Purvis in Canal Reach had asked Jackson if he could rewire the house for her – the estimate from the Electricity Board was quite *ridiculous*. Then there was that couple who'd just moved into Albert Street who wanted pelmets made for the windows . . .

Lewis listened and made his awkward notes. It was, he had to admit, pretty well as Morse had said it would be; and when he reported back to Kidlington the only thing that seemed to interest Morse was, of all things, Mrs Purvis's re-wiring.

'Rewiring, eh? I wonder how much Jackson knocked her back for that? My place needs doing and someone told me it'll cost about £250.'

'Well, it's quite a big job, you know.'

'£250 isn't really a lot these days, though, is it?' said Morse slowly.

'Not enough to keep Jackson quiet, you mean?'

'I keep telling you, Lewis – Jackson didn't write the letter!'

'Who do you think did, then?'

Morse tilted his head slightly and opened the palms of his hands. 'I dunno, except that he – or she! – is well enough educated to know how to *pretend* to be uneducated, if you see what I mean. That letter would have been just the sort *I'd* have written, Lewis, if someone had asked me to try to write a semi-literate letter.'

'But you're a *very* well educated man, sir!'

'Certainly so – and don't you forget it! And whilst we're on this education business, I just wonder, Lewis, exactly where Mrs Purvis went to school when she was a girl.'

It seemed to Lewis the oddest question that had so far posed itself to his unpredictable chief, and the reason for it was still puzzling him as he brought the police car to a halt in front of the bollards that guarded Canal Reach.

Chapter Thirty-one

She sat down and wrote on the four pages of a note-sheet a succinct narrative of those events

Thomas Hardy, *Tess of the D'Urbervilles*

Morse had known – even before he'd noticed the rows of paperback Catherine Cooksons and Georgette Heyers along the two shelves in the little sitting room.

'His name's Graymalkin,' Mrs Purvis had replied, looking down lovingly at the grey-haired Persian that wove its feline figures-of-eight round her legs. 'It's from *Macbeth*, Inspector – by William Shakespeare, you know.'

'Oh yes?'

Lewis listened patiently whilst Mrs Purvis was duly cosseted and encouraged, and it was a relief when Morse finally brought forward the heavier artillery.

'You know, you're making me forget what we called for, Mrs Purvis. It's about Mr Jackson, of course, and there are just a few little points to clear up – you know how it is? We're trying to find out a little bit more about the sort of odd jobs he was doing – just to check up on the sort of income he had. By the way, he was doing some work for you, wasn't he?'

'He'd finished. Rewiring the house, it was. He wasn't the *neatest* sort of man, but he always did a good job.'

'He'd finished, you say?'

'Yes – when would it be now? –'

'And you'd squared up with him?'

Mrs Purvis leaned down to stroke Graymalkin, and Lewis thought that her eyes were suddenly evasive. 'I squared up with him, yes, before . . .'

'Mind telling me how much he charged?'

'Well, he wasn't a *professional*, you know.'

'How much, Mrs Purvis?'

'£75.' (Why, wondered Lewis, did she make it sound like a guilty admission?)

'Very reasonable,' said Morse.

Mrs Purvis was stroking the Persian again. 'Quite reasonable, yes.'

'Did he often do jobs for you?'

'Not really. One or two little things. He fixed up the lavatory –'

'Did you ever do any little jobs for *him*?'

Mrs Purvis looked up with startled eyes. 'I don't quite see –'

'Mr Jackson couldn't write very well, could he?'

'Write? I – I don't know really. Of course he hadn't had much education, I knew that, but –'

'You never wrote a letter for him?'

'No, Inspector, I didn't.'

'Not a single letter?'

'Never once in my life! I swear that on the Holy Bible.'

'There's nothing wrong in writing a letter for a neighbour, is there?'

'No, of course there isn't. It's just that I thought –'

'Did you ever *read* a letter for him, though?'

The effect of the question on the poor woman was instantaneous and devastating. The muscles round her mouth were quivering now as two or three times she opened her lips to speak. But no words came out.

'It's all right,' said Morse gently. 'I know all about it, you see, but I'd like to hear it from you, Mrs Purvis.'

The truth came out then, reluctantly confessed but perfectly clear. The bill for rewiring the tiny property had been £100, but Jackson had been willing to reduce it by £25 if she was prepared to help him. All she'd got to do was to read a letter to him – and then to say nothing about it to anyone. That was all. And, of course, it was only after beginning to read it to him that she'd realized it must have been a letter that Ms Scott had left on the kitchen table when she'd hanged herself. There had been four sheets of writing, she recalled that quite clearly, although Jackson had taken the letter from her after she'd read only about half of it. It was a sort of love letter, really (said Mrs Purvis), but she couldn't remember much of the detail. It said that this man she was writing to was the only one she'd ever really loved and that whatever happened she wanted him to know that; and never to blame himself in any way. She said it was all her fault – not his, and ... But Mrs Purvis could remember no more.

Morse had listened without interruption as the frightened woman exhausted her recollections. 'You didn't do anything else for him – anything else at all?'

'No, honestly I didn't. That was all. I swear on the – '

'You didn't even try to find a telephone number for him?' Morse had spoken evenly and calmly, but Mrs Purvis broke down completely now. Between sobs Morse learned that she *hadn't* looked up a telephone number, but that Jackson had asked her how to get through to directory enquiries, and that she'd told him. It was only later, really, that she'd begun to realize what Mr Jackson might be up to.

'You're not very well off, are you, my love?' said Morse gently, laying a comforting hand on the woman's shoulder. 'I can understand what you did, and we're going to forget all about it – aren't we, Lewis?'

Rather startled at being brought so late into the action,

Lewis swallowed hard and made an indeterminate grunt that sounded vaguely corroborative.

'It's just that if you can remember anything – anything at all – about this man Ms Scott was writing to – well, we'd be able to tie the whole thing up, wouldn't we?'

Mrs Purvis nodded helplessly. 'Yes, I see that, but I can't – '

'Do you remember where he lived?'

'I'm sorry, but I didn't see the envelope.'

'Name? There must have been a name somewhere, surely? She must have written "Dear Somebody", or "My dear Somebody", or something? Please try to remember!'

'Oh dear!'

'It wasn't "Charles", was it?'

The light of redemption now beamed in Mrs Purvis's eyes, as though her certain remembrance of things past had atoned at last for her earlier sins. ' "My dearest Charles",' she said, slowly and quietly. 'That's what it was, Inspector: that's how she started the letter!'

Graymalkin's eyes watched the two detectives as they left – eyes that stared after them with indifferent intelligence: neither hostility against the intruders, nor compassion for the mistress. Now left in peace, the cat curled up on the armchair beside the fire, resting its head on its paws and closing its large, all-seeing eyes. It had been another interlude – no more.

That same evening Morse drove up to the JR2 in Headington, and spoke with the sister in the Intensive Care Unit. Silent-footed, they walked to the bed where Michael Murdoch lay asleep.

'I can't let you wake him,' whispered the sister.

Morse nodded and looked down at the boy, his head turbaned in layers of white bandaging. Picking up the chart from the foot of the bed, Morse nodded his ignorant head as his eyes followed the mountain-peaks of pulse-rate and temperature. The top of the chart read *Murdoch, Michael; date of birth: the second of Octo* – But Morse's eyes travelled no further, and his mind was many miles away.

The clues were almost all assembled now, although it was

not until four hours and a bottle of Teacher's later that Morse finally solved the first of the two problems that the case of the Jericho killings had presented to him. To be more precise, it was at five minutes past midnight that he discovered the name of the man who had killed Ms Anne Scott.

Chapter Thirty-two

A man without an address is a vagabond; a man with two addresses is a libertine

G. B. Shaw

Detective Constable Walters had experienced little glamour since his appearance on the stage in the first act of the Jericho killings, and his latest assignment, a hefty burglary in North Oxford, had made no great demands on his ratiocinative skills. An upper window had been left open, and the burglars (two of them, perhaps) had helped themselves to the pickings whilst the owners were celebrating their silver wedding at the *Randolph*. The only fingerprints that might have been left had disappeared with the articles stolen, a list of which Walters had painstakingly made late the previous evening. No clues at all really, except that one of the intruders had urinated over the lounge carpet – an attendant circumstance which had elicited little enthusiasm when reported to the path boys. In fact, even the suggestion that there were two of them had been entertained only because one of the neighbours thought she may have seen a couple of suspicious youngsters walking up and down the road the day before. No, it was going to be one of those unsolved crimes – until perhaps the culprits were caught red-handed, asking for umpteen other offences to be taken into consideration. It was, therefore, a pleasurable relief for Walters when Lewis walked in on Friday morning.

'You want to see the new super, sarge?'

'No. Actually, it's Constable Walters I'm after.'

'Your chief a bit sore about the promotion?'

'Sore? Morse? He looked like he'd won the pools when I last saw him.'

'Can we help you?'

'Morse says you looked into Ms Scott's early marriage, and found where her husband had been living before he was killed.'

'That's right.'

'You spoke to the landlady?'

Walters nodded.

'Tell me all about it,' said Lewis.

'Important, is it?'

'So Morse says.'

By the end of the morning, after a visit to the landlady, after inspecting the medical records in the Radcliffe Infirmary's Accident Department, and after matching his findings with the road accident records in the archives at Police HQ, Lewis knew it all. Yet he felt oddly frustrated about his three hours' research, for Morse – who would never stoop to such fourth-grade clerical stuff himself – had already told him what he'd find: that the other driver involved in the fatal accident with Anne Scott's former husband had been *Michael Murdoch*.

Back in Morse's office, Lewis began to recount his morning's findings, but his reception was surprisingly cool.

'Cut out the weasel words, Lewis! It was just as I said, wasn't it?'

'Just as you said, sir,' replied Lewis mildly.

'And why didn't that incompetent Walters take the trouble to put the landlady's address in his report?'

'I didn't ask him. He probably didn't think it was important.'

'Didn't *think*? What the hell's he got to think *with*?'

'He's only a young fellow –'

'And doubtless *you*, Lewis, with your vast experience, wouldn't have thought it very important either?'

'No, I don't think I would, sir,' replied Lewis, marvelling at his own intrepidity. 'And I know how much you value my own idea of what's important and what isn't.'

'I see.' But there was an icy note in Morse's reply that suddenly alerted Lewis to an imminent gale, force ten. 'I'd always thought, Lewis, that the job of a detective, however feeble-minded he may be, was to produce a faithful and accurate report on whatever facts he'd been able to establish – however insignificant those facts might appear.' The voice was monotonous, didactic, with the slow, refined articulation of a schoolmaster explaining the school rules to a particularly stupid boy. 'You see, it's often the small, seemingly insignificant detail that later assumes a new-born magnitude. You would agree with that, would you not?'

Lewis swallowed hard and nodded feebly. He was in for a carpeting, he knew that. But what had gone wrong?

'So your friend Walters was somewhat remiss, was he not? As you say, I respect your own judgement of what may or may not be important; though, to be honest, I'm disappointed that you don't expect a slightly higher standard of accuracy and thoroughness in your colleagues' reports. But let's forget that. Walters doesn't work for *me*, does he?'

'What have I done wrong, sir?' asked Lewis quietly.

'What have you done wrong? I'll tell you, Lewis. You're bloody careless, that's what! Careless in the way you've been writing your reports –'

'You know my spelling –'

'I'm not talking about your bloody spelling. Listen, man! There are half-a-dozen things here that are purely, simply, plainly, absolutely bloody *wrong*. You're getting *slack*, Lewis. Instead of getting better, you're getting a bloody sight *worse*. Did you *know* that?'

Lewis looked down at the desk and said nothing. He knew,

deep down, that he'd rushed a few things; but he'd tried so hard. Whenever Morse picked up his coat for the night and asked, as he often did, for 'a report in the morning', he could have had little idea of how long and difficult a job it was for his sergeant to get the sentences right in his mind, and then tick-tick away on the typewriter until late into the evening while his chief was sitting with his cronies in the local. No, it wasn't fair at all, and Lewis felt a sense of hurt and injustice.

'Let me just see what you mean, if you don't mind, sir. I know I – '

'There's this for a start. Remember it?' Morse's right forefinger flicked the statement taken by Lewis from Mrs Celia Richards. 'And with this one, Lewis, if I remember rightly – as you can be bloody sure I do! – I specifically asked you to take care. *Specifically*.'

Lewis looked down at the statement brusquely thrust across to him and he remembered exactly what Morse had said. He opened his mouth to say something, but Etna was still erupting.

'What the hell's the good of a sergeant who can't even get an address right? A sergeant who can't even copy three figures without getting 'em cock-eyed? And then look at this one here!' Morse had now picked up another sheet and was launching a second front somewhere else – but Lewis was no longer listening. This wasn't just unfair; it was *wrong*. The address on the statement he held was perfectly correct – he was convinced of that. And so he waited, like a deaf man watching a film of Hitler ranting at a Nuremburg rally; and then, when the reverberations had settled, he spoke four simple words, with the massive authority of the Almighty addressing Moses.

'This address is right.'

Morse's mouth opened – and closed. Reaching across the desk, he retrieved Celia Richards' statement, and then fingered through the other documents in front of him until he found what he was looking for.

'You mean to say, Lewis, that she lives at two-*six-one*, and that this address here' – he passed across a Xerox copy of the letter which had accompanied the parking-fine – 'is also correct?' The last three words were whispered, and Lewis felt a shiver of excitement as he looked at the copy:

Dear Sirs,

Enclosed herewith please find cheque for £6, being the penalty fixed for the traffic offence detailed on the ticket (also enclosed). I apologize for the trouble caused.

Yours faithfully,

C. Richards.

On the original letterhead, the address had been pre-printed at the top right-hand corner: *216 Oxford Avenue, Abingdon, Oxon.*

It was Lewis who spoke first. 'This means that Celia Richards never paid the fine at all, doesn't it, sir? This is *Conrad* Richards' address.'

Morse nodded agreement. 'That's about it. And I drove past the wretched place myself when . . .' His voice trailed off, and in his mind at that very moment it was as if a colossal flash of lightning had suddenly illuminated the landscape for a pilot flying lost and blind in the blackest night.

Morse's eyes were still shining as he stood up. 'Calls for a little celebration, don't you think?'

'No, sir. Before we do anything else, I want to know about all those other things in the reports where – '

'Forget 'em! Trivialities, Lewis! Minimal blemishes on some otherwise excellent documentation.' He walked round the table and his right hand gripped Lewis's shoulder. 'We're a team, we are – you realize that, don't you? You and me, when we work together – Christ! We're bloody near invincible! Get your coat!'

Lewis rose reluctantly from his seat. He couldn't really understand why Morse should invariably win, but he supposed it would always be so.

'You reckon you've puzzled it all out, sir?'

'Reckon? *Know*, more like. I'll tell you all about it over a pint.'

'I'd rather you told me now.'

'All right, Lewis. The fact of the matter is that we now not only know who killed Anne Scott, my old friend, but we also know who killed George Jackson. And you want the names? Want 'em now?'

So Morse gave the two different names. The first one left Lewis utterly perplexed, since it was completely unknown to him; the second left him open-mouthed and flabbergasted.

BOOK FOUR

Chapter Thirty-three

What shall be the maiden's fate?
Who shall be the maiden's mate?
Sir Walter Scott, *The Lay of the Last Minstrel*

'There are three basic views about human life,' began Morse. 'One of 'em says that everything happens by pure chance, like atoms falling through space, colliding with each other occasionally and cannoning off to start new collisions. According to this view there's nothing in the scheme of things that has sorted us out – you and me, Lewis – to sit here in this pub, at this particular time, to drink a pint of beer together. It's all just a pure fluke – all just a chancy set of fortuitous circumstances. Then you get those who reckon that it's ourselves, as people, who determine what happens – at least to some extent. In other words, its our own characters that affect the way things turn out. Sooner or later our sins will find us out and we have to accept the consequences. It's a bit like bowls, Lewis. When somebody chucks you down the green, there's a bias, one way or the other, and you're always going to drift in a set directior.. And then there's another view: the view that it doesn't matter a bugger what particular circumstances are, or what individual people do. The future's fixed and firm – just like the past is. Things are somehow ordained from on high – pre-ordained, that's the word. There's a predetermined pattern in life. What's going to be – is going to be; and whatever you do and whatever your luck is, you just can't avoid it. If your number's up – your number's up! Fate – that's what they call it.'

'What do *you* believe, sir?'

'Me? Well, I certainly don't go for all this "fate" lark – it's a load of nonsense. I reckon I come somewhere in the middle of the other two. But that's neither here nor there. What *is* important is what Anne Scott believed; and it's perfectly clear to me that she was a firm believer in the fates. She even mentioned the word, I remember, when – when I met her. And then there was that particular row of books just above the desk in her study – all those Penguin Classics, Lewis. It's pretty clear from the look of some of those creased black spines that the works of the Greek tragedians must have made a deep impression on her, and some of those stories – well, let's be more specific. There was one book she'd been re-reading very recently and hadn't put back on the shelf yet. It was lying on her desk, Lewis, and one of the stories in that book – '

'I think I'm getting a bit lost, sir.'

'All right. Listen! Let me tell you a story. Once upon a time – a long, long time ago, in fact – a handsome young prince came to a city and quite naturally he was entertained at the palace, where he met the queen of that city. Soon these two found themselves in each other's company quite a bit, and the prince fell in love with the beautiful and lonely queen; and she, in turn, fell in love with the young prince. And things were easy for 'em. The prince was a bachelor and he found out that the queen was a widow – her husband had recently been killed on a journey by road to one of the neighbouring cities. So they confessed their love – and then they got married. Had quite a few kids, too. And it would've been nice if they'd lived happily ever after, wouldn't it? But I'm afraid they didn't. In fact, the story of what happened to the pair of 'em after that is one of the most chilling and terrifying myths in the whole of Greek literature. You know what happened then, of course?'

Lewis looked down at his beer and reflected sadly upon his lack of any literary education. 'I'm sorry, I don't, sir. We didn't have any of that Greek and Latin stuff when I was at school.'

Morse knew again at that moment exactly why he always wanted Lewis around. The man was so wholesome, somehow: honest, unpretentious, humble, almost, in his experience of philosophy and life. A lovable man; a good man. And Morse continued in a gentler, less arrogant tone.

'It's a tragic story. The prince had plenty of time on his hands and one day he decided to find out, if he could, how the queen's former husband had died. He spent years digging out eye-witnesses of what had happened, and he finally discovered that the king hadn't died in an accident after all: he'd been murdered. And he kept working away at the case, Lewis, and d'you know what he found? He found that the murderer had been –' (the fingers of Morse's left hand which had been gesticulating haphazardly in front of him, suddenly tautened and turned dramatically to point to his own chest) '– that the murderer had been *himself*. And he learned something else, too. He learned that the man he'd murdered had been – *his own father*. And in a blinding, terrifying flash of insight, Lewis, he realized the full enormity of what he'd done. You see, not only had he murdered his own father – but he'd married *his own mother*, and had a family by her! And the truth had to come out – all of it. And when it did, the queen went and hanged herself. And the prince, when he heard what she'd done, he – he blinded himself. That's it. That's the myth of Oedipus.'

Morse had finished, and Lewis felt himself strangely moved by the story and the way his chief had told it. He thought that if only his own schoolteachers had been able to tell him about such top-of-the-head stuff in the way Morse had just done, he would never have felt so distanced from that intimidating crew who were listed in the index of his encyclopaedia under 'Tragedians'. He saw, too, how the legend Morse had just expounded linked up at so many points with the present case;

and he would indeed have been able to work it all out for himself had not Morse anticipated his activated musings.

'You can appreciate, Lewis, how Anne Scott's intimate knowledge of this old myth was bound to affect her attitudes and actions. Just think! As a young and beautiful undergrad here, she had met a man and married him, just as in the Oedipus myth Queen Jocasta married King Laius. Then a baby arrived. And just as Jocasta couldn't keep her baby – because an oracle had told her that the baby would kill its father – so Anne Scott and her husband couldn't keep theirs, because they had no permanent home or jobs and little chance of bringing up the boy with any decent prospects. Jocasta and Laius exposed the infant Oedipus on some hillside or other; and Anne and her husband did the modern equivalent – they found a private adoption society which took the baby off their hands immediately. I don't know much about the rules and regulations of these societies, but I'd like to bet that in this case there was a provision that the mother was not to know who the future foster-parents were going to be, and that the foster-parents weren't to know who the actual mother was. Now, Lewis! What would every mother be absolutely certain to remember about her only child – even if it was taken from her almost immediately after it was born. Face and features? Certainly not! Even after a few weeks any clear-cut visual memory would be getting progressively more blurred – and after a few months, certainly after a year, the odds are that she wouldn't even recognize her own offspring. So what's that one thing that she'll never forget, Lewis? Just think back a minute. Our friend Bell – *Superintendent* Bell – was quite right on one point. He believed that something must have happened the night before Anne Scott died that proved to be the *immediate* cause of her subsequent actions. He didn't do a bad job, either, because he came up with two or three very interesting facts.

'He learned, for instance, that the bridge evening happened to be its first anniversary, and whatsername had laid on some sherry for the occasion; and if you want to get non-boozers a bit relaxed fairly quickly, a few glasses of sherry isn't a bad bet. Doubtless tongues began to wag a bit more freely than usual, and we know a couple of the things that cropped up. Vietnam and Cambodia did, for a start, and I suspect that the only aspect of those human tragedies that directly impinges on your bourgeois North Oxford housewife is the question of adopting one or two of the poor little blighters caught up in refugee camps. All right, Lewis? I reckon *adoption* was a topic of conversation that night. Then Bell got to know something else – and bless his heart for sticking it down! They were talking about *birthdays* – and not unnaturally so, in view of the fact they were celebrating their own first birthday; and as I've just said, Lewis, there's one thing no mother's ever going to forget – and that's when her only baby was born! So this is how I reckon things were. That night at the bridge party, somebody who knew Mrs Murdoch pretty well got a fraction indiscreet, and let it be known to a few people – including, alas, Anne Scott – that Mrs Murdoch's elder son was an adopted boy. And then, in the changing circles of conversation, Anne must have heard Mrs Murdoch herself volunteering the information that her elder son, Michael, was celebrating his nineteenth birthday on that very day! What a quirk of fate it all was!'

'I thought you didn't believe in fate, sir.'

But Morse was oblivious to the interjection, and continued his fantastic tale. 'When Laius, Jocasta's husband, was killed, it had been on the road between Thebes and Corinth – a road accident, Lewis! When Anne Scott's husband died, it had also been in a road accident, and I'm pretty sure that she knew all about it. After all, she'd known the elder Murdoch boy – and Mrs Murdoch herself, of course – for more than a couple of years. But, in itself, that couldn't have been a matter of great moment. It had been an *accident*: the inquest had found neither party predominantly to blame. If experience in driving means anything, it means that you have to expect learner drivers – like Michael Murdoch – to do something daft occasionally; and in this case, Anne Scott's husband wasn't careful enough to cope with the other fellow's inexperience. But do you see how things are beginning to build up and develop,

Lewis? Everything is beginning to assume a menacing and sinister importance. Young Michael Murdoch was visiting Anne Scott once a week for special coaching; and as they sat next to each other week after week in Canal Reach I reckon that sheer physical proximity got a bit too much for both of 'em. The young lad must have become infatuated by a comparatively mature and attractive woman – a woman with a full and eminently feelable figure; and the woman herself, who had probably only been in love once in her life – and that with a married man who'd never been willing to run off with her – must surely have felt the attraction of a young, virile lad who worshipped whatever ground she chose to tread. She must have led him on a bit, Lewis; and sure as eggs are eggs, the springs on the old charpoy in the bedroom are soon beginning to creak pretty steadily. Then? Well, then the trouble starts. She misses a period – and then another; and she goes off to the Jericho Clinic – where they tell her they'll let her know as soon as they can. It must have been then that she wrote to Charles Richards pleading for a bit of help: a bit of friendly guidance, at the very least – and perhaps for a bit of money so that she could go away and have a quiet, private abortion somewhere. But, as we know, the letter never got through to Charles Richards at all. By some freakish mischance the letter was intercepted by Celia Richards – and that, Lewis, was the source of all the trouble. As the days pass – and still no reply from her former lover – Anne Scott must have felt that the fates were conspiring against her. Michael Murdoch was the very last person in the world she was going to tell her troubles to: he'd finished his schooling, anyway, and so there was no longer any legitimate reason for them seeing each other. Perhaps they met again once or twice after that – I just don't know. What is perfectly clear is that Anne Scott was growing increasingly depressed as the days dragged on. Life hadn't been very kind to her, and looking back on things she saw evidence only of her failures: her hasty adolescent marriage that had been short-lived and disastrous; her love for Charles Richards which had blossomed for a good many years but which had always been doomed to disappointment; other lovers, no doubt, who'd given her some physical gratification, but little else; and then Michael Murdoch . . .'

Morse's voice trailed off, and his eyes drifted along the other tables in the lounge bar where groups of people sat exchanging the amusing ephemera of a happier, if somewhat shallower, life than Anne Scott could ever have known. His glass was empty, and Lewis, as he picked it up and walked over to the bar, decided on this occasion not to remind Morse whose turn it was.

'So,' resumed Morse, lapping his lips into the level of his pint without a word of gratitude, 'Anne Scott's making a bit of a mess of her life. She's still attractive enough to middle-aged men like you and me, Lewis; but most of those are already bespoke, like you, and the ones that are left, like me, are a load of old remaindered books – out of date and going cheap. But her real tragedy is that she's still attractive to some of the young pupils who come along to that piddling little property of hers in Jericho. She's got no regular income except for the fees from a succession of half-wits whose parents are rich enough and stupid enough to cough up and keep hoping. She goes out quite a bit, of course, and occasionally she meets a nice enough chap but . . . No! Things don't work out, and she begins to think – she begins to *believe* – that they never will. She's got a deeply pessimistic and fatalistic streak in her make-up, and in the end, as you know, she abandons all hope. Charles Richards, as she thinks, doesn't give a sod about her any longer: just at the time when she desperately needs a friend, *he* can't even fork out an envelope and stamp. But she was a pretty tough girl, I should think, and she'd have been able to cope with her problems – if it hadn't been for that shattering revelation at the bridge evening.

'She'd been reading the Oedipus story again in the Penguin translation – probably with one of her pupils – and the ground's all naked and ready for the seeds that were sown that fateful evening. Adoption and birthdays – they were the seeds, Lewis, and it must have been the most traumatic shock of her whole life when the terrible truth dawned on her: *Michael Murdoch was her own son.* And as the implications whirled round in her mind, she must have seen the whole thing in terms of the fates marking her out as another Jocasta. Everything fitted. Her husband had been killed – killed in a road accident – killed by her own son – a son with whom she'd been having sex – a son who was the father of the child she was expecting. She must have felt utterly powerless against the workings of what she saw as the pre-ordained tragedy of her own benighted life. And so she decides to do the one thing that was left open to her: to stop all the struggling and to surrender to her fate; to co-operate with the forces that were now driving her inexorably to her own death – a death she slowly determines, as she sits through that long and hopeless night, will be the death that Queen Jocasta chose. And so, my old friend, she hanged herself ... And had she but known it, the curse had still not finally worked itself out. Michael Murdoch is in the Intensive Care Unit at the JR2, and he's blinded himself, Lewis – just as Oedipus did. The whole wretched thing's nothing less than a ghastly re-enactment of the old myth as you can read it in Sophocles. And as I told you, if there was one man guilty of Anne Scott's death, that man was Sophocles.'

The beer glasses were empty again and the mood of the two men was sombre as Morse took out his wallet and passed a five-pound note over to Lewis.

'My round, I think.'

It was a turn up for the books; an even bigger one when Morse insisted that Lewis kept the change.

'You've been far too generous with your rounds recently, Lewis. I've noticed that. But over-generosity is just as big a fault as stinginess, you know. That's what Aristotle said, anyway.'

Lewis was feeling a little light-headed in the rarefied air of these Greek philosophers and tragedians, but he was anxious to get one thing straight.

'You still don't believe in fate, sir?'

'Course I bloody don't!' snapped Morse.

'But you just think of all those coincidences –'

'What are you talking about? There's only one real coincidence in the business: the fact that Anne Scott should find that one of her pupils is her own son. That's all! And what's so odd about that, anyway? She's had hundreds of pupils, and Oxford's not all that big –'

'What about the accident?'

'Augh! There are millions of accidents every year – thousands of 'em in Oxford –'

'You exaggerate a bit, sir.'

'Nonense! And that's where the coincidences stop, isn't it? Anne Scott decided to hang herself – *she* decided that. It was a conscious human decision, and had nothing to do with those wretched fates spinning your threads or lopping 'em off or whatever else they're supposed to do. And the fact that Michael Murdoch squirted so much dope into himself and then did what he did – well, that was a sheer fluke, wasn't it? He could have done anything.'

'Fluke, sir? You seem to want to have it all ways. Flukes, coincidences, decisions, fates ...'

Morse nodded rather sadly. He wasn't quite sure where his own pervasively cynical philosophy of life was leading him, but the facts in this particular case remained what they were; for the life and death of Anne Scott had traced with awesome accuracy those murderous, incestuous, and self-destructive patterns of that early story ...

'Do you know, Lewis, I could just do justice to some egg and chips.'

Lewis was losing count of his surprises. 'I reckon I'll join you, sir.'

'I'm afraid you'll have to treat me, though. I don't seem to have any money left.'

Chapter Thirty-four

The great advantage of a hotel is that it's a refuge from home life

G. B. Shaw

The hotel room could have been almost anywhere: a neat, well-furnished room, with a white-tiled bathroom annexe, its racks replete with fluffy, white towels. A cosmopolitan room — a little antiseptic and anaemic, perhaps, but moderately expensive and adequately cosy. Two separate lights were affixed to the wall just above the head-board of the double bed, though neither was turned on as Charles Richards lay on his back, his left hand behind his head, smoking silently. He wasn't sure of the exact time, but he thought it must be about 7.30 a.m., and he had been awake for over an hour. Beside him, her back towards him, lay a young woman, the mauve-striped sheet draped closely round her naked body. Occasionally she stirred slightly and once or twice her lips had mumbled some somnolent endearment. But Charles Richards felt no erotic stirrings towards her that morning. For much of the time as he lay there he was thinking of his wife, and wondering sadly why it was that now, when she was willing to let him go, his thoughts kept drifting back to her. She had not cried or created any scene when at last the truth of his relations with Anne Scott had been forced into the open. But her eyes had betrayed her hurt and disappointment, and a hardness that made her face seem older and plainer; yet later she had looked so tender and so very vulnerable that he had almost found himself falling in love with her afresh. She had said little, apart from a few practical suggestions about the days immediately ahead: she was proud and wounded. He wondered where exactly she was at that moment. Almost certainly back home from Cambridge by now. And if she was, her bed would already have been made up neatly, the sheets stretched taut across the mattress and lovingly smoothed as she had always smoothed them . . .

And then there was Conrad – his dear and loyal brother Conrad – who had turned up the previous day and managed to book a single room in one of the cheaper hotels across the plaza. Outwardly Conrad seemed as calm as ever, yet underneath were indications of an unwonted anxiety. Which, of course, was all perfectly understandable, for Conrad had been left with a difficult choice. But, as Charles saw it, his brother had almost certainly made the wrong one. Why come out to Madrid? There was virtually no chance that the police could suspect Conrad of anything; so why hadn't he arranged some quiet little business trip in England? All right, he just *had* to get away, so he'd said – though Charles doubted even that.

There was a light knock on the door, followed by the rattle of a key in the bedroom lock, and a young, heavily moustached Spanish waiter brought in the breakfast tray. But the woman still slept on. And Charles was glad of that, for the previous morning she had suddenly jerked herself up to a sitting position, completely naked to the waist; and for some deeply innate reason, he had felt himself madly jealous as the waiter's dark eyes had feasted on her breasts.

For five minutes the tray by the bedside remained untouched, and then Jennifer turned over towards him, her long, painted fingers feeling inside the top of his pyjama jacket. He knew then beyond doubt that after breakfast he would be making love to her again, and momentarily he despised himself – despised that utterly *selfish* self of his that almost invariably sought some compensating gratification from every situation: just as he had sought out Jennifer Hills after Celia had learned the truth. He shook his head slowly on the pillow, and reached out for the coffee-pot; but the woman's fingertips were detouring tantalizingly towards his pyjama trousers, and he turned himself towards her.

'Can't you even wait till after breakfast?'

'No – o! I want you *now*.'

'You're a sexy bitch, aren't you?'

'Mm. Specially in the mornings. You know that . . .'

When the Spanish chambermaid came in to clean up at 10.30 a.m., she found the toast untouched, as it had been the previous morning; and smiling knowingly to herself she turned her attention to smoothing out the rumpled mauve-striped sheets.

Conrad Richards ate little breakfast, either, for he was a deeply worried man. He'd suspected the previous day that Charles had been most displeased to see him, and now he wished he'd never come. But he needed some advice and reassurance, and for those he had depended on his brother all his life. He walked across to the Tourist Office at nine o'clock and found that if he wanted to he could fly back to Gatwick that same afternoon. Yes, that would probably be the best thing: get back, and see Celia again, and face things . . .

But when, at 11 a.m., the brothers met in the cocktail bar of the Palace Hotel, Charles seemed his bright, ebullient self once more.

'Go back *today*? Nonsense! You've not even had a chance to look round. Look at that!' He pointed out across the plaza to the fountains playing beside the statue of Neptune. 'Beautiful, isn't it? We'll do a bit of sight-seeing together, Conrad. What do you say?'

'What about er – ?'

'Don't worry about her. She's flying back to Gatwick this afternoon – on my instructions.'

Celia, too, had been up early that morning, deciding as she had done to follow Charles's practice of putting some time in at the office on Saturday. The previous day, a measure of greatness had been thrust upon her, for she had found herself making decisions about contracts and payments without the slightest hesitation – and she'd enjoyed it all. Seated in Charles's chair, she'd dictated letters and memoranda, answered the telephone, greeted two prospective clients and one ineffectual salesman – all with a new-found confidence that had surprised her. Action! That's what she told herself she needed – and plenty of it; and she just said 'No, no, no!' whenever the waves of worry threatened to wash all other thoughts away. Indeed, for some brief periods of time she found herself almost succeeding in her self-imposed discipline. But the currents of anxiety were often too strong, and like her brother-in-law she felt the urgent need of having Charles beside her. Charles, who was so strong and confident; Charles whom, in spite of everything that had happened, she knew was the only man she could ever fully love.

She was still in the office when she took the call at ten-past twelve. It was from Madrid. From Charles.

She was at home two hours later when she received another call, this time from Detective Chief Inspector Morse, to whom she was able to report that her husband would be returning home on Monday morning, his flight scheduled to land at Gatwick at 10.40 a.m., and that she herself was driving up to meet him. If it was *really* necessary, yes, they could probably be back by about 2 o'clock – if the plane was on time, of course. Make it 2.30 then? Better still, 3 o'clock, just to be on the safe side. At the Richards' house? All right. Fine!

'Have you any idea where your husband's brother is?'

'Conrad? No, I haven't, I'm afraid. He's off on business somewhere, but no one seems to know where he's gone.'

'Oh, I see.'

Celia could hear the disappointment in the inspector's voice and was clearly anxious to appear co-operative. 'Can I give him a message – when he gets back?'

'No-o.' Morse sounded indecisive. 'Perhaps not, Mrs Richards. It was just – No, it doesn't matter. It's not important.'

Lewis had come into the office during the last part of the telephone conversation, and Morse winked at him broadly as he replaced the receiver.

'Monday, then! That's the big show-down, Lewis. Three

o'clock. And you know something? I reckon I'm looking forward to it.'

Lewis, however, was looking unimpressed, and something in his face spelled trouble.

'Aren't *you*, Lewis?'

'I'm afraid I've got some rather odd news for you.'

Morse looked up sharply.

'It was very irregular, they said, and Saturday morning's hardly the best time to make enquiries, is it?'

'But you found out?'

Lewis nodded. 'You're not going to like this much, sir, but the Scotts' baby was adopted by a couple in North London: a Mr and Mrs Hawkins. They christened the boy "Joseph", and the poor little fellow died just before his third birthday – meningitis.'

Morse looked utterly blank and his eyes seemed to stare down into some vast abyss. 'You're quite sure about this?'

'Quite sure, sir. You were right about Michael Murdoch being adopted, though. Same society. But his parents were both killed in a road accident just outside –'

But Morse was no longer listening, for if what Lewis had just told him was true ...

Yet Morse had not been so very far from the truth, and if only he had known it, the final clue in the Anne Scott case lay even now inside his jacket pocket, in the shape of the unopened letter he had so recently picked up from the front-door mat of 9 Canal Reach.

'Does this mean that we're back to the drawing-board, sir?'

'Certainly not!' said Morse.

'Will you want me tomorrow?'

'Sunday? Sunday's a day of rest, Lewis – and I've got to catch up with the omnibus edition of *The Archers*.'

Chapter Thirty-five

Sir: (*n.*) a word of respect (or disapprobation) used in addressing a man

Chambers's Twentieth-Century Dictionary

The up-swung door of the wide double garage revealed the incongruous collocation of the Rolls and the Mini as Morse walked across the crunching gravel and rang the bell. Clearly number 261 was in a different class from Conrad's house. It was Celia who answered the door.

'Come in, Inspector.'

'Plane on time, Mrs Richards?'

'A few minutes early, in fact. You know my husband, of course.'

Morse watched them carefully as they stood there, fingers intertwined as though some dramatic reconciliation had recently been enacted – or, at least, as though they wished to give *him* that impression. He nodded rather curtly.

'Afternoon, sir. I'd hoped that we could have a quiet little chat on our own – if, er, your wife – '

'I was just going, Inspector – don't worry. Why don't you go through into the lounge, Charles? You can let me know when you've finished – well, finished whatever you've got to discuss.' She sounded remarkably happy, and there was a spring in her step as she walked away.

'She's obviously glad to have you back, sir,' said Morse, as the two men sat opposite each other in the lounge.

'I think she is, yes.'

'Bit surprising, perhaps?'

'We're not here to talk about my personal affairs, I hope?'

'I'm afraid your personal affairs are very much involved, sir.'

'But not my private relations with my wife.'

'No. Perhaps not, sir.'

'And I wish you'd stop calling me "sir"!'

'My sergeant calls me "sir" all the time. It's just a sort of social formality, Mr Richards.' Morse slowly took out a cigarette, as if he were anxious to impose some leisurely tempo on the interview. 'Mind if I smoke?'

'Not a bit.' Richards took an ash-tray from the mantelpiece and placed it on the arm of Morse's chair.

Morse offered the packet across but Richards shook his head with a show of impatience. 'Not for the minute, thanks. It's about Anne Scott, isn't it?'

'Amongst other things.'

'Well, can we get on with it?'

'Do you know where your brother Conrad is?'

'No. Not the faintest.'

'Did he ring you – while you were in Spain?'

'Yes. He told me one of your men had taken his fingerprints.'

'He didn't object.'

'Why should he, Inspector?'

'Why, indeed?'

'Why *did* you take them?'

'I thought he might have murdered Jackson.'

'What *Conrad?* Oh dear! You must be hard up for suspects.'

'Yes. I'm – I'm afraid we are.'

'Do you want *my* fingerprints?'

'No, I don't think so. You see you've got a pretty good alibi for that night. Me!'

'I thought the police were always breaking alibis, though. In detective stories it's usually the person with the cast-iron alibi who commits the murder, isn't it?'

Morse nodded. 'Not in this case, though. You see, I happen to know exactly who killed Jackson – and it wasn't *you*.'

'Well, that's something to be grateful for, I suppose.'

'Did Conrad also tell you that we found the blackmail note in your desk?'

'No. But Celia did. I was a bit daft to keep it, I suppose.'

'But I'm very glad you did. It was the biggest clue in the case.'

'Really?'

'And Jackson didn't write it!'

'*What?*'

'No. Jackson couldn't have written that letter because – '

'But he *rang*, Inspector! It must have been Jackson.'

'Do you remember exactly what he said when he rang?'

'Well – no, not really, but – '

'Please try to think back if you can. It's very important.'

'Well – he seemed to know that er – well, he seemed to know all about me and Anne.'

'Did he actually *mention* the letter?'

'Do you know – I don't think he did, no.' Richards frowned and sat forward in his chair. 'So you think, perhaps, that – that the person who rang me ... But it *was* Jackson, Inspector! I know it was.'

'Do you mind telling me how you can be so sure?' asked Morse quietly.

'You probably know, don't you?' To Morse, Richards' eyes suddenly seemed to show a deeply shrewd intelligence.

'I don't really know anything yet.'

'Well, when Jackson rang, I decided to change things. You know, change the time and the place and all that. I thought it would give me a chance – '

'To follow him?'

'Yes.'

'How much money did you take with you?'

'£250.'

'And where did you arrange to meet him?'

'Woodstock Road. I left the money behind a telephone box there – near Fieldside – Fieldhouse Road, or some such name. I can show you if – '

'Then you waited, and followed him?'

'That's right.'

'In the car?'

Richards nodded. 'It wasn't easy, of course, but –'

'Did you take Conrad with you?'

'Take Conrad? What – what on earth – ?'

'How did Conrad follow Jackson? On his bike?'

'What the hell are you talking about? *I* followed Jackson – in the *car*. I just –'

'There's a folding bicycle in your garage. I just happened to er notice it as I came up the drive. Did he use that?'

'I just *told* you, Inspector. I don't know where you're getting all these cock-eyed notions from but –'

'Did you put the bike in the back seat or in the boot?'

'I *told* you –'

'Look, sir! There can be no suspicion whatever that either you or your brother, Conrad, murdered George Jackson. None! But I'm still faced with a murder, and you've got to tell me the *truth*, if only because then I'll be able to eliminate certain lines of enquiry – and stop meself wasting me bloody time! You've got to understand that! If I can get it quite clear in my own mind exactly what happened that night, I shall be on the right track – I'm certain of that. And I'm certain of something else, and that is that *you* involved Conrad in some way or other. It might not have been on a bike –'

'Yes, it was,' said Richards quietly. 'We put it in the back of the Rolls, and when I parked just off the main road, Conrad got it out. He'd dressed up in a gown and had a few books with him. We thought it would sort of merge into the background somehow.'

'And then Conrad followed him?'

'He followed him to Canal Reach, yes – last house on the right.'

'So?'

'So nothing, Inspector. We knew where he lived and we – well, it was me, actually – I found out his name.'

'Go on!'

'That's the finish, Inspector.'

'You didn't drive Conrad into Oxford the night Jackson was killed? The night you spoke at the Book Association?'

'I swear I didn't!'

'Where *was* Conrad that night?'

'I honestly don't know. I *did* ask him – after we'd heard about this Jackson business. But he said he just couldn't remember. Probably at home all night but –'

'He's got no alibi, you mean?'

'I'm afraid not.'

'Well, I shouldn't worry about that, sir – Mr Richards, I mean. I'd take it as a good sign rather than a bad one that your brother's a bit hazy about that night.'

'I see, yes. You know, it's not all that easy, is it, remembering where you were a week or so ago?'

'*You'd* surely have no trouble, though? About that night, I mean.'

'No, I haven't. I forget exactly when the meeting finished, but I know I drove straight home, Inspector. I must have been home by – oh, half-past ten, I should think.'

'Would your wife remember?'

'Why don't you ask her?'

'Hardly worth it, is it? You've probably got it all worked out, anyway.'

'I *resent* that, Inspector! All right, my brother and I probably acted like a pair of idiots, I realize that. I should have told the police about the letter and so on straightaway. All right! But please don't drag *Celia* into things! I've treated the poor woman shabbily enough without her having to –'

'I'm sorry! I shouldn't have said that; and it doesn't really matter *when* you got home that night. Why should it?'

'But it's rather nice when someone can confirm what you say, isn't it? And I'm quite sure that Celia –'

'Forget it, please! I think I've got the general picture, and I'm very grateful to you.' Morse stood up to go. 'We shall have to have a statement, of course. But I can send Sergeant Lewis along at some time that's convenient for you.'

'Can't we get it done now, Inspector? I've got a pretty hectic programme these next few days.'

'Not off to Spain again, I hope?'

'No. I'm off to Newcastle first thing in the morning, and I expect to be there a couple of days. Then I'm going on – '

'Don't worry about that. There's no rush. As I say, it's not really important. But you know all this bureaucratic business of getting things down on paper: getting people to sign things, and all that. And to be truthful, Mr Richards, we sometimes find that people change their evidence a bit when it actually comes down to having to sign it. Funny, isn't it? And, of course, the memory plays some odd tricks on all of us. Sometimes we find that we suddenly remember a particular detail that we thought we'd quite forgotten.'

'I'm not sure I like what I think you're trying to say,' said Richards, his voice a degree harsher now.

'No? All I'm saying is that it won't do any harm for you to think things over at your leisure. That's all.'

'Shall I write it all out, and post it to you?'

'No, we can't do that, I'm afraid. We shall need you to sign the statement in front of a police officer.'

'All right.' Richards seemed suddenly relaxed again and rose from his chair. 'Let's arrange something, shall we?'

'I should think the best thing is for you to give Sergeant Lewis a ring at the Kidlington HQ when you've finished your business trips. One day early next week, shall we say?'

'Monday? Will that be all right?'

'Certainly. Well, I'll be off now. I'm sorry to have taken up so much of your time.'

'Would you like a cup of tea?'

'Tea? Er, no thank you – I must be getting back. Please give my regards to Mrs Richards.'

The two men walked to the front door, and Morse asked if he could have a quick look at the Rolls.

'Beautiful!' was his verdict.

'And here's the famous bike,' said Richards ruefully.

Morse nodded. 'I've always had pretty sharp eyes, they tell me.'

They shook hands and Morse walked down to the road where Lewis sat waiting with his usual placid patience.

'Well?' said Morse.

'It was just as you said, sir.'

Morse sat back contentedly as they drove past the last few houses in Oxford Avenue. 'Well, I've thrown in the bait, Lewis. We just sit back now, and wait for the fish to bite.'

'Think he will?'

'Oh, yes! You should have heard me, Lewis. A bloody genius, I was!'

'Really, sir?'

'Why do you call me "sir" all the time?'

'Well, it's just a sort of convention in the Force, isn't it? Just a mark of respect, I suppose.'

'Do you think I deserve some respect?'

'I wouldn't go so far as that, but it's a sort of habit by now and I don't think I could change in a hurry – sir!'

Morse sat back happily, for things were going extraordinarily well. At least on one front.

Chapter Thirty-six

A vauntour and a lyere, al is one
Geoffrey Chaucer, *Troylus and Criseyde*

As instructed, the sister had telephoned Kidlington HQ when the time seemed to her most opportune; and the following evening at 8 p.m. Morse and Lewis sat waiting in a small ante-room just off Dyne Ward in the Eye Hospital at the Radcliffe Infirmary in Walton Street, whither Michael Murdoch had now been transferred. Edward Murdoch, after just leaving his brother's bedside, looked surprised and somewhat flustered as he was ushered into this room and told to sit down. There were no formalities.

'Can you spell "believe"?' asked Morse.

The boy swallowed hard and seemed about to answer when Morse, thrusting the blackmail note across the table, answered the question for him.

'Of course you can. You're a well educated lad, we know that – No! Please don't touch it, Edward! Fingerprints all over it, you see – but whoever wrote that letter couldn't spell "believe", could he? Just have a look at it.'

The boy shifted awkwardly in his chair, his eyes narrowing over the writing in the long, uncomfortable silence that followed.

'Did you write it?' asked Morse slowly. 'Or was it your brother?'

The boy shook his head in apparent bewilderment. 'You must be joking!'

It was Lewis who spoke next, his voice flat and unconcerned. 'You didn't write it yourself – is that what you're saying?'

'Of course I didn't!'

'That's all I wanted to know, Mr Murdoch,' said Lewis with polite finality. He whispered something into Morse's ear; and Morse, seemingly faced with a decision of some delicacy, finally nodded.

'*Now*, sir?' asked Lewis.

Morse nodded again, and Lewis, taking a pen from his breast pocket and picking up a sheaf of papers from the table, got up and left the ante-room.

Morse himself picked up a copy of *Country Life*, turned to the crossword, and had finished it in eleven minutes – minutes during which Edward Murdoch was showing increasing signs of agitation. Two or three times his mouth had opened as if he were about to speak, and when Morse wrote in the last word he could stay silent no longer.

'What *is* all this?'

'We're waiting.'

'Waiting for – for *him* to come back?'

Morse nodded. 'Sergeant Lewis – that's his name.'

'How long will he be?'

Morse shrugged his shoulders and turned over a page to

survey the features of the Honourable Fiona Forbes-Smithson. 'Difficult to say. Some people are co-operative – some aren't.'

'He's gone to see Michael, hasn't he?'

'He's got his duty to do – just like the rest of us.'

'But it's not *fair*! Michael's *ill*!'

'He's a lot better. Going to see a bit, so they tell me.'

'But it's not – '

'Look, lad!' said Morse very gently and quietly. 'Sergeant Lewis and myself are trying our best to solve a murder. It takes a lot of time and patience and we have to do an awful lot of things we'd rather not do. But if we're lucky and people try to help us – well, sometimes we manage to get to the bottom of things.'

'But I've *told* you, Inspector, I never – '

'You *lie*!' thundered Morse. 'Do you honestly believe it was *my* wish for Sergeant Lewis to go and disturb your brother? You're *right*. He *is* ill. Do you think I don't know all about him? Do you think I'd risk his chances of getting over all this trouble if I didn't *have* to?'

Edward Murdoch did a very strange thing then. Like some frenetic pianist banging away at the same chords, he pressed the fingers of both his hands all over the letter in front of him, and sat back breathing heavily with a look of triumph in his eyes.

'Not *really* very sensible,' said Morse mildly. 'You see, I'm going to have to ask you why you did that, aren't I? And, I'll tell you something, lad, you'd better think up something pretty good!'

'You're trying to trick me!' shouted the boy. 'Why don't you just – ?'

'I'm not trying to trick you, lad. I don't need to. You're making enough mistakes without needing me to do much about it.'

'I *told* you. I didn't – '

'Look! Sergeant Lewis'll be back any minute now, because I can't really believe your brother's as stupid as you are. And when he comes in, we'll have a statement, and then we'll take you up to Kidlington and get one from *you*. It's all right. You didn't write the letter, you say. That's fine. All we've got to do is to get it down in writing, then typed up, and signed. It won't take all that long, and I'll give your mum a ring and tell her –'

'What's it got to do with her?'

'Won't she be a bit worried about you, lad? You're all she's got at home now, you know, and she's had one hell of a time this last few weeks, hasn't she?'

It was the final straw, and Edward Murdoch buried his head in his hands and wept.

Morse quietly left the room and beckoned to Lewis, who had been sitting for the last quarter of an hour on a bench at the end of the corridor, making steady progress with the Coffee-Break Crossword in the *Daily Mirror*.

The sordid little story was soon told. It had been Edward who had seen the letter to Charles Richards underneath a pile of books in the study, unsealed but ready to post, with the envelope addressed and stamped. In it Anne Scott had begged for advice, support, and money. She was sure she was pregnant and the father could only be Charles Richards because she had never made love with any other man. She pleaded with Charles to contact her and arrange to see her. She knew he would agree because of what they had meant to each other for so many years; and so very recently, too. She held out no threats, but the very fact that such a thing had crossed her mind served only to show how desperate she was feeling. If he could be her lover no longer, at least he could be a friend – *now*, when she needed him as never before. She treasured all the letters he had written to her, and re-reading them was about the only thing that gave her any hope. She would burn them all – as he'd often asked her to – if only he would help her. If he wouldn't – well, she just couldn't say what she would do.

As best he could remember it, that was the gist of the letter that Edward had read before hastily replacing it as he heard Anne climbing the stairs; and that was the gist of what he'd told his brother Michael the same evening. Not in any fraternal, conspiratorial sort of way. Just the opposite, in fact; because Michael had frequently boasted about making love to Anne, and – yes! – he, Edward, had been angry and jealous about it. But Michael had laughed it off; after all it wasn't much good her appealing to *him* for any money, was it? He couldn't even afford a decent fix every now and again. Then Anne had died; and soon after hearing of her death, Michael had asked Edward whether he could remember the name and address of the man Anne had written to. And that's how it started. Just a joke, really – that's what they'd thought, anyway. There was a chance of some money, perhaps, and money for Michael was becoming an urgent necessity, because (as Edward knew) he'd been on drugs for almost a year. So, almost in a schoolboyish manner, they had concocted a note together – and, well, that was all. The next day Michael had been rushed off to hospital, and Edward himself had felt frightened. Was still frightened – and agonizedly sorry about the cheap thing he'd done and all the trouble he'd caused. He'd never rung up Charles Richards, and he'd never been down to the willow trees to see if anything had been left there.

Whilst Lewis was laboriously scrawling the last few sentences, Morse wandered off and walked into the ward where Michael lay, a large white dressing over his right eye, his left eye, bruised and swollen, staring up at the ceiling. 'Your brother just told me that between you you wrote a letter to Charles Richards. Is that right, Michael?'

'If Ted says so. I forget.' He seemed nonchalant and unconcerned.

'You don't forget other things, perhaps?'

'What's that supposed to mean?'

'You'd always remember getting into bed with Ms Scott, surely?'

To Morse the look that leaped into the single eye of Michael Murdoch seemed distastefully crude and triumphant but the boy made no direct reply.

'Real honey, wasn't she?'

'Phew! You can say that again.'

'She – er – she took her clothes off, you mean?'

'You kidding? Beautiful body that woman had!'

Morse shrugged his shoulders. 'I wouldn't go so far as that myself. I only saw her after she – after she was dead, but ... you can't really say she had a beautiful body, can you? With that great birth-mark on her side? Come off it, lad. You can't have seen many.'

'You don't notice that sort of thing too much, though, do you, when – ?'

'You must have noticed it sometimes, though.'

'Well, yes, of course, but – '

'What a cheap and sordid little liar you are, Murdoch!' The anger in Morse's voice was taut and dangerous. 'She had no birth-mark anywhere, that woman! She had one big fault and only one; and that was that she was kind and helpful to such a spineless specimen as you, lad – because you're so full of wind and piss there's room for nothing else!'

The eye was suddenly dull and ashamed, and Morse turned away and walked out. In the corridor he stood at the window for a few minutes breathing heavily until his anger subsided. Perhaps he was a cheap and sordid liar himself, too, for he had seen Anne Scott once – and once only. At a party. Fully dressed. And, as it seemed to him now, such a long, long time ago.

Whilst Morse and Lewis were still at the Eye Hospital, passengers arriving on a British Airways scheduled flight from Madrid were passing through the customs hall at Gatwick, where onlookers might have seen two plain-clothes men walk up on either side of a middle-aged, broad-shouldered man, his dark hair greying at the temples. There was no struggle, no animated conversation: just a wan, helpless sort of half-smile on the face of the man who had just been arrested. Indeed, the exchanges were so quietly spoken, so decorous almost, that even the bearded customs man a few yards away had been able to hear only a little of what was said.

'Mr Conrad Richards?'

The broad-shouldered man had nodded, unemotionally.

'It is my duty as a police officer to arrest you on a charge of murder: the murder of Mr George Jackson of 9 Canal Reach, Jericho . . .'

The customs man frowned, his chalk poised in mid air over the next piece of luggage. Arrests in the hall were commonplace, of course; but Jericho, as it seemed to him, sounded such a long, long way away.

Chapter Thirty-seven

I never saw a man who looked
  With such a wistful eye
Upon that little tent of blue
  Which prisoners call the sky
Oscar Wilde, *The Ballad of Reading Gaol*

Morse had heard of the arrest the previous evening after returning to Kidlington HQ at about 9.45 p.m. He had been pleasurably surprised that things had developed so quickly, and he had promptly despatched a Telex of thanks to Interpol. His decision had been a simple one. The HQ building was non-operational as far as cells were concerned, and he had ordered the police car to drive direct to St Aldates, where a night's solitary confinement might well, in Morse's view, prove beneficial for the prisoner's soul.

The next morning, Morse took his time; and when Lewis drove into the crowded St Aldates' yard it was already 9.45 a.m.

'I'll see him alone first,' said Morse.

'I understand, sir.' Lewis appeared cheerfully indifferent. 'I'll nip along and get a cup of coffee.'

Richards was seated on a narrow bed reading the *Daily Express* when the cell-door was closed behind Morse with a thumping twang.

'Good morning, sir. We haven't met before, have we? I've met your brother several times, of course – but never you. I'm Morse – Detective Chief Inspector Morse.'

'Charles has told me about you, Inspector.'

'Do sit down, please. We've er we've got quite a lot to talk about, haven't we? I told the people here that you were perfectly free, of course, to call your lawyer. They told you that, I hope?'

'I don't need a lawyer, Inspector. And when you let me go – which won't be long, believe me! – I promise I shan't even complain about being cooped up for the night in this wretched cell.'

'I do hope they've treated you reasonably well?'

'Quite well, yes. And it's good to get back to some English food, I must say. Perhaps a prisoner's life isn't too bad – '

'It's pretty grim, I'm afraid.'

'Well, I think you've got a bit of explaining to do, Inspector.'

'Really? I was hoping *you* were going to do all that.'

'I've been accused of murdering a man, I understand?'

'That's it.'

'Don't you think you owe me just a little explanation?'

'All right. Your brother Charles told you about the blackmail note he received, and asked you for your co-operation. You've always been a kindly and good-hearted fellow, and you said you'd do what you could. Then your brother had a phone call about the note – or at least a call he *thought* was about the note – and he arranged to meet the blackmailer, Jackson. He drove his Rolls into Oxford, and he took you with him. When you got near the rendezvour that night, you crouched down in the back seat, and Charles carefully kept the car away from the lighted road whilst you quietly got out, taking Mrs Richards' folding bicycle with you. Then you waited – and you followed the man you'd seen take the money. Luckily he was on a bicycle as well, and you tailed him down to Jericho, where you saw him go in his house. And that was the night's work successfully completed. Charles was waiting for you at some pre-arranged spot and – '

'The Martyrs' Memorial, actually.'

'You – you're not going to deny any of this?'

'No point, is there? It's all true – apart from the fact that I've got a folding bike of my own.'

'Ah well! Even the best of us make little mistakes here and there.'

'Big ones, too, Inspector – like the one I suspect you're about to make. But go on!'

'The plan had worked well, and you decided to repeat it. Charles had agreed to speak to the Oxford Book Association and he took you with him that Friday night. He probably dropped you somewhere near St Barnabas' Church and arranged to pick you up at about a quarter-to-ten or so.'

Richards shook his head in quiet remonstration. 'Look, Inspector. If you really – '

'Just a minute! Hear me out! I don't think you meant to murder Jackson. The idea was that you – '

'I *can't* listen to this! You listen to *me* a minute! You may be right – you probably are – in saying that Charles meant to go and see Jackson. Knowing Charles as I do, I don't think he could have let a thing like that go. He'd like as not have gone to see Jackson and scared the living daylights out of him – because you mustn't underestimate my brother, Inspector: he's as tough and unscrupulous as they come – believe me! But don't you understand? Something put a whacking great full stop to any ideas that Charles may have had. And you know perfectly well what that something was: *Jackson was murdered*. And that, from our point of view, was that! We just felt – well, we needn't worry about him any more.'

'So you didn't go to Jackson's house that night?'

'I certainly did *not*.'

'Where were you that night, sir?' (Had the 'sir' crept in from conditioned reflex? Or was Morse feeling slightly less sure of himself?)

'I don't know,' replied Richards in a hopeless voice. 'I just don't know, Inspector. I don't go out much. I'm not a womanizer like Charles, and if I do go out it's usually only to the local.'

'But you didn't go to the local that night?'

'I may have done, but I can't remember; and it's no good saying I can. If I had gone, it would only have been for an hour or so, though.'

'Perhaps you stayed at home and watched the telly?'

'I haven't got a telly. If I was home that night I'd have been reading, I should think.'

'Anything interesting?'

'I've been reading Gibbon recently – and reading him with infinite pleasure, if I may say so –'

'Which volume are you up to?'

'Just past Alaric and the sacking of Rome. Volume Four.'

'Don't you mean Volume Three?'

'Depends which edition you're reading.'

Morse let it go. 'What was the *real* reason for your visit to Jackson's house that night?'

Richards smiled patiently. 'You must have a pretty poor opinion of my intelligence, Inspector.'

'Certainly not! Any man who reads Gibbon has got my vote from the start. But I still think no one actually *intended* murdering Jackson, you see. I think he was after something else.'

'Such as?'

'I think it was a letter – a letter that Jackson had found when he pushed his way through into Anne Scott's kitchen that morning. At first I thought it must have been a letter she'd written for the police – a suicide note – telling the whole story and perhaps telling it a bit too nastily from your brother's point of view. But now I don't think so, somehow. I think the letter Jackson found had probably been received through the post that very morning – a letter from your brother telling Anne Scott that he couldn't and wouldn't help her, and that everything between them was over.'

'Have you got the letter?' asked Richards quietly.

'No,' said Morse slowly. 'No – we haven't.'

'Aren't you going to have to do a bit better than this, Inspector?'

'Well, your brother was looking for *something* – in that shed at the bottom of Jackson's garden. Or was that *you*, sir?'

'In a *shed*?'

Morse ignored the apparent incredulity in Richards' voice and continued. 'That letter would have been a bad thing for your brother, sir. It could have broken up his marriage if –'

'But Celia *knew* about Anne Scott.'

'Only very recently, I think.'

'Yes, that's true.'

'Do you love your sister-in-law?'

Richards looked down sadly at the concrete floor and nodded. 'I shall always love her, I suppose.'

Morse nodded, too, as if he also was not unacquainted with the agonies of unrequited love.

'Where does this leave us, Inspector?'

'Where we started, I'm afraid, sir. You've been charged with the murder of Jackson, and that charge still stands. So we'd better get back to thinking about where you were on the night when –'

Richards got up from the bed, a new note of exasperation in his voice. 'I've told you – I don't *know*! If you like, I'll try – I'll try like hell – to get hold of somebody who may have seen me. But there are millions of people who couldn't prove where they were that night!'

'That's true.'

'Well, why pick on *me*? What possible evidence – ?'

'Ah!' said Morse. 'I wondered when you were going to ask me about the evidence. You can't honestly think we'd have you brought here just because no one saw you reading Gibbon that night? Give us a *little* credit!'

Richards looked puzzled. 'You've *got* some evidence? Against *me*?'

'Well, we're not *absolutely* sure, but – yes, we've got some evidence. You see there were several fingerprints in Jackson's bedroom, and as you know I asked my sergeant to take yours.'

'But he *did*! And I'll tell you one thing, Inspector, my

prints could quite definitely *not* have matched up with anything there, because I've never been in the bloody house – never!'

'I think you've missed my point, sir. We didn't really get a chance of matching up your prints at all. I know it's our fault – but you must forgive Sergeant Lewis. You see, he's not very well up in that sort of thing and – well, to be truthful, sir – he mucked things up a bit. But he's a good man, and he's willing to have another go. It's important, don't you think, to give a man a second chance? In fact he's waiting outside now.'

Richards sat down on the bed again, his head between his hands. For several minutes he said nothing, and Morse looked down at a man who now seemed utterly weary and defeated.

'Cigarette?' said Morse.

Richards took one, and inhaled the smoke like a dying man gasping at oxygen.

'When did you find out?' he asked very quietly.

'Find out that you weren't Conrad Richards, you mean? Well, let me see now . . .' Morse himself inhaled deeply on his own cigarette; and as he briefly told of his discoveries, the same wan and wistful half-smile returned to the face of the man who sat on the edge of the narrow bed.

It was the face of Charles Richards.

Chapter Thirty-eight

Fingerprints are left at the scenes of crime often enough to put over 10,000 individual prints in the FBI files. Even the craftiest of perpetrators sometimes forget to wipe up everywhere

Murder Ink

'When did you find out, Morse?' asked the ACC that afternoon.

'Looking back on it, sir, I think the first inkling *should* have come when I went to the Book Association and learned that it had been Anne Scott who had suggested to the committee that Charles Richards should be invited along to talk about the small publishing business. Such a meeting would attract a few people, the committee felt, especially some of the young students from the Polytechnic who might be thinking of starting up for themselves. But "small" is the operative word, sir. In a limited and very specialized field the Richards brothers had managed to run a thriving little concern. But who had heard of them? Who – except for Anne Scott – *knew* them? Virtually no one in Oxford, that's for certain – just as virtually no one would recognize the managing directors even of your big national publishers. And, remember, the Richards brothers had only just moved into Oxfordshire a few months earlier – half a dozen miles *outside* Oxford itself – and the chances that anyone would recognize either of them in a small meeting were very slim indeed. The only person who *would* have known them both was dead: Anne Scott. So they laid their plan – and decided to follow the same routine as the one which had proved so successful earlier in the week, when it was *Conrad* Richards who drove the Rolls to Oxford and *Charles* Richards who followed Jackson to Canal Reach.

'Perhaps from the little we've learned about the two brothers' characters this wasn't surprising: it was Conrad who'd always been ready to play second fiddle, and Charles who'd always been the more dynamic. So they decided to swap roles again for the Friday evening, with Conrad taking his brother's place in a talk which – very much at the eleventh hour – had been brought forward, thus almost certainly cutting down what would have been a meagre audience at the best of times. Charles had already written out his notes for the speech, and Conrad probably knew more about the workings of the business, anyway. Conrad, I'm sure, was quite happy to do this; what he adamantly refused to do was to go down to Canal Reach. As ever, in his own mild way, he was quite willing to co-operate wherever he felt he could – but it had to be *Charles* who went to face Jackson. Now, I'm fairly sure in my own mind, sir, that although Charles Richards wasn't reckoning on murder, he was determined to get that letter back – or else. He tried to scare Jackson and pushed him around from room to room as he tried to find what he wanted – the letter which would implicate him deeply in Anne Scott's death, and pretty certainly put paid to his marriage – and possibly his business, too. And when they got to the bedroom he got so exasperated that he literally shook the life out of Jackson against the bedpost. At that point Charles Richards was in a tight spot. He knew his own name was likely to crop up somewhere in police enquiries into Anne Scott's death, and he realized how vital it was that Conrad, who was at that very moment talking to an audience under the alias of 'Charles Richards', should be given an utterly unassailable alibi. So he rang up the police – and then he got the hell out of Jericho and waited at the Martyrs' Memorial for Conrad to pick him up.'

'He didn't find the letter?'

'So he says – and I'm inclined to believe him.'

'What about the change of date for the meeting? Was that deliberate?'

'I don't really see how it could have been, sir: there wasn't the time, I don't think. No. Charles had to go to Spain on business some time this month, and it so happened that one of his girl friends told him that she could get away, too, and join him. But only during that week. So Charles pleaded urgent business, the meeting was changed, and the brothers took full advantage of – '

'Lucky for them, wasn't it? Keeping the audience down, I mean.'

'Luckier than you realize, sir. Miss Universe or World or something was on the telly that night and – '

'I'm surprised *you* weren't watching it, Morse.'

'Did they pick the right girl, sir?'

'Well, personally I'd have gone for Miss – Go on!'

'I should think things must have looked pretty black as they went home that night and talked over what had happened. But very soon one thing must have become increasingly clear to the pair of them. Perhaps all would be well, *if only they could keep up the pretence*. The real danger would come if the police, in connection with Anne Scott's death, discovered that the "Charles Richards" of the OBA talk was not Charles Richards at all – but his brother Conrad, because *the speaker* that night had an alibi that no one in the world could shake. So the brothers made their decision. Celia Richards had to be brought into the picture straightaway, and Charles had no option but to tell her everything about his affair with Anne Scott and to plead with her to take her part – a pretty big part, too – in the deception that followed.'

The ACC nodded. 'Ye-es. You'd better tell me how they worked that.'

'To an outsider, sir, I think that one thing about this case would seem particularly odd: the fact that Sergeant Lewis and myself had never been *together* when we'd met Conrad Richards; and, at the same time, we'd neither of us met the two brothers when *they* were together. Let me explain, sir. I met Charles Richards – or rather the man I *thought* was Charles Richards – for the first time at the OBA, when his physical appearance was firmly fixed for me *as* Charles Richards. As it happened, I did ring up the *actual* Charles Richards the next day, but the line, as I well remember, was very poor and crackly, and we ended up almost shouting to each other. In any case, I'd only heard him speak the once – and it just didn't occur to me that the man I was speaking to was any other than the man I'd sat listening to on the back row. Then, a day or two later, I rang Charles Richards again; but he was out at the time and so I left a message with his secretary for him to ring back. As we now know, sir, the two brothers were able to solve that little probiem without too much trouble. When Charles received the message, he got *Conrad* to ring me back. Easy. But I asked for a meeting with him the next day, and that took a bit more organization. When I called at Charles Richards' office I was treated to a neat and convincing little charade by Celia – acting as the receptionist – and by Conrad – playing the part of Charles. It was, by the way, sir, at that point that I should have taken more notice of one very significant fact. Celia asked *me* for a cigarette that day – something she surely would never have done if the man who was with her was really her husband, because I was later to learn that Charles Richards was a heavy smoker. Anyway, I suspected nothing at the time, and the three of them must have felt encouraged about keeping up the pretence if the police were to bother them again.

'Then we were a bit unlucky. Lewis and myself paid a *surprise* visit to Abingdon one afternoon, to get Conrad's fingerprints. But I didn't join him for a start, sir. I had another er lead to follow up, and so I wasn't with Lewis when he called at the office and met Conrad – the same man who'd twice passed himself off to me as *Charles*. We had reason to believe that Conrad might have been involved in things somehow, and we wanted to find whether his prints matched those found in Jackson's bedroom. So Lewis got the prints – Conrad's prints – and of course they matched nothing, because it had been *Charles* who had been in Jackson's house. That same afternoon we returned to the Richards' firm – but we were too late. We searched the offices that the brothers used, and as you know we found the blackmail note in Charles's desk. But the real clue I missed, I'm afraid. It was pretty clear from the ash-trays full of stubs that Charles was virtually a chain-smoker, but in Conrad's room there was no physical sign whatsoever of smoking and not the faintest smell of stale tobacco. Then we made a final visit to Abingdon, when Celia and Conrad – this time with ample warning – put on another little performance for me, playing the parts of a reconciled couple very cleverly. But they were wasting their time, I'm afraid. You see, there were two reasons for my visit. First, to get the man I'd been interviewing to the front door so that Lewis could see him and so corroborate what we'd suspected – that the man I'd been meeting all the time was in fact *Conrad* Richards.'

'But why all the clever-clever stuff, Morse? Why didn't you just arrest him there and then and get it over with?'

'We'd have run the risk of letting the big fish get away, sir, and that was the second reason for my going that day. I had to lay the bait to get Charles Richards back in England, and so I told Conrad that we had to have a statement from him and that it was going to be *Sergeant Lewis* who would take it down. You see, Lewis *knew* the real Conrad Richards: he'd taken his fingerprints. And so any statement would have to be made by the *genuine* Charles Richards; and to do that he'd have to get back from Spain fairly quickly. As, in fact, he did, sir.'

'And he walked into our men at Gatwick – and then you walked into *him* at St Aldates.'

'Yes. Once I'd mentioned that we needed to take his prints again and that Sergeant Lewis was going to try to do a better job this time, he realized the game was finally up. Lewis had never taken *his* prints at all, you see – and, well, Charles could see no point in pretending any longer. I offered him a cigarette – and that was that!'

'How kind of you, Morse! I suppose, by the way, the prints *were* Charles Richards'?'

'Er, well, as a matter of fact they weren't, sir. I'm afraid I must have been just a little careless er myself when I examined the head-board and –'

The ACC got to his feet and his face showed pained incredulity. 'Don't – don't tell me they were –'

Morse nodded guiltily. 'I'm afraid so – yes, sir: *they were mine*.'

Chapter Thirty-nine

The troubles of our proud and angry dust
  Are from eternity, and shall not fail.
Bear them we can, and if we can we must.
  Shoulder the sky, my lad, and drink your ale
A. E. Housman, *Last Poems*

Apart from a few small details the case of the Jericho killings was solved, but Morse knew as he sat in his office the following morning that it wasn't yet quite the time to pack away the two box files on the shelves of the Record Office. There were two things really that still nagged at his brain. The first was the realization that his Sophoclean hypothesis about Anne Scott's suicide had been largely undermined by Lewis's patient enquiries . . . (Where was Lewis, by the way? Not like Lewis to be late . . .) The second thing was that the letter Charles Richards had written to Anne Scott had still not been found. Was that important, though? Beyond much doubt it had led directly to Anne's death, but it wasn't difficult to guess at its contents; not difficult to reconstruct the events of that morning when Anne had received one letter from the clinic saying, yes, she *was* pregnant, and another from Charles Richards saying, no, he *wasn't* going to see her again.

Morse nodded to himself: it had been the post that morning that had been the final catalyst – not the previous night's talk at the bridge club of birthdays and adoptions. But why should Anne have been up so early that morning? Usually, as he'd learned, she would stay in bed until about lunch-time on a Wednesday, after getting to bed so very late after bridge. And, then again, why had she cancelled her lesson with Edward Murdoch? Had Anne Scott *really* had a morbid sense of the gods' ill-favour as they played their sport with men and women? If not, what had she done when she got home early that morning? What if ... ? Ye-es. He'd been assuming that she'd stayed awake that terrible night largely because the bed had not been slept in. Or so it had appeared. But surely she *could* have gone to bed? Gone to sleep, got up early, made the bed, and then ... But *why* had she got up so early that morning?

Morse shook his head. It wasn't quite adding up, he knew that, and he needed to talk to Lewis. (Where the hell *was* Lewis?) Morse reached for another cigarette and his mind wandered back to the night when he had met Anne ... the night when but for some miserable ill-luck that had taken him away ... when Lewis had come in and dragged him off ...

'Morning, sir!' Lewis looked as bright and cheerful as the golden sunlight outside. 'Sorry to be a bit late, but – '

'*Bit* late? You're *bloody* late!' Morse's face was sour.

'But you said – '

'Got your car here?'

'Outside.' Lewis permitted himself a gentle smile and said no more.

'I want to take a last little look at Jericho, Lewis. There's that bloody letter from Richards for a start. Bell's lot looked for it; *you* looked for it; Richards himself looked for it – and nobody can find it, right? So it's about time *I* had a look for it! You all swear it's not there, but the trouble is you've probably all been looking in the wrong *place*. I'm not saying I know where the right place *is*, but I'll be surprised if I don't do a bit better than the rest of you. Can't do worse, can I? You need a bit of *imagination* in these things, Lewis ...'

'As you wish, sir.'

Morse was unusually talkative as they drove down the Woodstock Road and turned down the one-way Observatory Street towards Jericho. 'Beautiful morning, Lewis! Almost makes you feel glad to be alive.'

'I'm always glad to be alive.'

'Really?' Morse vaguely looked along the stuccoed fronts of the terraced houses and then, as Lewis waited to turn into Walton Street, he suddenly caught sight of the Jericho Tackle Shop, and a beautiful new idea jumped across the threshold of his mind.

'Jackson was buying his new rod from there, wasn't he?' Morse asked casually.

'That's right.'

Lewis parked the police car by the bollards at Canal Reach. 'Which key do you want first, sir?'

'Perhaps we shan't need either of them.'

The two men walked up the narrow little street, where Morse led the way through to the boat-yard before turning right and climbing over the fence into the back garden which the late George Jackson had fitfully tended. The shed door was still secured only by the rickety latch that Morse had opened once before, and now again he looked inside and surveyed the vast assortment of Jackson's fishing tackle.

'Is that the new rod?' he asked.

'Looks like it, sir.'

Morse carefully disconnected the jointed sections and examined them. 'You see, Lewis? They're hollow inside. Just the place to hide a letter, wouldn't you say? Just roll the letter up into a cylinder and then ...' Morse was busily peering and feeling inside the sections, but for the moment, as Lewis stood idly by, he could find nothing.

'It's here, Lewis! It's here somewhere. I know it is.'

But a quarter of an hour later he had still found nothing. And however Morse twisted and pulled and cursed the collection of rods, it soon became clear that no letter was concealed in any of them.

'You've not been much bloody help!' he said finally.

'Never mind, sir – it was a good idea,' said Lewis cheerfully. 'Why don't we nip over the way and have a noggin? What do you say?'

Morse looked at his sergeant in a peculiar way. 'You feeling all right, Lewis?'

'Well, we've solved another case, haven't we? It'll be a little celebration, sort of thing.'

'I don't like these loose ends, though.'

'Forget it, sir!' Lewis led the way through the back yard and out once more into Canal Reach, where Morse stopped and looked up at the bedroom window of number 9. Still no curtains.

'I wonder . . .' said Morse slowly.

'Pardon, sir?'

'You got the key, you say?'

Lewis fiddled in his pocket and found it.

'I was just wondering,' said Morse, 'if she had an alarm clock in her bedroom. Can you remember?'

'Not off hand, sir. Let's go and have a look.'

Morse opened the door and suddenly stopped. *Dejà vu.* There, on the inside door-mat, was another brown envelope, and he picked it up and looked at it: 'Southern Gas Board' was printed along the bottom of the cover.

'Just nip upstairs then, Lewis, and bring the alarm clock down – if there is one.'

When Lewis had left him, Morse put his hand inside his breast pocket and pulled out the envelope he had previously found – and until this moment forgotten about. Slitting open the top in a ragged tear he took out a single typed sheet of paper:

SUMMERTOWN CURTAINING 8th Oct

Dear Ms Scott,

I am sorry that we were unable to contact you earlier about your esteemed order for curtaining and pelmeting. Unfortunately it proved impossible for our fitters to come as agreed on the 3rd inst., since our suppliers let us down over the yellow material for the study and the front bedroom, and we thought it more sensible to do the whole house in one day rather than doing the jobs in two bits. We regret the inconvenience caused.

I am now able to inform you that all materials are ready and we look forward to hearing from you as soon as possible about a convenient time. We confidently expect, as before, that all the work can be completed in a single day and we shall be happy to begin work at about 9 a.m. if this is again suitable to you.

Yours faithfully,
J. Burkitt (Manager)

As Morse finished reading Lewis was standing beside him, a small, square, black alarm-clock in his hand. 'Anything interesting?'

Morse pondered the letter once more, then pointed to the clock. 'I think we've probably got another loose end tied up, yes – if that thing's set for about half-past seven.'

'Quarter-to-eight, actually, sir.'

'Mm.' Morse stood still just inside the door, his mind reconstructing the scene that must have taken place in that very room. He seemed sadly satisfied.

'You know that letter from Charles Richards, sir? Don't you think she probably burnt it with the one from the clinic? Perhaps if we get the path boys to have a look at those ashes in the grate – '

Morse shook his head. 'No. I buggered that up when I started poking around, Lewis. It's no good now.'

'You think he *did* write a letter to her, sir?'

'Well, not in direct answer to hers, no. Celia Richards intercepted that, as we know. But I think she must have got in touch with him somehow, after she'd heard nothing; and I think he wrote to her – yes, I do.'

'He says he *didn't*, though.'

'Pretty understandable, isn't it?'

'You mean he's got one death on his conscience already?'

Morse nodded. 'Not the one you're thinking of, though, Lewis. I don't believe he gives a sod about what he did to Jackson: it's the death of Anne Scott that he'll have on his conscience for ever.'

'I'll get them, sir,' said Lewis as they walked into *The Printer's Devil*. 'You just sit down and read that.' He handed Morse an envelope which had quite clearly been rolled into a tight cylindrical shape. 'I came here this morning, and I found it inside the new rod, sir. I hope you'll forgive me for not telling you before, but it's not the letter *you* were looking for.'

Lewis walked over to the bar, and Morse sat down and immediately saw the name on the grimy envelope: it was his own.

For Chief Inspector (?) Morse
Thames Valley Police
Absolutely Private, and for the
attention of no one else.

Inside the envelope was a single sheet of writing, together with a further envelope, itself already opened, and addressed 'Charles Richards'. Morse took the single sheet and slowly read it:

Dear Inspector Morse,

Perhaps you will have forgotten me. We met once at a party when you had too much to drink and were very nice to me. I'd hoped you'd get in touch with me – but you didn't. Please, I beg you, be kind to me again now – and deliver the enclosed letter personally and in the strictest confidence. And please, please don't read it. What I am going to do is cowardly and selfish, but somehow I just can't go on any more – and I don't want to go on any more.

Anne Scott

Lewis had brought the beer over and was sitting quietly opposite.

'Have you read this, Lewis?'

'No, sir. It wasn't addressed to me.'

'But you saw who it was addressed to?'

Lewis nodded, and Morse passed it over.

'You didn't read this one, either?' asked Morse, taking out the envelope addressed to Charles Richards.

'No, sir. But I should think we know roughly what's in it, don't we?'

'Yes,' said Morse slowly. 'And I think – I think I ought to do what she asked me, don't you?' He passed the envelope across. 'Seal it up, Lewis – and see that he gets it straightaway, please.'

Was he doing the right thing? Charles Richards would find

the letter terribly hurtful to read – there could be little doubt of that. But, then, life *was* hurtful. Morse had just been deeply hurt himself . . . 'I'd hoped you'd get in touch with me', she'd said, 'but you didn't'. Oh! If only she'd known . . . if only she'd known.

He felt Lewis's hand on his shoulder and heard his kindly words. 'Don't forget your beer, sir!'

Epilogue

Jericho has altered little since the events described in these chapters, although the curious visitor will no longer find Canal Reach marked upon the street map, for the site of the narrow little lane in which Ms Scott and Mr Jackson met their deaths is now straddled by a new block of flats, in which Mrs Purvis (together with Graymalkin) is happily resettled, and where one of her neighbours is the polymath who once regaled Morse on the history of Jericho and who is now a mature student reading Environmental Studies at London University. Some others, too, who played their brief parts in the case have moved – or died; but many remain in the area. Mrs Beavers, for example, continues to run the corner post office, and Mr Grimes to sit amongst his locks and burglar-alarms. And the Italianate campanile of St Barnabas still towers above the terraced streets below.

In the wider confines of Oxford, a few small items of information may be of some interest to the reader. Michael Murdoch, a jauntily-set black patch over his right eye, was able to make a late start to his university studies in the Michaelmas Term, whilst Edward Murdoch's German master confidently predicted a grade 'A' in his Advanced level examination. The bridge club flourished pleasingly, and Gwendola Briggs was heard to boast of twenty-two signatures on the wreath purchased for old Mr Parkes, cremated on the very day that Charles Richards was found guilty at Oxford Crown Court of the murder of George Jackson. Somewhat surprisingly, Detective Constable Walters made up his mind to leave the police and to join the army – a decision which displeased, amongst others, Superintendent Bell, a man who finds his talents now more profitably employed in administration than ever they were in detection. In late November Sergeant Lewis's eldest daughter produced a baby girl, and Mrs Lewis was so overjoyed that she bought a modestly expensive bottle of red wine to accompany her husband's beloved egg and chips.

And what of Morse? He still walks to his local most evenings, and would appear to take most of his calories in liquid form, for no one has seen him buying cans of food in the Summertown supermarkets. In mid-December he was invited to another party in North Oxford; and as he waited in the buffet queue his eyes caressed the slim and curving bottom of the woman just in front of him as she leant across the table. But he said nothing; and after eating his meal alone, he found an easy excuse to slip away, and walked home.